GIVING UP THE GHOST

Marilyn Levinson

Cover Art Design by: Kelly Moran/Rowan Prose Publishing
Photo Credit: Adobe Images/Deposit Photos
Second Edition
ISBN: 978-1-961967-68-7
Rowan Prose Publishing, LLC
www.RowanProsePublishing.com
Published in the United States of America

PRAISE for Marilyn Levinson

"A master of the mystery and suspense genre."
Midwest Book Review

"A 'spirited' start to a fun new mystery series that kept me guessing to the end."
Booklist

"Plenty of red herrings and amusing characters."
Kirkus

Dedication:

For my dear friend, Paula Goldbaum, who read and enjoyed this book so many years ago. Many thanks for your support and belief in me as a writer.

Acknowledgements:

How lucky I was when I told my beloved and now late agent, Dawn Dowdle, that I needed someone to update my website. She told me to contact Kelly Moran. I did—and Kelly redid my website that very day.

Shortly after, Kelly, an author in her own right, launched Rowan Prose Publishing—another lucky day for me! She published Come Home to Death, the first adult novel I ever wrote, and republished many of my mysteries that never really received the attention I felt they deserved. She gave them fresh, eye-catching covers and smart, effective publicity that have brought me many new readers.

I've been fortunate to have Shakera Blakney as my editor. Though all my books had been previously edited, Shakera made each one shine. Giving Up the Ghost, the first mystery I wrote—and still one of my favorites—is a perfect example.

Thank you, Kelly and Shakera!

CHAPTER ONE

Gabbie stepped out of her car and regarded the place she was to call home for the rest of the school year. In the gloom of early nightfall, the weatherbeaten cottage held as much charm as the *House of Usher*.

Her bout of shivers came from the raw January wind as well as from her sense of isolation. Woods on either side separated her from her nearest neighbors—both summer people, according to the real estate agent—and the overgrown bushes hid the cottage from anyone driving down this godforsaken road. Why, a gang of ruffians could commandeer the place, and no one would hear her screams!

She let out a humorless bark of laughter as she realized *the pièce de résistance* camouflaged a potential danger as well: the spectacular view of the Long Island Sound that had driven her to haggle with Mary Hanley until she lowered the rent to one Gabbie could afford. Beyond the straggly row of scrub oaks bordering the back lawn, the land fell away...into a thirty-foot drop to the beach.

Where was her common sense? Her grasp on reality? By taking this teaching job, she'd allowed herself to follow another rash impulse like the one that had led her to marry Paul Montebello.

And that had proven to be the most egregious mistake of her life.

"Enough!" she scolded aloud, refusing to fall prey to the pattern of negative thinking that always left her spent and depressed. She had to put distance between herself, and everything connected to Paul. Get away from Westchester County, Paul's sphere of influence, though currently he resided further north: in prison. She'd been lucky to find a district in need of an English teacher in the middle of the school year, one whose administrators were willing to hire her though she hadn't taught in years. As for this cottage, it was a better choice than her only alternative, a hole-in-the-wall apartment above a dry-cleaning establishment in a neighboring town.

If only it wasn't so dark! Grabbing a suitcase in each hand, Gabbie inched cautiously along the snow-covered path to the front door. Once inside, she switched on the light in the small hall and wrinkled her nose as a dank, musty odor filled the air. Mary had claimed the odor would disappear once the place was aired out. "It had better," Gabbie muttered as she turned up the thermostat. She welcomed the low roar as the heating system came to life, followed by a blast of warm air from a nearby vent. *Good!* At least she wouldn't freeze.

She glanced to her left, at the living room crowded with musty, old furniture. *It's only till the end of June,* she reminded herself and focused on the fact that her drive to the high school was seven minutes flat.

She retrieved the rest of her things from the Volvo and was about to carry them upstairs when a shudder ran up her spine. Stopping to take a breath, and see if she could hear any movement, Gabbie quietly put her things down. She couldn't put it into words, not even to herself, but she didn't feel alone. She didn't hear a sound, but the hairs on her neck rose all the same—chilled by something or someone that shouldn't have been there. She got the feeling she wasn't alone. Someone was watching!

Gabbie spun around to peer into the darkened den across the hall from the living room. "Who's there?"

Silence.

She flew up the steps, her heart pounding. "You're doing a great job of scaring yourself," she muttered. "Get a grip or you'll be a total wreck in no time. Everything feels weird because it's a strange house and new surroundings." She grabbed all she could carry and went upstairs, as fast as she could climb.

In the larger of the two bedrooms, she made up the queen-sized bed and put her clothes in the closet and bureau. She was setting her toiletries on the bathroom counter when the sound of whistling froze her where she stood. Gabbie took two deep breaths, grabbed her hair spray—the only weapon she could think of—and braced herself at the head of the stairs.

"Who's there?" she repeated, fear turning her voice harsh. Had Paul hired someone to follow her and kill her? He considered disloyalty a sin and turning him in to the authorities had to strike him as the most grievous sin of all.

A bantam-sized man in his late sixties came into view. He wore workman's boots, a plaid flannel shirt and a deerstalker hat that left his face in shadow.

"Hello, there." He looked up at Gabbie. Was he smiling or leering? "Didn't mean to frighten you, but I knocked and knocked and nobody answered. I'm Reese Walters, by the way. I own Walters' Floor and Appliances, half a mile east of town."

Gabbie descended two steps, voice sharp. "How'd you get in?"

"With a key." He removed it from his pocket and held it up to prove his point. "Mary Hanley said to come look over the kitchen and see what needs doing. It's in pretty bad shape."

Relief and irritation vied for dominance. Irritation won. "She had no business giving you the key after I signed the lease."

Reese Walters held out both palms in a conciliatory gesture. "Now don't go blaming Mary when all she wants is to see you comfortable. Besides, Roland Leeds gave me the key. He asked me to keep an eye on things after...well, after."

"After what?"

He waved away her question. "Here's what I'll do," he said expansively, the way he probably did when he wanted a customer to believe he was cutting her a special deal. "Tomorrow I'll have my men replace the microwave and oven and measure for a new kitchen floor. I should've taken care of it months ago, only I didn't expect anyone would be renting so soon. Not since..." His voice faltered, then he quickly changed direction. "I should say, not till the spring."

Gabbie eyed him warily. "Is something wrong with the cottage? Something I should know about, like the roof leaks?"

"No, ma'am, the place is sound enough. Roland's grandfather built it with his own two hands. The thing is, not many folks come to Chrissom Harbor in the dead of winter."

His answers didn't sit right with her, though she couldn't quite put her finger on what was wrong. Even so, there was no point in being rude. She descended to the hall and offered her hand. "I'm Gabbie Meyerson," she said, pleased to be using her maiden name again. "I've come to teach English at the high school."

Reese shook her hand. "Pleased to meet you, Gabbie. Mary mentioned you'll be taking over for Lydia Ketchem while she recuperates from her operation."

Gabbie pursed her lips. Had the agent repeated every single word of their conversation?

"Welcome to Chrissom Harbor. They're sure lucky to have found you."

"Why do you say that?"

He gulped, then spoke rapidly. "Because half the school year's over, isn't it? Hard to get replacements. Anyway, your kitchen and living room lights are all working. No burned-out light bulbs. Want me to take a look upstairs?"

"No, it's fine, but I noticed there's a TV in the den. Would you mind checking to see if it's connected?"

Reese's eyes darted to the room across the hall and then peered down at his watch. "Is that really the time!" he exclaimed in exaggerated surprise. "I best be going. My wife expected me home half an hour ago." He edged toward the door.

"Tell you what," he continued before she could squeeze in a word, "I'll have my men look at the TV tomorrow to make sure it's in working order."

"Well, all right."

He tilted back his hat, and his gray eyes met hers. "And make sure you keep your doors locked. People around here are decent and hard-working, but times are different now, if you get what I mean."

"Er...of course."

Not certain if he meant this as a general caution or that a rapist roamed the woods, Gabbie heeded his advice and double-locked the door behind him. *My first visitor,* she mocked as she climbed the stairs to finish the business of settling in. Still, now that she'd been promised a working kitchen, she found herself feeling more kindly disposed toward the cottage. Plus, Reese had been friendly enough, though his insinuations of danger and problems left her a bit uneasy.

He's probably one of those gossipy people who likes to come across as mysterious and knowing she decided, then placed a pile of her favorite novels on the nightstand and put him out of her mind.

A crash sent her flying down the stairs. Nothing seemed to be out of place in the kitchen or the dining room. She stood in the entranceway to the den and looked about. A large ashtray lay at her feet. Gabbie gasped. It hadn't been there before. It must have fallen, but how?

Reese Walters probably brushed against it when he was here. It was the only logical explanation. But how to explain the scent of male cologne wafting through the room?

Stop imagining things, she told herself. She went upstairs to finish putting away her clothes.

Half an hour later, her possessions in place, Gabbie realized her stomach was growling. She was ravenous and for good reason, as her last bit of nourishment had been a muffin and a cup of coffee before noon. She went to the kitchen and opened cupboards. Plenty of cooking and eating utensils but nothing to eat. *Of course there wasn't any food. Why would she expect to find food in an empty house?*

She considered driving into town, but felt too exhausted to make the effort. Instead, she finished off the crackers and package of cheddar cheese she'd brought and boiled water for tea. Tomorrow she'd stock up at the supermarket.

She yawned as she cleared the table, and a wave of exhaustion nearly knocked her off her feet. It had been a long and arduous day of transition, but eight-thirty was too early to crawl into bed.

The den was the perfect place to veg out. In the warm glow of lamp light, the room had an inviting appearance. Still, a tingle at the nape of her neck made her pause before entering the room.

Silly! she told herself. *There's nothing to be afraid of.*

A cold draft, strong enough to ruffle her hair, sent her to the sliding glass door to make certain it was locked. It was, but as an added precaution against chills Gabbie closed the vertical blinds and shut out the night. Even so, a current seemed to undulate the air. To offset her uneasiness, she strode about and scrutinized the room.

The den appeared to be a recent addition to the cottage and had been furnished for masculine comfort, judging by the brown leather couch and recliner. A bronze Roman soldier stood on a wall unit shelf guarding the TV, Blu-ray player, and stereo system.

Gabbie approached the built-in bookcases on either side of the entertainment unit to scan the books that half-filled the shelves. There were several suspense novels and the rest dealt with investing, money, and the economy.

This was her home for the next few months, she reminded herself.

It was time to stake her claim and add a feminine touch, she decided as she placed her snow scene paperweight—a gift from a favorite aunt—on the oversized desk in the far corner. This simple act seemed to dissipate the tension in the room.

Feeling more at home, she sank back into the recliner and, remote in hand, clicked her way through channels without finding anything of interest. Not surprising, since she couldn't remember the last television program she'd seen. But it was nice to know the TV worked, which meant the Blu-ray player probably did as well. And the telephone would be connected in a day or two.

She turned off the set, closed her eyes, and curled on her side, burrowed deeper into the oversized chair. *Mmm, comfy.* The leather, buttery and well-padded, lulled her into a state of deep relaxation. Considering all she'd recently accomplished, Gabbie allowed herself a moment of self-congratulation. She'd found a temporary job and was on her way to putting her past behind her.

Half asleep, she murmured. "This place isn't so bad."

An amused male voice interrupted, "Think so? I wouldn't bet money on that, honey."

CHAPTER TWO

Gabbie leaped to her feet, a hand pressed against her thumping heart. "Who's that? Who's there?"

She glanced about the room, raking the corners, but saw no one.

"The police! I'll call the police!" She strode to the desk where a phone rested beside the lighted lamp. But as she reached for the phone, she remembered the line wasn't connected. No doubt she was the only person in America who didn't own a cell phone. Well, she had owned one, but in her efforts to pare down expenses, she'd given it up.

Even if she reached the police, what would she say? That she was drifting off to sleep in her new rental and heard someone—some invisible male—make a wise-crack comment? Gabbie grimaced. She had a pretty good idea what the officer would suggest: she was dreaming or letting her imagination run wild.

A man's voice coming from her bedroom sent her scurrying toward the stairs. Then she heard music. Relieved, Gabbie strode into the room and turned off her clock radio. She must have accidentally set it to go off when she was plugging it in. "That's what I heard before, the radio," she uttered. "It had to be."

Reason told her she'd misunderstood what the voice had said, it couldn't have been speaking to her. Which didn't keep her from tossing and turning for most of the night. She finally slept and was awakened by the shrill sound of the old-fashioned alarm, which she'd set instead of the clock radio.

She showered and dressed quickly, eager to leave the cottage, and drove to Chrissom Harbor High School.

It was an old, three-storied brick building, surrounded on three sides by parking lots, playing fields and courts. A considerable distance beyond were woods, farms, and what appeared to be a new housing development.

Gabbie parked in a visitor's spot and headed for the Main Office where Lydia Ketchem was waiting for her. The English chairperson was a sturdy, no-nonsense woman in her mid-fifties, with short iron-gray hair and a warm smile. Gabbie was grateful to have the job, but now that she'd met the woman she was replacing, she was sorry Lydia had to undergo surgery on her rotator cuff, followed by months of rehabilitation.

"Let's go to the classroom and I'll explain what I've been doing. They're good kids, most of them. You'll know who the troublemakers are before the first day's over."

They walked along a narrow, locker-lined corridor made more dismal by flickering florescent lights. Gabbie winced. She felt it was the middle of the night though she knew outside the sun was shining.

Lydia noticed and laughed. "Dreary, I know. From the looks of things, you'd think this place dates back to the Puritans. The Board's talking about finally building a new middle-high school. They'll put it to a vote in May, but I'm afraid most of the old-timers and summer people will come out and nix it. They don't want their taxes to go up."

"Is that a new development of houses beyond the playing fields?" Gabbie asked.

"Oh, yes. They're sprouting up all over the place. And new houses mean more kids. So, we'll get a new building one of these years, most likely after I retire." She rubbed her shoulder. No doubt the torn rotator cuff was causing her pain.

They turned left and continued along another corridor and heard raucous laughter before two boys came into sight. Both were slender, but the taller, older of the two dwarfed his friend by several inches. He shrugged his shoulders repeatedly, clearly a nervous tic. Each of the boys wore black pants and a black sweatshirt under a black trench coat. Their hair, dyed shoe-leather black, hung down their backs in skinny ponytails.

Lydia stepped in their path, her nostrils bristled with fury. "Todd! Barrett! You both were suspended, which means you spend the day in Dr. Jordan's office. And you know the rules: no black trench coats. Put them away in your lockers now!"

The boys glanced at each other in mock amazement and brayed with laughter. The older, taller boy fixed his pale blue eyes on Lydia. "We told Dr. Jordan we were cold, and he let us get our jackets."

Lydia glared at them. Gabbie felt the intensity of her anger and the effort it cost her to speak civilly. "Jackets, yes, not trench coats. Or would you like me to extend your suspension?"

The other boy shrugged. "So? We don't mind hanging out in the office. Mrs. Green lets us collate papers."

"Go to your lockers, and don't let me see those trench coats ever again."

They laughed but the taller boy replied, his voice soft, almost caressing. "We'll try to remember not to wear them in school, Ms. Ketchem, but we might when we're riding around. Say, down Rostoff's Lane, to check out the animals." They shrugged out of their trench coats, tossed them over a shoulder, and walked on.

Gabbie was glad to see them go. They were an obnoxious, insolent pair. She turned to ask Lydia a question then stopped when she saw her face was still livid with fury... and fear.

"Bastards," she muttered. "How dare they threaten me!"

"What do you mean?"

"I live on Rostoff's Lane with my cats, Tiger and Fluffy. Good thing I've got protection against the likes of them."

Gabbie shivered. "You mean a gun?"

"That's exactly what I mean."

"Isn't that a bit—" She bit her lip. "Drastic?"

Lydia shook her head decisively then winced in pain. "Talk to Darren Rollins, our local lawman. He's pretty sure they kidnapped and shaved that poor little Yorkie he found wandering on the beach last winter." She grimaced. "Not to mention the kids they torment, kids who attend school under our jurisdiction and protection."

They continued walking. Gabbie said, "Please tell me I don't have either of them in class."

"Sorry, but Barrett Connelly's in your English Twelve. He's ice cold through and through."

I only have to get through till June. Still, having a student like Barrett Connelly was unnerving. She suddenly remembered Reese Walters' comment last night, about the school being lucky to get her. Which brought back in full force his inferences about the cottage and her unsettling experience in the den.

"Lydia, I'd like to ask you something."

"Certainly. That's why I arranged for us to get together this morning."

Gabbie smiled as she shook her head. "I've plenty of questions about the curriculum and the kids, but this is about the cottage I rented. It belongs to someone named Roland Leeds." She drew a deep breath. "Is there something I should know about it that no one's telling me?"

Lydia eyed her speculatively before nodding.

"Roland's brother, Cameron, lived in the cottage. Last May he was killed. He fell to the beach and broke his neck."

"Oh, how awful!" Gabbie shuddered. As she'd feared, the drop from the bluff was dangerous!

"I'm sorry to have upset you," Lydia said kindly, "but you asked, and someone would have told you sooner or later."

"No, I'm glad you told me," Gabbie said quickly. "It's just so shocking."

"An unfortunate accident."

An accident, Gabbie told herself, but it didn't explain the vibes she'd picked up in the den, much less the voice—if that was what she'd heard.

"He didn't die in the house?"

"Not according to the articles in the newspaper. Why?"

Gabbie hesitated, unwilling to appear foolish.

Lydia patted her arm. "Did you sense Cam's presence in the cottage?"

"Maybe. I'm not sure."

"It can happen, you know. After my mother died, I felt her with me for two days."

This, coming from the practical woman Lydia seemed to be, allowed Gabbie to admit, "I did sense something." Curious, she asked, "What kind of a man was Cameron Leeds?"

Lydia grinned. "Sexy. Edgy. First cousin to Lucifer himself. Women adored him, and men liked him, too, as long as they didn't get burned in one of his business schemes. Best friends with our police chief since they were kids.

"And here we are!" She stopped and unlocked her classroom door and invited Gabbie to enter. "Now," she said before Gabbie could pose another question, "let's get down to business."

For the next hour and a half Gabbie listened, asked questions, and took notes as Lydia filled her in on the three classes she'd be teaching. Lydia was a pro, no doubt about it. Besides telling Gabbie exactly what she was up to in each class, she gave her a thorough rundown of every student: who were the trouble-makers, the work-shirkers, the kids with serious problems.

Lydia paused to down two pills with a cup of bottled water. "I'll be glad when the surgery's behind me and I don't have to live with this pain. Anyway, on to whom you can count on for support and help with discipline problems.

"Suzanne Lindstrom, the foreign language chair, is taking over my administrative duties. If you have an English-type question, talk to Cindy West. I'd steer clear of Tim Jordan, our illustrious principal. He'll listen intensely to your problem and promise intervention, but he's terrified of lawsuits and lets most issues 'settle themselves,' as he puts it. Mac Debrowski, the assistant principal is a screamer. He shouts at the little darlings, then he lets them go. If you want tough backup, call on the guidance counselors. Or Dr. Joe Miller, our superintendent, but only if you're at the end of your rope."

Gabbie bit her bottom lip. "It sounds ominous."

Lydia waved her hand as she laughed. "I was talking worst case scenario. Most of the kids are nice enough. Just a bit spoiled and lazy. We've only a handful like Barrett and Todd. And Todd Ross was merely a hyper kid who got into the usual mischief until Barrett moved here two years ago."

The bell rang, indicating Lydia's two free periods were up. At her request, Gabbie stayed while the third period students piled into the room. Lydia introduced her to the twenty-eight kids who would be her students starting tomorrow. Gabbie smiled nervously, then took a seat in the back of the room.

Lydia led the students in a discussion of the chapter in *The Great Gatsby* that they'd read for homework. She coaxed, cajoled, scolded, and made every attempt to engage their interest and deepen their understanding of what they'd read.

Toward the end of the period, Gabbie gathered the textbooks Lydia had given her, and left the room as unobtrusively as she could. She returned to the Main Office, where Mrs. Green, the head secretary, had her fill out forms and gave her an earful of the school's many rules and regulations.

CHAPTER THREE

I t was close to noon when Gabbie drove out of the parking field, eager to make the most of her last day of freedom. She had chapters to read and lesson plans to prepare. Lydia had made things easy for her by assigning *The Great Gatsby* to all three classes. Her schedule was good, too. She'd be teaching periods three, four, and six, and free to leave school at twelve-forty.

Main Street in Chrissom Harbor consisted of three long blocks that curved like a fat C. The stores on both sides of the street appeared to be fifty years behind the times and not very appealing. The Harbor Diner, with its chrome-colored art deco trim, stood in the middle of the curve, between a bait shop and a bridal gown shop that displayed two garish-colored bridesmaid's dresses—one burnt orange, the other chartreuse—in the window.

The diner needed a complete overhaul, Gabbie decided. She sat down at the only booth whose vinyl seats weren't patched with duct tape and ordered a tuna on rye and coffee. When her order arrived, she bit into her sandwich and was pleasantly surprised to taste white tuna, a trace of mayonnaise, and no celery. The coffee was freshly brewed. No wonder the place was quickly filling up.

Gabbie turned to Chapter One of *The Great Gatsby* and started reading. Having studied the book in college and seen the movie wasn't the same as having the material fresh in her mind so she could discuss plot, character and symbolism with her students. She paused occasionally to jot down what she considered pertinent observations.

"Hello, there."

Gabbie looked up, into chocolate-brown eyes.

"I—I didn't hear you," she said to the grinning police officer who had slipped into the seat across the table. She told herself her heart was racing because he'd startled her, not because he looked downright gorgeous in his brown uniform.

"Glad to know I haven't lost my touch." He thrust forward a hand. "Darren Rollins, police chief of Chrissom Harbor. And you're Gabriela Meyerson, our new English teacher."

She shook his hand. It was calloused and strong. "News travels fast around here."

"That's because not much happens in CH during the winter. Things get livelier when the summer people arrive and boats sail in and out of the harbor."

She nodded and was about to take another bite of her sandwich when he said, "Word has it you've rented Roland Leeds' cottage."

Gabbie bristled. "I don't appreciate Mary Hanley telling my business to everyone in town."

His expression turned solemn. "Mary knows I take a personal interest. My good buddy used to live there."

She was instantly contrite. "I'm sorry—I just heard about what happened to Cameron Leeds last spring."

Darren nodded. "I'm willing to bet Mary didn't offer that bit of information. She's been working like a demon to rent the place, though Roland said not to bother trying 'til the spring. But Mary insisted the sooner someone's living there, the better." He winked. "I hope you got it for a good price. It's kind of rough in spots."

Gabbie laughed. "You could say that again. But Reese Walters stopped by yesterday. He'll be fixing up the kitchen."

"The den's the most comfortable room in the cottage. Cam added it on about six years ago."

Gabbie suppressed a shudder as she considered the room Reese Walters refused to enter, where she thought she'd heard a male voice, and smelled a man's cologne. Not to mention the fallen ashtray and the cold draft. Too many incidents to ignore, when you added them up. She wanted to tell Darren about it, but surely, he was a man of logic and hard facts. There was no point in making him think she was a ditz.

"Lydia Ketchem told me Cameron Leeds was your best friend," she said instead.

"Yep. Since we were kids." Darren cleared his throat. When he spoke again, his voice was hoarse with emotion. "It happened eight months ago, and I still find it hard to believe he's gone. Cam had more life to him than any five people." He smiled. "He was a charmer. Our town Romeo. His animal magnetism drove the women wild."

Gabbie factored in what he told her, then she shook her head. "What I don't understand is how he could have fallen from the bluff. I mean, I saw there's no fence, and that line of straggly trees is hardly a barrier, but he lived there for years. Was it late at night when it happened?"

Darren's face closed like a shuttered window. "No, the report said it was around sunset, as a matter of fact." He eased out of the booth in one graceful motion. "Well, time to go. It was nice meeting you."

She'd offended him with her probing questions. When would she learn to curb her curiosity and her tongue? "Sorry. I didn't mean to pry. It's just that the cottage is so isolated in winter. And then finding out that someone died there." She gave a nervous laugh. "You can understand if I'm uneasy."

Darren stood beside her as he seemed to think this over.

Gabbie quivered. She hadn't been this close to a man in months. With her pulse skittering, she reached for her pen—and jostled her coffee mug, sending it clattering over. Quick as a bullet, Darren pulled napkins from the dispenser and mopped up the liquid before it could damage her books.

"Thanks." She averted her eyes, not wanting to see his expression of exasperation, and began to babble. "I'm sorry. I didn't get much sleep last night. I'm not usually such a klutz." But when she looked up, he was smiling.

"I'm good at cleaning up messes. At least according to my ex-wife."

"That's good to know," she said, responding to both his cleaning abilities and the fact that he had an ex-wife instead of a wife.

"Not really, since she considered it my only virtue."

Darren rested his hand on the booth behind her. "I can imagine how it must feel, coming to live in a new town and discovering that the guy who owned the place you're renting died. But let me put your mind at ease on that score. Cam was dead drunk when he fell to his death. A totally senseless waste of a good man."

Gabbie felt chastened, knowing he'd been reluctant to share this last piece of information. But Darren mistook her silence for worry.

"You're safe at the cottage, but to put your mind at rest, my deputy and I will patrol the area twenty-four, seven. Call the station if you see anything suspicious." He reached inside his shirt pocket and handed her a card. "Here are my home and cell numbers. Call any time."

Gabbie was about to ask if he gave these numbers out to everyone, but he was already halfway to the cash register. He paid, shook hands with the owner, then sauntered out the door.

"Nice package, Chief Rollins," she muttered, "but I'm taking a long sabbatical from men."

Her teeth chattered in the bone-chilling cold as she hurried to her car. She drove to the end of Main Street, turned right onto Cove Street, then continued past two churches, several auto body shops and the new, modern library. Five minutes later she arrived at the supermarket, where she bought enough groceries to last her a week.

With regret, Gabbie bypassed the frozen lobster tails and Belgian chocolate-covered cookies. There was less than five hundred dollars in her account, which had to last her, if she was careful, until she received her first paycheck. She would not put herself in the position of having to borrow from her mother or her sister, each of whom, in her own insidious way, would make her feel like a fool: her mother, for having blown the whistle on her husband; Dina, for marrying Paul in the first place. Gabbie chased away thoughts of her family and her past. Instead, as she drove slowly back to the cottage, she reviewed everything she'd learned about Cameron Leeds.

My God, you're becoming obsessed! she berated herself, and immediately giggled because of the ludicrous way she was casting him in the role of a romantic figure. A cross between Antonio Banderas and Robin Hood. A ploy, no doubt, to keep her anxieties regarding her new job at bay.

When she arrived home, Gabbie tucked a bag of groceries in each arm and maneuvered around a van bearing the logo of Reese Walters's store parked smack in front of the cottage. She frowned as she passed through the front door left wide open to the elements, and kicked it closed when she got inside.

"Sorry about that, ma'am."

She glanced up at a burly man, his Yankees' cap turned backwards, walking towards her. The young Black man behind him gave her a quick smile.

The large man, clearly the job foreman, said, "We just hooked up your new oven and microwave. They're in fine working order."

"Thank you." Gabbie followed them into the kitchen, where she inspected the new appliances. "They look great."

"They're top of the line," he continued proudly and slapped the pile of folders on the counter. "Here are the brochures explaining everything. Read them when you have a few minutes."

"I will," Gabbie assured him though she doubted she'd have time to do anything of the kind.

"That's about it, then." He moved toward the door then turned. "Oh, and your phone's working."

"Thanks again."

"Reese said to tell you he's sorry, but he can't put down the new floor for you till next week. The installer's out sick, and he's behind schedule. He'll call to tell you when."

Gabbie smiled. "Please tell Reese I appreciate his getting me the appliances so quickly."

"Sure enough. My pleasure."

Gabbie saw the men out. She was glad Reese had proved to be a man of his word about getting the kitchen in working order. Still, as she double-locked the front door she made a mental note to ask for his key after the new floor was installed.

She put away the groceries, retrieved the satchel of schoolbooks from the Volvo, then changed into old jeans and a sweatshirt. Her plan was to spend the rest of the afternoon—or longer if necessary—preparing for her first day of school.

Her fears swarmed up like locusts as she started down the staircase. What if she'd lost the knack of teaching after so many years? Would she learn the kids' names quickly? Could she maintain discipline without coming off as an ogress?

Gabbie took a deep breath and focused on her objective: to improve her students' reading and writing skills. She felt excitement well up as she determined to turn her students' experience of reading *The Great Gatsby* into an intriguing adventure. And she'd accomplish that by emphasizing the human condition, she decided as she paused outside the den. After all, every novel was about people. People driven by their emotions—their desires, their loves, their hates, their ambitions.

She found herself standing in the hall, reluctant to cross the den's threshold. The room appeared innocuous, even inviting, backlit by the afternoon sun. Still, there was no denying the energy she'd sensed last night, or the mocking voice she'd heard or thought she'd heard.

Maybe she'd felt Cam's presence, as Lydia put it, because he'd died a violent death. Exasperation forced her to move. "I can't stand here all day," she blurted. "I have to get to work."

She entered the room and looked around. Nothing seemed unusual. No sudden drafts or sense of energy or otherworldly presence. *See,* she told herself. *It's only a large, pleasant room.* Relieved, she sat down in the recliner and began to read.

CHAPTER FOUR

An hour later, Gabbie's muscles ached from working in a cramped position. She stretched her arms overhead and decided it was time for a break. In the kitchen, she poured water into the teapot and set it on her new range to boil. The stove, though a beautiful appliance, was wasted on her as she had no intention of doing much cooking or baking. She'd stick to preparing simple fish and chicken dishes, and not even that tonight. Her dinner would be an omelet or a cheese sandwich.

She returned to the den with a mug of tea, which she placed on the table beside the telephone. She'd no sooner sat down and opened *The Great Gatsby* when a male voice said, "Looks like you're settling in nice and comfy."

She leaped up. The book went flying.

"Who's there? Where are you?" she demanded, her voice hoarse as her eyes swept the room.

At first, she saw nothing, which was terrifying in itself. Then, in the far corner by the sliding doors, she caught a flutter of movement. She spun around in time to watch the figure of a man grow more solid until it appeared almost, but not quite, a three-dimensional living person.

"No, it's impossible!" she moaned sinking into the chair, where she huddled, mouth agape, watching him slowly cross the room.

"You're not! You can't be Cameron Leeds." The name escaped her lips as if it had a life of its own.

"That's me, all right. Cameron Franklin Leeds. In the spirit if not the flesh." He leaned against the edge of the desk, his arms crossed in a casual pose.

Mesmerized, Gabbie stared at the ghost of a man whose striking good looks outstripped her imagination. Khaki shorts and a short-sleeved rugby shirt showed off his lean, athletic build. Black hair framed a square face of even features that reminded her of Warren Beatty in his heyday.

He flashed her a grin. "Hey, relax. I'm one of the good guys."

One of the good guys? It was like a macabre joke. She wanted to run from the room, but she couldn't move. She remained frozen where she sat.

She drew her lips into a tight line. "That's good to kno w..." she said softly, then shook her head, her voice cracking. "Only—I wish you weren't here." She sank deeper into the recliner, eyes wide. "You aren't here. You can't be. You're not—"

Her voice failed her.

She closed her eyes, praying she was in the middle of a dream and that he'd disappear. But when she opened her eyes, he was still perched against the desk, waiting patiently for her attention.

Was she losing her mind? No, she was hallucinating—creating the image she thought she could see, because of what she'd been told about the man who had died while living in this cottage. Except that idea wouldn't fly.

Last night, when she'd sensed his presence and heard his voice, she'd known nothing about Cameron Leeds. How bizarre and unnerving. But at least he showed no signs of being hostile.

"Are you a ghost?" she finally ventured.

"I suppose. Or we might use another term if you prefer: phantom, wraith, apparition, specter. All euphemisms, wouldn't you agree?"

Now that her terror had abated, Gabbie was surprised by how quickly she was adjusting to the reality of her situation: the ghost of Cameron Leeds was haunting—or whatever the right word might be—her cottage. Still, she remembered what Lydia and Darren had said about his reputation with women and could even see how any susceptible female might fall victim to his charms.

Yes, she was shaken by his ghostly appearance, but totally impervious to his appeal! This certainly broke the spell that had rooted her, and she was free to move.

"I'm going to make myself a cup of tea," she declared as she strode out of the room.

"You have one on the table," he called after her. When she didn't answer, he said, "Please come back."

She caught the urgency in his voice and spun around. "Look, I need to be by myself."

"But I have to talk to you."

Oddly enough, he made no attempt to follow her but stood hovering just inside the den. "At least tell me your name," he shouted.

"It's Gabbie. Gabbie Meyerson."

"Are you coming back? Please come back to the den so we can talk."

"Please, Gabbie."

She took three steps and realized he couldn't follow her! He could only manifest inside the den! Though Cam continued to call to her, she didn't respond. Eventually he fell silent.

In the kitchen she braced herself against the sink and breathed deeply to regain her equilibrium.

"There's a ghost in the den waiting to talk to me," she said aloud to get some sort of grasp on the situation.

It sounded weird. It was weird.

She'd heard of people who communicated with spirits and with the dead, but certainly no one she'd ever known. Yet, beneath the strangeness of it all, she sensed exhilaration. Questions swirled in her head, questions that demanded answers.

Though curiosity tugged at her, Gabbie was reluctant to return to the den. After a year and a half of upheaval, she was finally starting over—and all she wanted now was a little peace. Gabbie had had enough excitement in her life these past eighteen months. She longed for a quiet life.

But her need to know finally propelled her back to the den. She hoped to find no sign of Cam. She hoped she'd fallen asleep while preparing for her class and that he'd been a part of an unusually vivid dream.

She hadn't been dreaming. He stood in front of the bookcase. Was it her imagination or was he more transparent? At any rate, he was eager to see her.

"I'm glad you came back, Gabbie. I need to talk to you."

"Why? You don't even know me."

He waved that away. "I know you now. And I can tell you're intelligent and resourceful, as well as a stunning, sexy woman."

"No personal remarks," she warned, "or I'm out of here. Don't tell me I'm the only one you've made contact with."

Cam sighed and nodded. "You are. I wasn't about to scare the women from the cleaning service half to death."

"But you didn't mind scaring me," she said wryly.

"Only because I desperately need to talk to you." To emphasize his urgency he moved closer, crowding her space. Again, she felt a chill in the air.

Gabbie leaped back and upset the table beside the recliner, spilling her tea.

"Sorry—sorry. I didn't mean to frighten you."

"It's the cold," she said, hugging herself.

"I'll try to remember. This is so weird for me."

"That makes two of us," she murmured. "But what did you need to talk about? Why have you come back?"

"To find out who murdered me."

CHAPTER FIVE

Gabbie hugged herself, gripping her upper arms in an attempt to control her trembling body. Murder was a vicious, life-taking act of deliberation. For months after she'd testified against her husband, she'd lived in fear that he might try to kill her. Now she shook her head to deny the possibility of what Cam had just told her.

"Are you sure? Darren said you were drinking heavily and you fell to your death. They found your body on the beach."

Cam gave her a knowing grin. "Darren, eh? Where and when did the two of you have this informative conversation?"

"In the diner," she said stiffly. "When I was having lunch."

"Is that a fact? I see my good buddy lost no time making your acquaintance. I'd beware of the Loving Lawman, if I were you."

"Let's stick to the subject." Gabbie glanced away so Cam wouldn't notice her red ears. Though why she should blush because she'd only just met Darren Rollins was too ridiculous for words.

Then she remembered, "From what I hear, you're the one with the Don Juan reputation."

"Trust me, Darren was never a slouch in that department. But he used to be smart enough to separate business from pleasure." Cam's face tightened with anger. "For once our police chief wasn't as thorough as he should have been."

"What do you mean?" Gabbie asked. It felt surreal, talking to a ghost about his murder.

Cam pointed toward the beach. "Darren knows better than anyone how many times I scrambled down that cliff when we were young. Hell, we both did! We had some great contests, which is how one Saturday night in our senior year I broke my leg, and he sprained his wrist. Pissed off our coach for keeping our basketball team out of the finals.

"And that ancient has-been who examined me afterward missed every sign that I was struck down, right here in this room."

"Darren said they found you down at the beach."

"Yes, but it happened right here."

Gabbie opened her mouth to argue when she remembered the den's piercing coldness the night before when Cam first appeared. Just now, he hadn't followed her into the kitchen because he couldn't. The den was the only room in the cottage where he could appear.

"I understand," she said slowly, wondering at the same time at her use of logic to support what a ghost was telling her about his death. "What isn't very clear is since you know that it happened here in this room, why don't you know who did it?"

"Because," he said slowly, as if explaining to a child, "I was struck from behind."

"Oh." Gabbie sank onto the couch to absorb this latest revelation. She was vaguely aware Cam had started pacing several feet away. He seemed to be waiting for her to speak.

"Who do you think might have done it?" she finally asked.

Cam stopped and scratched his forehead. He looked embarrassed. "It could be any one of a handful of people."

Gabbie gulped. "A handful? You mean like, I don't know, two?"

He cleared his throat. "More like four. Six on the outside."

"Six! Six mortal enemies? You must have been a real upstanding citizen."

"I was what you'd call an entrepreneur," Cam said modestly.

Gabbie tossed back her head of curly auburn hair and let out a rip-roaring guffaw. "A wheeler-dealer, was what I was told."

"That's a bit harsh."

"But accurate, I bet. I know your type. I just divorced the king of connivers."

"And how is he managing without you?" Cam asked.

"He's in jail where he belongs. I helped put him there."

"Oh," Cam said, after a moment of silence.

Gabbie was pleased to note the new note of respect in his voice when he said, "You're a formidable woman."

"I certainly hope so," she answered, with more confidence than she felt. Paul's arrest, trial, and the subsequent divorce had knocked the stuffing out of her, and she was just beginning to feel like herself again.

"Jill Leverette's another formidable woman. She was furious with me the last time we were together, though I don't think she'd actually kill me."

"Was she your lover?"

Cam nodded. "And married to that idiot Fred, whom she should have divorced years ago. Anyway, I was leaving town, and Jill got it into her head she was going with me. Foolish girl. She was so sure she was coming with me, she told Fred about her plans."

"But you didn't want her along."

He grimaced. "She nearly had a stroke when I told her I didn't think it was a good idea for her to leave her daughter."

Gabbie snorted. "Translation, you didn't want her cramping your style."

Cam gave her a wounded look. "That's not it at all. I had a few business stops to make, then I was off to the Cote d'Azur with no definite plans after that. I had no idea where I'd end up. My intention was to get away from CH for while—until things settled down."

"What things?"

Cam rubbed the back of his neck. "Just some leftover mess from a couple old business things. Nothing serious."

"Specifically?" she pressed.

He cleared his throat. "There was one deal in particular that gave me grief. Over a year ago, I bought up connecting plots of land from some local guys and sold them to a builder. He got the official okay to put up a housing development. I saw the plans. Real beauties: five-bedroom Victorians with a front porch, basement, on acre plots."

Gabbie tilted her head slightly, trying to make sense of what he'd just said. "You said you bought the land over a year ago. Why would anyone wait to kill you several months later?"

"Frankly, it's hard to imagine. But seeing the project get off the ground, with signs advertising the new development all over the place, inflamed their resentment. Made it fresh in their minds all over again. Reese Walters was pissed something awful. And Don Terranova threatened to shoot me on sight." Cam snorted "As if he could hit the side of a barn these days."

Gabbie heard what he was really saying. "So, you bought cheap and sold high. Did the dirty on a bunch of your cronies."

Cam shrugged. "Cronies, acquaintances... call them what you like." He laughed. "I found the builder. I practically designed the development, for God's sake. And those four lugs know damn well they're fifty thousand dollars richer than they would have been if they'd held on to their bits of land."

"But they didn't make out as well as you did on the deal," she said sarcastically.

"Don't worry. I made it up to them. Or would have—" He stopped abruptly as a thought occurred to him.

She cocked her head. "Go on. What were you about to say?"

Cam shook his head. "No. Nothing for you to be concerned about. I am—I was—a businessman. Believe me, I honored my debts."

She sighed, exasperated. "If that's the case, then none of them would have been angry enough to kill you, would they?"

"I certainly hope not. Those guys were my friends."

Interesting how quickly his acquaintances gained the status of friendship. Gabbie shut her mind to Cam's discrepancies for the present and concentrated on the facts. "Getting back to that afternoon, tell me what you remember."

He furrowed his brow as he thought. "Let's see… I finished packing around four-thirty and was sitting there in my lounger drinking my favorite gin." He gave a little laugh. "I was kind of fuzzy by then. I went outside to-er 'use the facilities' as they say, then returned to my desk to do some last-minute paperwork. I was trying to make sense of some document when a terrible pain struck the back of my head. I blacked out, thought I came to, and blacked out again. When I woke up, I was dead."

"I am sorry," Gabbie said, trying to take in the enormity of what he'd just told her.

"Which is why I need you to help me, Gabbie."

"Oh, no!" Gabbie raised her palms to ward off his preposterous demand.

"I can tell you're resourceful, and you're good with people. Precisely the type of woman capable of finding out who did the deed."

"I can't, Cam! I won't!"

"Come on, Gabbie. I need you! You're my link to this town. To the world!"

"Look," she said desperately, "I'm terribly sorry someone killed you, but I've come to Chrissom Harbor to recover from the traumas in my own life. I can't get involved in a murder investigation." She stood, ready to flee.

"Gabbie, don't go!"

She paused when she saw the anguish on his face.

"I hate to be melodramatic, but I'll shriek and carry on until you agree to find out who killed me." He proved his point by letting out an ear-piercing noise. Gabbie clapped her hands over her ears.

"Stop it! I get your message, but honestly, there's nothing I can do."

"Just talk to these people." His words came faster and faster. "They'll know you're staying here at the cottage. It's human nature for you to show an interest in my death. Wonder aloud if I had enemies, if my death wasn't an accident. And if someone acts weird or his story doesn't jive, tell Darren. Only don't let him know I started you off on this. He'll cart you right over to the local nut house."

"Cam, I really don't—"

"It's easy enough. All you have to do is go to Logan's Place. It's that log cabin-looking restaurant-bar on the far end of Main Street. Everyone in town goes to Logan's, sometime or another. In fact, Jill often eats there Monday nights with her husband and daughter."

"No, no, no." Gabbie covered her ears and walked out of the den.

He followed her to the doorway and called after her as she climbed the stairs. "Jill works part-time as bookkeeper for Reese Walters, and she does volunteer work, teaching reading to immigrants."

Both amused and exasperated, Gabbie returned to the hall and shook her head at him. "I'll think about it. It's the best I can offer."

"All right." He gave her a heartbreaking smile. "I appreciate whatever you're willing to do. Even if it's just to have dinner at Logan's tonight, to hear what people have to say about me." He paused. "The food's really good."

Suddenly she was hungry and not in the mood to prepare dinner, not even an omelet. Maybe going to Logan's wasn't a bad idea. She could meet some of the townsfolk and find out what they were saying about Cam.

"I might go to Logan's, after all." When that brought on a huge smile, she quickly added, "But that doesn't mean I'm going to play detective. I still have to think it over."

"When will you let me know?"

"As soon as I've decided. Please don't nag. I'm here to teach English, remember? I'll be lucky if I keep one chapter ahead of the kids."

Cam dismissed her concerns with a flick of his wrist. "A piece of cake. I can tell you're a pro."

Gabbie bit her lip. The anxiety she'd been holding at bay, swept over her like a tsunami.

"I'm glad you have confidence in me because I'm terrified. I haven't stepped foot inside a classroom in years."

CHAPTER SIX

L ogan's Place resembled the kind of log cabin Abe Lincoln was supposed to have grown up in, except the restaurant-bar blazed with still-hanging Christmas lights. It stood back from the corner, allowing patrons to park on all four sides of the rectangular-shaped building. Gabbie pulled into one of the few available spots. She tugged open the rough-hewn wooden door and was enveloped by the heavenly aroma of shrimp scampi.

She stood in the tiny vestibule feeling like *Alice in Wonderland* as she debated which of the two doors to open next. The one to her right led to the dimly lit bar. Gabbie peered in. Several patrons sat on stools or leaned against the long counter. The drone of the six o'clock news emitting from the overhead TV seeped through the door.

Maybe later, she decided, and opted for the larger, brighter dining room where couples and families sat at tables covered with red and white checked tablecloths.

The kitchen doors at the back of the room swung open, and a buxom blonde woman in her late forties emerged. She smiled as she approached Gabbie. "Dinner for one?"

"Yes," Gabbie said.

"Follow me, please."

The woman led her to a small table flush with the side wall farthest from the bar. Gabbie sat down on a gingham cushioned chair.

"We have no menus. Tonight, we're serving shrimp. Fried shrimp, shrimp diablo, shrimp sautéed, and shrimp scampi. But we always have burgers and salads, if that's your pleasure."

She disappeared, quickly replaced by a pretty, college-aged waitress in a red-and-white uniform. "Hi, I'm Sarah," she said brightly, then recited the evening's options again—this time with a cheerful reminder: unlimited shrimp, but no doggie bags.

"I'll go with the scampi," Gabbie said, forsaking the cheeseburger she'd planned to order.

"Mashed, french-fried, home fries or rice?"

"Er... home fries."

Sarah grinned. "My favorite. You also get soup and a salad. All for sixteen ninety-five."

"This has to be the best bargain in town."

"Oh, it is," Sarah agreed, "and everyone knows it."

Gabbie ordered Manhattan clam chowder and the blue cheese dressing. Certainly not dietetic, but she'd start an exercise routine once she got settled. Sarah returned a minute later with her soup.

"I made sure it's nice and hot," she told Gabbie.

"Well, thank you." Gabbie replied, touched by the young woman's thoughtfulness. It had been some time since anyone had bothered to please her. She took a spoonful of soup and sighed. It was scrumptious. Plenty of clams and not overly salty.

While she waited for her salad, Gabbie studied her fellow diners and felt a pang of disappointment that none fitted Cam's description of the Leverettes. Sarah served her salad then the main course. The shrimps were huge and succulent, the sauce zesty but not too spicy. The portion was large enough for two, but so delicious, she was determined to finish it all. Who in the world could possibly have room for refills?

She ate leisurely, comfortable with her own company, for once not self-conscious about dining alone. The hum of conversation gave her a sense of community without the obligation of joining in, though Sarah stopped by from time to time to see how she was enjoying her meal.

The people at the next table left. A bus boy cleared it in record time, and the hostess seated one of the many parties that now waited near the entrance. They were a couple in their late thirties, early forties and their sullen teenaged daughter—a tall, slender girl with long brown hair. Gabbie's pulse quickened. Maybe this was Jill Leverette and her family. The woman was pretty and shapely, but her most striking feature was the wavy blonde hair that cascaded halfway down her back. Her companion, a bearlike, lumbering man, wore an intelligent though perplexed expression, as if his mind were miles away resolving a difficult problem. The three sat in silence until Sarah came to take their orders.

Full as she was, Gabbie couldn't resist ordering a peach cobbler to go with her coffee. While she was on her second cup, the party of three finished their main course and prepared to leave. They'd hardly spoken a word, except for the few times the mother asked her daughter a question and was rebuffed with a terse one-word answer. *Poor woman!*

"Was everything to your satisfaction?" the hostess asked as Gabbie stepped up to pay.

"Everything was delicious," Gabbie answered with a grin. "I'll be back soon."

The woman handed Gabbie her change and returned her smile. "I'm Monica. My husband Mike and I own Logan's."

Gabbie put out her hand. "Gabbie Meyerson. Pleased to meet you, Monica."

"We're the closest you'll get to home cooking in CH. Wednesday night's pasta, Thursday's meat loaf, Friday's fish, and Saturday's a surprise. Sunday and Tuesday nights you'll have to fend for yourself."

"Sounds good to me," Gabbie said. She stopped in the vestibule and took a deep breath as though she were about to swim under water. *Here goes. Miss Marple on the trail,* she thought, half-mocking, half-eager to begin. *I'll order a beer and finish it, no doubt, before I think of something pertinent to ask the patrons at the bar.*

The door to the bar swung open and a man held it for her, giving her no choice but to enter. She blinked in the dim light and noticed most of the tables as well as the bar stools were now occupied. The TV was muted as a dreamy sixties song filled the room.

"Over here, Gabbie," she heard someone call.

Gabbie squinted toward the rear of the bar where Reese Walters was waving to catch her attention. She hesitated, then approached the round table where he sat with two men. All three smiled at her, expectant.

"Gabbie Meyerson, meet Terry Lopez and Jack McMahon. Fellas, Gabbie's the new English teacher I told you about. Gabbie, why don't you sit down and have yourself a beer?"

Startled, she paused for a moment, wondering at the ease with which she was achieving her goal. But was that what she wanted, to start asking questions on behalf of a ghost? The thought suddenly struck her as hilarious, and she had to cover her mouth to contain her laughter as she headed for the vacant seat between Reese and Terry.

"Hello, everyone. Reese, thanks for putting in the new appliances so quickly." A pang of guilt prodded her to add, "I'll start using them when I'm settled and find the time to prepare meals."

Reese shrugged. "Use them or not as you please. I'll get to the floor just as soon as I can."

The handsome Latino in his mid-forties turned to her and offered his hand. "Pleased to meet you, Gabbie. I'm Terry, in case you're wondering who is who."

"And I'm Jack." The Jolly Green Giant in his rumpled flannel shirt smiled, showing the gap between his front teeth. Though he looked to be about fifty-five, there was something childlike in his expression. Size-wise they looked like Papa Bear, Mama Bear, and Baby Bear, Gabbie thought, with Reese, the oldest, being the baby.

Terry squared his shoulders. "Welcome to CH. And just in case you happen to need a new car, I'll give you a fantastic deal on a new Camry." He lowered his voice in mock modestly. "I was named Chrissom Harbor Motors Best Salesman two years in a row."

The other men laughed good-naturedly. "Give her a break, Terry," Reese said. "She only moved in yesterday."

"Yeah," Jack agreed. "I bet Gabbie needs a new car like she needs me to deliver more furniture over to Cam Leeds' cottage."

Gabbie felt a stab of anxiety as the three men turned to stare at her. Then she realized they were waiting to see her reaction. She'd give them one, all right, and learn as much as she could by pretending to know nothing. "Cam? I thought the owner's name was Roland Leeds."

The air around the table crackled with energy.

"Both brothers owned it," Reese explained, "but it was Cam who lived there till he died. Happened last May."

"Oh? That's too bad. Was he ill long?"

Reese sent her a look of apology. "I didn't want to say anything last night, with you just moving in and all."

But you didn't mind making enough innuendos to frighten any sensible person, she thought.

"Fell over the cliff to the beach below," Jack said. "Dead drunk when it happened."

Gabbie's hand flew to her heart. "My God, how awful!"

Terry smirked. "Lots of folks 'round here think it's for the best."

Gabbie's outrage was genuine. "How can you say that about a man who's dead!"

Terry shrugged. "A man who lived to make deals, some of them as crooked as the curve of this beer bottle."

Reese grimaced. "Cam used people, even his friends. He pulled all kinds of shenanigans—as long as he ended up with more cash in the bank."

Jack reached out a meaty hand to pat Reese on the shoulder. "You gotta stop chewing at that like a dog on a bone. What's done is done. And you're in good company."

"Right you are, Jack, but I can't get over how you, me, Don and Terry would have made a bundle if that skunk hadn't—"

"Good evening, miss. And what's to be your pleasure?"

Gabbie turned to the publican. He stood broad and solid, most likely a former football player who had managed to keep in shape.

"I'll have a Bud light."

He rejected her order with a disparaging shake of his bald head. "Logan's has choices for the discerning beer drinker. What about a Bass Ale or a Stella Artois? And I have Kilians on tap."

"Oh," Gabbie said, flustered that he'd seen through to her humble opinion of the establishment. "In that case, make it a Stella Artois."

"Stella Artois it is." He winked like she'd passed some unspoken test—pleased with her selection. "I'm Mike, by the way.

And you're the new English teacher who's renting the Leeds place."

"Gabbie Meyerson." She put out her hand and he shook it. "I see there are no secrets around here."

Mike roared with laughter. "News travels fast. As for secrets, CH has more skeletons in the closet than boats in the marina—during the summer months, that is."

He left as a chubby man dropped into the chair between Terry and Jack. He was panting as if he'd been running. Reese made the introductions.

"Gabbie Meyerson meet Don Terranova. Gabbie's come to teach English at the high school."

"She's renting the Leeds cottage," Terry added. "We're filling her in about Cam."

Don Terranova's smile turned into a leer. "Gabbie, you're lucky the guy's six feet under. He'd try to screw you one way or the other."

"Watch your language. There's a lady present," Mike admonished. "Here you are, Gabbie. Glass and beer properly chilled."

She sipped and nodded her approval. "Perfect," she declared. Mike smiled and disappeared. Gabbie returned her attention to the four men, eager to find out more. "Are you saying Cameron Leeds swindled the four of you?" she asked.

"And managed so it was all legal and above board," Terry added, a steely tone to his voice. "He convinced each of us to sell him our adjoining parcels of land over by Miller's Pond. We'd bought them ten years ago as a lark. Cam kept after us how it was marshy land and no one in his right mind would ever want it. Said he'd pour dirt into it, maybe develop it someday down the road."

"And he lied!" Reese's face turned red with fury. "He turned it over, quick as a fox, to a builder. Now they're putting up million-dollar houses on one-acre plots. He bought low, sold high."

Gabbie was delighted with the way things were going. Getting them to talk was as easy as riding a bicycle. "And you didn't know a builder wanted to buy the land?"

Jack shook his head. "We hadn't a clue. At the time we thought selling was a good thing to do, being the land's a bit marshy and the taxes were just hiked up. And I, for one, could make good use of the fifty thou he paid us each."

"Cam was probably responsible for the tax hike, too," Don said. "He was on the tax exploratory committee, remember?"

"Come on," Terry said. "He wasn't that powerful."

"He was a scoundrel, all right." Reese shook his head mournfully. "I'll never forgive him for the way he treated Jill. Plenty of times she came to work with red eyes. The foolish girl thought he'd marry her, but he only brought her grief."

"Jill's problem was taking Cam seriously," Jack said. "He was a great one for living it up. He must have been a nice change from her stick of a husband. Adele says Fred thinks more about his work at the lab than his wife."

"Still, Jill should have known better," Terry said bitterly. "Cam always went after the married women." He tilted back his chair and took a deep pull on his beer before he spoke again. "All in all, the scum bucket got what was coming to him. You gotta admit, there's some justice in the world."

"Yeah," Don agreed. "Good thing he died, or maybe someone would have arranged it for him."

The eyes of the other men shifted pointedly away from Don. Terry and Reese drank their beer. Jack rummaged through his wallet.

So, Gabbie thought, *Cam nailed Don's wife and maybe Terry's.* She'd have to ask Cam. Now was the perfect opportunity to pop the question she'd been dying to ask. She gave a little laugh.

"Are you sure nobody pushed him off the cliff? It sounds like half the town had reason to want him dead."

The four men exchanged worried glances.

Terry spoke first. "Hey, Gabbie, no one killed Cam. The guy may have pulled a few dirty tricks, but he was our friend. The greatest drinking buddy. The most fun guy around."

"Don't get the wrong impression," Reese said. "We're just letting off steam."

"Besides,' added Jack, "Darren got the coroner to examine the body, and old Doc Bradley said it was death by misadventure."

"Who's Darren?" Gabbie asked, glad the light was dim.

"Darren Rollins – CH's police chief and Cam's best friend," Don said. "If there was the slightest chance of foul play, believe me, he'd have been on the case in a minute."

Gabbie was debating where to take the discussion from here, when the matter resolved itself. She yawned. Even her bones felt tired, dragging her toward sleep. She longed to crawl into bed and shut off the light. She rose to her feet. "Sorry to cut it short, but these last few days have exhausted me. It was nice meeting you, gentleman."

As she reached into her pocketbook Jack covered her hand with his. "Our treat tonight, Gabbie. Welcome to Chrissom Harbor."

"Why, thank you," she said, touched despite herself.

The men nodded as though they'd come to an unspoken agreement. Reese said, "We're here most weeknights round about this time, so join us whenever you feel like a bit of company." He laughed. "Mind you, we extend this offer to very few women besides our wives. Though the truth is, my Jane rarely comes down."

"I'm honored," Gabbie said.

Don wagged a stubby finger at her. "Make sure you stop by Tessa's Salon on Elm Street ASAP. Owned and operated by me and my wife. I'll see that you get good head – er, a good haircut and blow dry."

Gabbie patted her mop of curly hair. The man was as coarse as Kosher salt, but she was long overdue for a haircut. Besides, a salon was the ideal place to pick up local gossip. Women were obliged to sit still while beauticians attended to their hair, with little else to do but chat with their neighbors. *Yes!*

"I just might do that." She slipped into her parka and headed for the door.

She drove slowly back to the cottage, sorting through the grievances the four men held against Cam. She found herself sparked with anger on their behalf. Cam had ill-used them, even cuckolded some of them, and these were men he'd known most of his life! She felt sorry for Reese, Terry, Jack, even Don, and hated being put in the position of having to consider that one of them might have killed Cam.

She turned into the rutted driveway and shut off the ignition. Of course, someone else might have killed Cam. Jill? Fred? The murderer might turn out to be a person Cam hadn't thought to tell her about. Gabbie shook her head. So many possibilities, and each and every one of them had a good reason for offing him!

"I can't believe it!" Gabbie facepalmed as reality stuck her like a slap in the face. She was still a sucker. After her ordeal with Paul, she still hadn't learned to protect herself from devious con artists. She'd no sooner heard Cam's sad tale and off she went to Logan's at his so-called innocent suggestion, rushing headlong into playing detective.

Well, she wasn't equipped to play detective. It was sad if someone had killed Cam, but he'd made a slew of enemies. However, her sense of justice prevailed. Murder was serious business. If someone had murdered Cam, that person deserved to be punished. If only there were some way she could convince Darren Rollins to reopen the case.

She let herself into the cottage and started climbing the stairs. Cam called out to her, wanting to know what she'd learned.

"Just that half the town is still mad at you. We'll talk tomorrow. Good night."

"But Gabbie—"

Gabbie closed her bedroom door so she wouldn't have to listen to his plaintive pleas. Tomorrow she'd repeat what his pals had said. Right now, she had to get a good night's sleep.

CHAPTER SEVEN

The alarm awakened Gabbie from a deep sleep. She peered out the window, at the light snow blanketing the back lawn in lacy white. A dart of nervous excitement zipped through her body and settled in her stomach. Today was her first day of school.

She showered, put on the woolen slacks and sweater she'd set out the night before, and went downstairs to eat a light breakfast of coffee and a bagel. Too late, she remembered she'd left her briefcase of school papers and books in the den. As she entered, Cam materialized, blocking her path. Gabbie drew back. One more step and she would have walked right through him!

"Don't do that!" she snapped.

"My, we're testy today." Cam settled comfortably on the couch. "Don't tell me you have first day jitters."

The briefcase was beside the lounge chair. Gabbie reached for it, felt an icy touch on the back of her neck, and nearly jumped.

"Aren't you going to tell me what transpired last night? I've been waiting for your report with bated breath."

He exuded two clouds of frost. Despite herself, Gabbie grinned as she knew he'd intended her to.

"That's right. Loosen up. I'd give you a back rub if I could."

"I'm sure. No doubt step three of your seduction routine. Things will go better if you delete all such comments, okay?"

She hid her grin as a shamefaced expression crossed his handsome features. He'd reacted like a human. He *was* human, except for the fact that he wasn't flesh and blood... and he was dead. Gabbie shivered. It was surreal how quickly she had adapted to conversing with a ghost.

"I met your four ex-cronies Reese, Jack, Don, and Terry," she went on. "They all hate your guts, especially Don for screwing—er, sleeping with his wife."

Cam laughed, clearly delighted. "You found out all that, did you? And in one evening. You're one terrific sleuth, Gabbie. I knew I could count on you."

Damn it, despite his wolflike tendencies, his charm came naturally. His admiration stroked her.

"I bet they cursed me out and griped and groaned, but the truth is, deep down each of them wishes he could've pulled off what I did."

"Pulled it off," she said wryly, "but didn't quite make it home and free."

His voice went soft, almost tender. "I want you to meet Jill and get to know her. She wouldn't harm me, even though I hurt her bad. But maybe Fred did the dirty deed and confessed to her after sleepless nights."

Gabbie had to grin at that. "You loved her, didn't you?" She let loose a chuckle. "And you're first finding it out."

Cam slumped back against the couch, his hands dangling between his knees. "I should have let her come with me. Then maybe we'd be together now—happy in some beautiful place."

"Not necessarily," Gabbie said bluntly. "Where does Jill do her volunteer teaching?"

"At the library, a couple of afternoons a week."

"I'll try to stop there later." Gabbie glanced at her watch. "I have to go. I'll let you know if I learn anything."

"Hold on! Does that mean you've officially decided to find my murderer?"

She thought a moment, surprised that she had. "It means I'll do my best to find out what I can. I can't promise any results."

"Thanks, Gabbie. That's good enough for me. One more thing!" he called out as she walked into the hall. "I wish you'd tell Jill that I miss her."

"And end up in a psych ward? Now don't go soppy on me."

But when she went outside, she felt a pang of sympathy for Cam's ghostly state.

The temperature had fallen to the low twenties, and the cold air made her gasp. The sun reflected brightly on the snow, which covered everything in sight. A postcard view of beauty. Even outdoors in frigid, wintry weather like this, it was wonderful to be alive.

Gabbie spent the first two periods of the morning in the faculty room, meeting various members of the staff. She wished she hadn't drunk those three cups of coffee as she chatted and reviewed her class plans, because when the bell rang, informing her it was time to teach her first class, her stomach felt like a trampoline full of jumping beans.

She walked down the hall to her classroom and stood self-consciously beside her desk while her twenty-eight students sauntered in. They barely glanced at her as they mulled around, chatting. Though the second bell rang, indicating the start of the period, they continued talking.

Gabbie frowned. It was time to instill order. "Take your seats and quiet down!" she said, a few decibels louder than she'd intended.

Most of them looked at her like she was a crazy woman, but at least they obeyed.

"As you know, I'm Ms. Meyerson, your new English teacher." This time her voice came out timidly. Gabbie cleared her throat and continued in a stronger tone. "Mrs. Ketchem told me what you've covered, and we'll continue on from there."

"Where's Mrs. Ketchem?" a tall boy called out from the back of the room. "Out on maternity leave?"

That brought a roar of laughter. Gabbie glanced down at the seating chart. Just as she'd thought—the wise-guy of period three.

"Jeff Borden," she announced, looking straight into the boy's laughing eyes. "Since you're so adept at amusing the class, may I assume you're eager to write a five-page report on humor in American literature?" She flared her nostrils. "And no plagiarism—which means no copying from any book or web site—or you might be brought up on criminal charges."

The boy's face turned white in outrage. "You can't do that! All I said was—"

She cut across his whining. "I heard what you said. And I asked if I might assume you'd like to write a five-page report?"

Jeff looked down at the floor without speaking.

Gabbie smiled. "Is that a 'yes'? Because unless you answer me, that's what you're going to do."

With his gaze still on the floor, he mumbled. "No."

"What's that?" Gabbie kept at him. "I couldn't hear your answer."

Jeff face shot up, flushed with embarrassment and fury. "I said I don't want to write the damn, I mean, the paper on humor."

"Then behave yourself," Gabbie said in a conversational tone, "and we'll get along fine." She looked around at the other students, who were watching her avidly. "The same goes for the rest or you. I've no time or patience to waste on anyone who doesn't want to learn."

Heads nodded.

Gabbie smiled. "Good. Now that we understand each other, I'll take attendance, then we can discuss Chapter Three of *The Great Gatsby.*"

The chapter, as Gabbie knew from having read it the night before, took place at one of Jay Gatsby's parties. She encouraged them to talk about the extravagance of his entertainment, allowing them to stray off the subject and compare it to parties they'd read about out in the Hamptons and in Hollywood. Once she had their attention, she asked questions about Jay Gatsby: How did Nick meet him? What kind of a host is he? Why are all sorts of wild rumors flying around about him?

She smiled as the discussion grew animated, as most of the students caught on to Jay's bland personality. "When he makes a date with Nick– is he just being a friendly neighbor or does he have an ulterior motive?" she asked. "And what about Nick and Jordan?"

She assigned them homework: to write three pages about Nick, Jay Gatsby or Jordan Baker, always backing up their assertions with statements from the text. "Or you might discuss the parties. Who's invited, who shows up. What kind of host Jay Gatsby is. Why you think he might be hosting these parties."

"Remember," Gabbie ended with a wink, "a good book has its secrets and its mysteries. So far, you know only what Fitzgerald wants you to know. But give it your best shot. Just don't go too far afield with speculation and conjecture. Stick to the presented facts."

They were intrigued. They were hooked. When the bell rang, many of the students called out, "Good-bye, Ms. Meyerson. See you tomorrow."

One down, two to go, she thought as she waited for the next class to begin.

This class was smaller—only twenty-two students—and not as chatty. They took their seats and stared at her, waiting. Gabbie thought back on the four years she'd taught English, before she'd married Paul and gave up her tenure to manage one of his offices. Each class was unique and had its own personality.

Her fourth period sophomores listened politely as she explained she was here for the rest of the term because Mrs. Ketchem was out on health leave and that she hoped the transition of teachers would be as smooth as possible. Then she took attendance. She tried to associate each student's face with his or her name. It would take a few days, maybe a week before she got them down cold.

"Theodosia Leverette?"

Gabbie's heart leaped in her chest as the tall girl who'd sat at the table next to hers last night at Logan's raised her hand. She was Jill's daughter. And the silent couple with her were her parents.

"Present. And it's Theo."

It was an order rather than a request. "Certainly," Gabbie said smoothly. "Everyone, please let me know the name by which you'd like to be called."

That brought a titter of laughter, which Gabbie found a refreshing change from the dull silence up till now.

"Charles Russell?" she called out and looked around the room.

A small elf of a boy raised his hand halfway. "Here, miss."

The phrasing of his response inspired laughter. Its mocking tone made Gabbie frown. "We can laugh in here, but never at anyone's expense. Do you prefer to be called Charlie?"

"Yes, I do. Thank you, miss."

This time she heard the twang in his speech and grinned. "Charlie, tell me, have you ever lived in South Carolina?"

There was no mistaking the pride that drew back his shoulders and lifted his gaze. "Born and bred, miss, until we moved here three years ago."

Gabbie felt a warm rush of affection for Charlie Russell. She finished taking attendance and began discussing Chapter Three of *The Great Gatsby.*

When the period ended, she went to the teachers' cafeteria and bought the lunch of the day: spaghetti with meatballs, a salad, and coffee. She sat down at a table with three female teachers. They introduced themselves then went back to discussing their upcoming winter vacation plans. Having nothing to contribute, Gabbie excused herself as soon as she finished eating and returned to her classroom. Her two sophomore classes had gone as well as she could have hoped. One more period, and she was through for the day.

According to Lydia's instructions, five of her seniors had yet to read their essays aloud. This might take up a period or two, depending on absenteeism and whether or not the students had completed the assignment. Lydia had advised her to review grammatical points as they were used both correctly and incorrectly in each essay presentation.

By the time the second bell rang, only five students were present. During the next five minutes, seven more ambled in, each bearing an excuse from a guidance counselor or murmuring they got back late from lunch because they had trouble finding parking spaces close by.

When the thirteenth student showed up, Gabbie introduced herself and announced that she expected them to come to class on time or their grades would reflect their tardiness. An overweight girl, whose tangled shoulder-length hair looked like it hadn't been combed for a month, cracked her gum.

"And no gum chewing," Gabbie said angrily.

"Mrs. Ketchem let us," the girl whined.

"Right, Lynne," a pretty girl who'd arrived on time said. "As long as we chew quietly."

Lynne made a face at her. "You're such an AK, April."

"That's enough, Lynne!" Gabbie glared at her. She hated playing policewoman, and she didn't want to antagonize the class, so she said, "You can chew gum, but crack it one more time and there's no gum chewing for you or anyone in the class."

She took attendance and noticed that Barrett Connelly was one of the three absentees. She checked the grade book to see who still had to read essays, then glanced at the seating plan. "Lynne?" She eyed the gum chewer. "Looks like we're ready to hear your essay. Would you rather stand at your seat or come to the front of the class?"

Lynne flipped frantically through a notebook, spilling loose papers onto the floor. "Oh, no!" she moaned. "Where is it? I know it's here."

"My rules are the same as Mrs. Ketchem's. If you don't have your essay when I call on you, your mark goes down a grade."

"That makes it an F for sure," one of the boys commented. The others burst out laughing.

Red blotches appeared on Lynne's face as she searched through her book bag. Gabbie took pity on her. "While you're looking, we'll hear from Heather."

Heather stood at her seat and began reading her essay "Why High School Students Should Take a Year Off Before Starting College." It was full of platitudes and clichés and soon had the other students yawning and doodling in their notebooks. When she finished, Heather looked up and smiled in anticipation of praise.

"Now that was logical and made its point," Gabbie said. "Any comments?"

The same boy who'd said Lynne would get an F raised his hand. "It's boring!"

Heather's nostrils flared. "Thanks, a lot, Andy. Some friend you are."

"Enough!" Gabbie interjected. "We're here to learn and to critique each other with consideration. Now, writing—fresh, original writing—is difficult to create, so we often take the easy way out by using well-worn expressions. Heather's essay has a good deal of merit. Let's take some of her points and rephrase them so that they sound exciting and new."

April raised her hand. "She could mention one country, like Mexico, for example, and say she wants to spend time there so she can learn the language and get to know the people."

"Very good," Gabbie said.

"Nah. She should fly to Colombia and become the first female drug lord... I mean, lady of the land." A maniacal giggle followed.

All eyes turned to Barrett Connelly standing in the doorway. He tossed a note on Gabbie's desk then strolled to the back of the room, where he sprawled out in the last seat of the middle row.

Gabbie looked at the slip of paper. It was from the principal's office, permitting Barrett back in class. The time stamped on it was fifteen minutes ago. "You're fifteen minutes late," Gabbie said. She noticed he was wearing a black polo and black jeans.

"I had to get my essay from my locker," Barrett said. "The damn thing was jammed, so I went to the custodians' office, but no one was there. I ran into Eddie, and he opened my locker."

His lie was so brazen, Gabbie knew he was challenging her, waiting to see if the new teacher caved. "You'll read your essay after Lynne."

"Oh, did I leave out that part? My essay's missing. Someone must have stolen it."

Gabbie shivered as he let loose another maniacal giggle. When he was done, she met his gaze. "Your grade is an F, unless by some miracle you happen to find it and read it in class tomorrow. The highest grade you may receive is a C, as you've already failed to bring it to class before today."

She shifted her attention to Lynne. "Have you found your essay?"

"Yep." Lynne stood up and began to read "Why Movie Stars and Sports Heroes Aren't Necessarily Good Role Models."

Gabbie listened, consciously ignoring Barrett's fixed stare, which he focused on her breasts when he wasn't writing feverishly in a small notebook. She ignored, too, his occasional giggle, having decided that reprimanding him would only bring him the attention he so clearly desired. The other students seemed unaffected by his presence and were quick to offer their comments as soon as Lynne finished reading her essay.

When the bell rang, Gabbie contained a sigh of relief that the period was over. Barrett was the last student to leave the room. As he passed her desk, he said softly, "Never make an enemy of the person in power."

"What?"

He walked out as if neither of them had spoken.

Shaken, she remained in her seat until students started coming in for the next class. *I'll speak to Tim Jordan about him*, she told herself.

But when she got to the principal's office, the door was closed, indicating he was in conference. Barrett's guidance counselor was occupied as well. She'd speak to one of them tomorrow, she promised herself, as she headed to her car.

CHAPTER EIGHT

G abbie was glad to see it was no longer snowing. The inch or two that had accumulated overnight was melting under sunny skies. The early afternoon brightness cheered her.

She told herself she'd done well her first day of school. She'd taught her lessons and controlled her classes. The kids were fine, except for Barrett Connelly, and she refused to let herself get spooked by some weird kid with a maniacal laugh.

It was one-thirty. The rest of the day spread before her. For a moment she was tempted to stop at the diner for a cup of coffee on the off chance that Darren Rollins would be there. Her heartbeat quickened as she considered pumping him for information that might help her find Cam's murderer. Or perhaps he could give her some vital information about Barrett Connelly.

Bad idea. She sped past the diner. Darren Rollins was the last thing she needed on her plate. Instead, she headed for the public library.

The building was surprisingly modern. To the right of the circulation desk was a prominent display of the latest best sellers. Several older men, probably retirees, sat in the well-lit reading area, poring over magazines and newspapers. Behind the glass that ran along the side of the main room, she saw five or six carrels, each equipped with a computer. The children's section, she noticed, was downstairs, along with rooms used for exercise classes and community meetings.

The process of getting a library card took longer than she'd expected, as she hadn't thought to bring her lease with her. The head of circulation called over the director of the library, a vibrant, attractive woman in her forties. Gabbie explained to Barbara McIntlock that she was a new teacher at the high school and wanted to do research. She was issued a temporary library card and requested to bring a copy of her lease the next time she came in.

"Enjoy our facilities, Ms. Meyerson," the director told her with a smile.

Gabbie thanked her and headed for one of the computers, intent on checking out articles on Fitzgerald and *The Great Gatsby*. One link led to another, and she printed out whatever she found of interest. She soon amassed a good deal of information to share with her students.

It was only when Gabbie felt an urgent pressure on her bladder that she realized she'd been hard at work for over an hour. She turned off the computer, retrieved her library card, and asked for directions to the ladies' room.

"Down the steps, go past the community rooms, then turn left."

Gabbie thanked the librarian and headed for the wide staircase. Downstairs, she passed a large room, its walls filled with an art exhibit of oil paintings. The sign to the rest rooms led her to a narrow hallway with two small rooms on either side. They were set up like classrooms, each furnished with a table and two chairs. One room—its door cracked open—held a young Chinese man and a woman with long blonde hair, their heads close together. The young man read aloud from a book in faltering tones.

When he stopped, the woman smiled at him. "Very good, Richard." She patted her student's shoulder. "Do you understand what you've been reading?"

He nodded slowly. "I think so." He proceeded to paraphrase in stilted English.

"Yes, that's correct."

Gabbie recognized the woman who had sat at the next table in Logan's the evening before with her husband and her daughter, Theo. *Jill Leverette!*

Her heart began to pound. Pieces were beginning to fall into place. *Don't be so dramatic*, she told herself. *This was a small town. Besides, Cam had told her Jill tutored in the library.*

Jill must have sensed Gabbie behind her, because she opened the door. "Did you want something? We have the room for another five minutes."

"Oh—no, sorry." Gabbie's words tripped over each other. "I was on my way to the... I heard someone reading, and being a teacher, I couldn't help—"

Jill flashed a dazzling smile, letting Gabbie know that her bumbling explanation was a perfectly good reason for having stopped to listen. Her smile lit up her face. *She is beautiful!* Gabbie stood staring at the woman Cameron Leeds had loved. Still loved, she corrected herself with an unexpected pang of jealousy.

"I'm not a certified teacher, but I help out with the literacy program."

Gabbie nodded and smiled. "Please excuse the interruption. I'll let you get on with the lesson."

In the ladies' room, she took her time brushing out her curly hair. It was getting unmanageable. She was in dire need of a haircut. Gabbie freshened her lipstick and powdered her shiny nose, thinking with rising excitement that Jill might very well show up after she ended her session with her student, which should be just about now.

Or she wouldn't. Gabbie made a disparaging face at her image in the mirror, then started for the door. It flew open and Jill walked toward her.

"I was hoping you'd still be here," she said by way of a greeting. "After you left, it dawned on me who you are."

Gabbie held out her hand. "Gabbie Meyerson, your daughter's new English teacher."

Jill's grip was firm, her blue eyes sad and wary. "I heard you're renting the Leeds cottage."

Gabbie gave her a wry smile. "And you're about to tell me one of the owners fell to his death there last spring. I didn't know it when I signed the lease, but everyone is quick to fill me in."

"Yes. Cameron Leeds." Jill set her briefcase on the floor and headed for one of the two stalls. When she emerged, she said, "I still can't believe it was an accident."

Gabbie's heart beat double-time. *Go slow*, she told herself. "There's no fence but a row of scrawny trees along the edge. And the drop is pretty steep, at least two stories, wouldn't you say?"

Jill answered over the sound of running water as she washed her hands. "Cam lived and played at that cottage most of his life." She gave a humorous laugh. "And it wasn't the first time he went over the bluff."

"I heard he and Darren Rollins both did – when they were in high school."

Jill nodded. "True enough. Do you know why?"

Gabbie laughed as she shook her head. "Give me time. I've only been living here since Sunday."

"They were fighting over a girl. Rosetta Davis, my sister Janice's friend. Rosetta's married now with three kids."

"Fighting over a girl? I thought Darren was Cam's best friend," Gabbie said. She opened the door, and they walked single file down the narrow hall.

"Best friend and avid competitor. In most things," Jill added softly.

But not where you're concerned, Gabbie mused. They climbed the steps without speaking. The pause in their conversation felt natural to Gabbie. Though she and Jill were strangers, Gabbie sensed the ease she felt in Jill's presence was mutual. *I like this woman*, Gabbie decided.

She stopped at a table displaying books labeled "favorites" while Jill continued on to the circulation counter. Gabbie selected a mystery she'd been meaning to read, then went to stand behind Jill who was having a problem checking out a book. The clerk—a wisp of a woman, as devoid of color as her gray sweater and skirt—was insisting Jill couldn't take it out because she hadn't returned *How to Be Happy*, which was now overdue.

"Sonia, I returned that book a week ago." Jill spoke slowly, as though to a child. "You can look it up on the computer."

"The computer's down," she snapped, "and we're too short-handed to send someone into the stacks to verify that you've returned it."

"How absurd!" Jill fumed. Ignoring the "Employees Only" sign, she marched through an open door that led to offices and called out. "Barbara! Could you please come out here. I need your assistance with another problem."

Barbara McInlock appeared immediately. Gabbie watched the director and Jill exchange knowing glances. Jill explained her problem, ignoring the blatant way Sonia eyed her maliciously as she spoke.

"Sonia," the director said, glancing at the clerk like this wasn't the first time they'd had this talk.

"Yes, Barbara?" Sonia's expression was now as bland as her tone of voice.

"Please check this book out for Jill. We can take her word that she's returned *How to Be Happy*."

Sonia nodded and did as she was told. Jill gave a huff of exasperation and headed for the exit. *What's in store for me?* Gabbie wondered as she handed Sonia her temporary library card.

The piece of paper fluttered to the floor. Sonia bent to pick it up. "But this address is the Leeds cottage! No one lives there."

Gabbie reined in her impatience. Did everyone in this town have to comment on her residence? "I live there now and will continue to do so for the next few months."

"Oh." Sonia's ears were red as she checked out the book and handed her the receipt indicating the due date.

Outside, the sun was slipping behind the trees. The temperature must have dropped at least twenty degrees. Gabbie pulled up the hood of her parka and hurried to her car. Two spaces away, Jill was closing the trunk of her car.

"That Sonia! Did she give you a hard time, too?"

"Not really. She just commented on where I was staying—like everyone else in this town."

Jill sighed. "She hates me, though for the life of me, I can't imagine why."

"She certainly was rude. I wonder why they don't fire her."

"CH is a small town. Everyone knows Sonia's story and feels sorry for her."

"What do you mean?"

Jill moved closer and lowered her voice. "Sonia was a year behind me in school. She was a wimp from the day she was born.

The kid the bullies always picked on." Her voice dropped to a whisper. "When she was in eleventh grade, she was raped."

Gabbie shivered. "Oh, how awful. Did they find the guy who did it?"

Jill sighed. "The rumor is some boys a couple of towns from here invited her to a party. They picked her up in a van and took turns with her. Sonia never said who they were. When the cops finally went to talk to her, she claimed she couldn't remember any of the details."

She bit her lip. "At the time, some people thought she was afraid to name names because the boys were from CH, but I don't believe it."

"The poor thing!" Gabbie exclaimed. "To have something that awful happen when you're sixteen or seventeen." She shivered as she suddenly thought of Cam the womanizer and wondered if he could have been the unnamed rapist.

"I feel bad for her, but Sonia's her own worst enemy. She's as difficult and nasty as they come." Jill frowned. "And I run the risk of seeing her sour puss every time I open my front door."

"How come?" Gabbie asked.

"She's my next-door neighbor. Lucky me." Jill shook her head and flashed her beautiful smile. "But enough negativity. I'm pleased to have met you, Ms. Meyerson."

"Gabbie."

"And I'm Jill." She waved and got into her car.

Gabbie drove home, rehashing every fact Jill had told her. No mention of her husband, Fred. Had Fred killed Cam? It seemed a bit farfetched and melodramatic, given that he and Jill were still living together as a couple. But maybe Fred had killed Cam so he and Jill would still be a couple. Although, judging from last night, they were barely on speaking terms. Surely, Jill wouldn't stay with Fred if she knew he'd murdered Cam, the operative word being "knew."

There were too many suspects, Gabbie mused as she un-locked the front door. Besides, how was she supposed to open up a murder investigation when Cam's best friend, the town's police chief, had ruled his death an accident? Obviously, she had to find evidence or proof or something that would convince Darren Rollins he'd been wrong. And how was she supposed to perform this amazing feat?

Thank goodness Cam wasn't around. Gabbie changed into jeans and a polo before preparing her dinner. With some trepidation, she headed to the den after finishing her meal and tidying the kitchen. She had prep work to do, and while Cam was the proverbial albatross around her neck, she owed him a report of what she'd learned so far, though it amounted to nothing.

She'd gotten half an hour's worth of reading and note-taking completed, when a draft of cold air chilled the room. This time she wasn't surprised when Cam materialized beside the glass doors.

"Hello, Gabbie. How was your first day of school?"

"Fine." She grinned. "I met Jill this afternoon. In the library."

"How is she? How does she seem?"

"Nice. Unhappy. We got to talking. She strikes me as a kind person."

"And that surprises you?"

"Kind of," Gabbie admitted.

"You expected a big, brassy blonde. What other type of married woman would have a longstanding affair with the town sex machine? But it just happened, Jill and me. If you knew Fred, you wouldn't wonder why."

She laughed. "I saw him at Logan's last night. He hardly said a word all through dinner."

Cam stretched out on the couch and narrowed his eyes. His expression turned forbidding, giving Gabbie an idea of the tough businessman he must have been. "Believe me, he's more toxic than the bland, boring persona he assumes."

Gabbie raised an eyebrow. "Quite the psychiatrist, aren't you?"

Cam laughed, delighted by what he considered a compliment. "You have to know how people think if you're going to outwit them."

He was sharp and surprisingly easy to talk to—for a ghost—but she wasn't in the mood for small talk. "Jill finds it hard to believe your death was an accident."

"I'm glad," he said quietly. She sensed the effort it took not to ask what else Jill had said about him. "Now to get Darren to see it that way. If we found one shred of evidence that pointed to murder, he'd reopen the investigation in a flash."

Gabbie gazed around the den. "One shred of evidence," she echoed. "The trouble is this room was never treated as a crime scene. Everything's been trampled on and handled."

Cam grimaced. "And Mary Hanley had some pretty thorough cleaners in here. I wasn't exactly the best housekeeper in town."

Gabbie forced herself to bring up the next subject. "Jill told me Sonia Russell was raped when she was in high school."

He sat up to stare at her in obvious surprise. "How did that happen to come up in the conversation?"

Gabbie sat down at the desk chair. She shook the snow scene paperweight and watched the snow settle before going on. "Sonia was clerking at the circulation desk. She gave Jill a hard time."

Cam chuckled. "That's Sonia, all right. She has her ways. Does it to make herself feel important."

Gabbie gave him a searching look. "I was just wondering. You didn't have anything to do with... that business."

Cam's hand flew to his heart. "Dammit, Gabbie, what do you take me for? I never forced a girl or woman for as much as a kiss. In fact—" He stopped, suddenly deep in thought.

"In fact, what?"

His voice drifted back to old memories. "It was Darren and I who found Sonia that night on the beach a couple of miles from here. It was early April, and cold as a witch's – er – nose. Must have been spring recess or something, because I was home from college."

"Anyway, Sonia was dressed in a frilly party dress. Some cheap rayon-type of material with ruffles—nothing the girls we dated would be seen dead in. We noticed right away it was dirty and torn. She must have heard us call to her, but she just sat there, hunched up on the sand, hugging herself and moaning.

"We got her into the car and Darren was all for going to the police. That's when Sonia suddenly found her voice and started screaming and cursing, telling us to take her home. She said her father was out drinking, and he'd kill her if he found out she'd left the house against his orders, even if it meant the boys who hurt her didn't get punished."

"That's when you knew she'd been raped?"

Cam nodded. He was growing transparent, she noticed. Their conversation would be ending soon.

"She denied it at first. Then the story came tumbling out: how she met two of them outside the candy store in town, and was flattered when they flirted with her. They invited her to a party. Said they'd come and pick her up. Sure, they did, only the party turned out to be four of them and poor Sonia in a van. Real scuzzes from two towns over. We made her promise to go to the doctor."

"And the scum got away with it." Gabbie snorted. "How typical."

"As far as the police were concerned." Cam grinned. "But let's see, by the time June rolled around, two of them had smashed noses, one a broken arm, and the other ended up in the nut house after we scared him half to death." He chuckled. "We snuck into his house one night. Dressed as ghosts, actually."

Gabbie pressed her lips together to keep from laughing. "Did Sonia find out?"

"Darren and I let her know we took care of the bad guys, but she never said one word. Not 'good' or 'thanks, fellas.' After that night she was weirder than ever. At least nobody bothered her again. If you don't count the beatings her father gave her till he died a year or two later. A nighttime hit-and-run got him when he was staggering home drunk. No one mourned him – not Sonia or any of his three sons."

Gabbie shuddered. "Poor Sonia."

"Just another sad CH story. There are plenty of 'em."

Gabbie looked at her watch. "I hate to chase you, Cam, but I've still some work to do."

"Just one more thing." Cam gnawed at his lower lip. "If you're going to keep on playing Sherlock Holmes, I'd better tell you about the money."

"What money?"

"The half million dollars arranged in neat piles that filled the bottom drawer of the desk you're sitting at. My traveling money, you might call it."

She stared at him. "My God, Cam. Did you usually keep sums that large in the cottage?"

"Of course not. I'm a great believer in making your money work for you—invest and wisely. This was cash from a deal that suddenly came my way. When I—er came back, it was gone." He chuckled. "Not that it matters. Like they say, you can't take it with you."

Gabbie thought a minute. "Did you come back immediately?"

"Time passed. About a week, I'd say."

"Then how do you know Darren didn't find the money and hand it over to your brother?"

"I was completely disoriented at the time – don't ask me why. I couldn't have drunk that much, but I remember hearing someone—the murderer—rifling through the drawerful of money. Next thing I knew he was finishing me off."

Gabbie was livid. She stared at his fading figure. "Damn you, Cameron Leeds, you might have told me this up front. Whoever killed you, did it for the money. It's as simple as that."

"Now that's precisely why I didn't tell you. I knew you'd jump to that erroneous conclusion, right off the bat. Most likely, someone came after me for an entirely different reason."

"No doubt for being the most infuriating, maddening creature that ever lived!"

She grabbed up her books and papers and flew out of the room. "I won't be back for days," she shouted from the hall. "Maybe a week. And I'm beginning to think that whoever killed you did the world a favor!"

CHAPTER NINE

Gabbie spread out her schoolbooks and papers on the kitchen table. She was so engrossed in what she was doing that the ring of the doorbell had her leaping up from her seat.

"Who's there?" she demanded through the wooden door.

"It's Chief Rollins. Darren. May I come in?"

Her heart fluttered as her fingers fumbled with the lock. "Hi. Anything wrong?"

"Nope." He grinned, bringing in the scent of cold night air and a trace of tangy aftershave. "I was doing my nightly surveillance, and decided I needed a break. Was hoping for a friendly cup of coffee and a pit stop."

"Sure. Go on." She gestured upstairs. "I'll put on the kettle."

He came thundering down the stairs five minutes later and joined her in the kitchen. He glanced at her schoolbooks on the table. "Hope I'm not interrupting."

"You're not, since you're only staying till you finish your coffee."

"I see you're a woman who sets boundaries." His tone was admiring rather than offended.

"I have to," she said, hoping he wouldn't ask why. Darren didn't. She set the steaming mug in front of him. "I've milk and sugar, but no cake."

"I take it black with three teaspoons of sugar."

"I'll remember that," she said and sipped her tea.

She liked the way he drank – neatly, without slurping or making weird noises. He cupped his hands around the mug, grateful for the warmth it gave off. Her gaze rose and she saw he was studying her.

"The place feels cozy with you here," he said.

She shrugged. "It's the new appliances. I haven't done a thing but buy some supplies and move in."

Darren smiled. "I know this cottage as well as the house I grew up in. Cam and his little brother, Roland, used to stay with their grandfather summers and holidays. He used to say it was like staying with Santa Claus."

"Why? Were his parents poor?"

"One parent – his mother – if you can call her that. His father took off after Roland was born. And she was poor, all right. Drank and gambled what little money she earned as a waitress."

"No wonder," Gabbie mused.

"No wonder what?" He sent her a questioning glance.

Gabbie felt her cheeks grow warm. "I've heard a few stories about Cam, how he was always making business deals. I suppose he wanted to make sure he never was poor again."

"That's a reason, not an excuse," Darren said brusquely.

Gabbie was pleased that he didn't share Cam's easy morality.

"Anyway," Darren continued, "when Cam was about twelve, Gramps died. He left the cottage to the boys, to be turned over to them when Cam turned twenty-one. Cam's mother moved them into the cottage full-time, along with her second husband.

A few years later she wanted to sell it. The boys said no, so she fought them for possession in court. Said her father must have been touched in the head to leave his cottage to kids instead of his own daughter, but the judge held firm. She and her third husband moved to Arizona a few years after that." Darren grimaced. "Not that it mattered. After their grandfather died, Cam and Roland brought themselves up. Joyce Leeds wasn't meant to be a mother."

Gabbie nodded. It was interesting to learn about Cam's childhood, but she needed to focus on more recent events. "You must miss him a lot."

"Miss him?" Darren snorted. "Not a day goes by when I don't curse him roundly for depriving me of his company. We were soul brothers, Gabbie. I'll never have a friend like that again."

"I know he fell to his death."

Darren jutted his chin in the direction of the Sound. "The fool tumbled down to the beach below. He'd been drinking. You could smell it a mile away."

Gabbie propped her elbows on the old wooden table. "Did you ever consider the possibility that it wasn't an accident?"

His eyes crinkled as he smiled at her. "You mean, do I think someone pushed him over? You never saw Cam. He stood six foot four and was strong as the proverbial ox." His smile disappeared. "There were no signs of a fight or a struggle anywhere on the body."

She was treading dangerous territory, challenging his professional expertise, but she owed it to Cam to find out everything she could. "What did the medical examiner find?"

His eyes narrowed. "Old Doc Bradley, our coroner, examined the body. He determined all wounds and contusions resulted from the fall."

Gabbie frowned. "Old Doc Bradley? What is he, a veterinarian?"

"A GP who cares about people. The kind of doctor you'd want taking care of you, whether you caught pneumonia or were hit by a car." Darren stood, legs apart, glaring at her.

Shooting stance, she thought, shivering. If he had a gun in his hand, which of course he didn't.

"Doc Bradley was a medic in Vietnam. He's seen more bodies, dead and alive, than any two MEs anywhere."

Gabbie nodded, pretending to accept Darren's defense of the old doctor. But Darren was wrong. Someone had killed Cam, and the old doctor had overlooked the cause of his injuries. Now the question was: did Darren truly believe Cam had fallen drunk to his death?

Or—the horrible possibility sprang up like a jack-in-the-box—did Darren deserve an Oscar for his performance of outraged innocence because he murdered Cam?

She closed her eyes, intent on making the preposterous thought disappear. Darren was a cop. An honest cop. *How do you know?* a small voice threw back at her. *Because he made you think so.* When she opened her eyes, he was setting his mug in the sink.

"It's time I got going."

Darren moved toward the door. She hurried after him. "I'm sorry. I didn't mean to push your buttons. It's just—"

"I know." He touched her shoulder, sending a rush of tingles through her body. "When civilians find out about accidents like this, they often assume it was murder. At any rate, I shouldn't have gotten so uptight about your questions."

"He was your best friend," she murmured.

"That he was."

She drew in breath, relieved he was no longer angry at her. He lowered his head toward her, and for one crazy moment she thought he was going to kiss her.

Instead, he winked. "Good night, Gabbie. Thanks for the coffee."

The next morning, Gabbie leaped out of bed, eager to leave the cottage. She didn't mind the icy wind that stung her face as she cleared the windshield or the slippery drive to school. It was a relief to get away from a nagging ghost and tempting thoughts of a sexy cop who just might have murdered his best friend.

A few of her students waved as she passed them in the hallway. She returned many smiles and "good mornings" to the staff. She stopped at the guidance office, noticed that Barrett's counselor wasn't in his office. The psychologist's door was closed. *I'll try later.*

Her third and fourth period classes went smoothly. She had students read their homework assignments aloud and used them as springboards for a lively discussion about how the various characters had influenced the story's plot so far. Then she read to them from chapter four until the bell rang.

Finish the chapter for homework and write a two-to four-page summary," she said, her tone light. "Keep it in the present tense and give it a good once-over when you're done." She smiled. "I might count it as a grade—or maybe we'll just talk about it in class tomorrow. Who knows? Maybe even a little quiz." She added, "Our first one together."

There were groans, but plenty of students calling "Bye, Ms. Meyerson!" and "See you tomorrow!"

She was disappointed that neither Theo nor Charlie were among the students warming up to her. As she left the room, she found them waiting for her out in the hall.

"Is the Photography Club meeting this Friday afternoon?" Theo asked. "There wasn't a notice in this week's announcements."

Gabbie swallowed. She'd agreed to be the advisor of the Photography Club as part of her job. It had all but slipped her mind. "Well, I hadn't planned on holding a meeting yet."

"But we always meet the second Friday of the month." For once Theo sounded upset rather than angry.

"Sometimes the last Friday, too," Charlie added. He was bouncing up and down on the balls of his feet. *Must be a nervous tic*, Gabbie thought.

She smiled at each of them, but neither smiled back.

"I suppose we could meet this Friday. I've been so busy with schoolwork, I haven't given it much thought. It's kind of late to put a notice in this week's announcements."

"Don't bother," Theo said. "Just a few kids besides us come anymore."

"Lots of other kids used to come," Charlie explained. "Until Barrett—"

"Charlie!" Theo elbowed him.

Gabbie felt a prickling between her shoulder blades. "What happened?"

"Nothing happened," Theo said gruffly. "Let's go, Charlie, or we'll be late to class."

"Let the other kids know we're meeting this Friday," Gabbie called after them. "And don't forget to bring your cameras."

Charlie spun around. "That's great, Ms. Meyerson. Will we meet in our English room like always?"

"You got it."

"Thank you." Theo's words came out strangled. Sullen though she was, her mother's lessons in manners were clearly something she couldn't ignore.

"See you tomorrow," Gabbie called after them, more cheerfully than she felt. She knew zip about photography. It looked like she'd be spending another afternoon in the library, this time learning the ABCs of photography.

Once in the teachers' lounge, Gabbie reached for the cup she'd brought in the day before and filled it with coffee from the half-full carafe.

"Coffee klatch is five dollars a month," said a tall, skinny Ichabod Crane-type.

"Do I pay you?" Gabbie asked, reaching into her pocketbook.

"If you like. Give me two dollars, seeing half the month is gone."

"I'm Gabbie Meyerson." She handed him two singles and watched him jot down her contribution in a tiny note pad. When pad and pen were back in the breast pocket of his tweed blazer, he stuck out his hand.

"Oscar Tweeney, Science. Welcome aboard."

Gabbie sat down on one of the two worn couches and sipped her coffee. Two women teachers came in and smiled at her then resumed their conversation. Gabbie joined their discussion about New Mexico, an area she'd visited with Paul a few years ago. At the end of the period, she rose with the others, rinsed out her cup, then walked back to her classroom. As she passed through the doorway, she realized she'd forgotten to speak to anyone about Barrett.

Only Barrett and another student had to read their essays aloud. Gabbie didn't know how long this would take, so she'd planned to have the class spend the remainder of the period writing on one of several topics she'd chosen.

Her seniors straggled in after the bell, some with coffee, others with soda and snacks. *Entitlements of the graduating class. Well, she'd see about that!* When they were seated, she told them they could bring in food if they liked. They could even sit in a circle. But coming in after the bell would count against them.

"How, Ms. Meyerson?" April asked.

Gabbie nodded. "I suppose a minute a point would be too harsh."

"How about you start counting five minutes after the bell?"

Gabbie met the dark liquid eyes of a tall, broad-shouldered black boy with riveting good looks. Byron Stokes. Quarterback, center forward, and quite the ladies' man among all the girls, or so she'd heard.

Gabbie considered. "All right, Byron. A five-minute starter and not one second more or it counts against you. But be warned, I start when the period begins, so don't come whining to me if you've missed the homework assignment or a test announcement because you decided to dawdle in the halls with your friends or sweetie of the moment."

She busied herself with her grade book, pretending not to hear their reactions, until too many curse words sullied her ears.

"One more thing," she said conversationally. "No curse words, and I mean none, beginning with damn and hell."

"How will that count against us, Ms. Meyerson?" Heather asked.

Gabbie smiled. "You'll find yourself writing all sorts of papers."

"But curse words are part of our language, Ms. Meyerson," Barrett said.

Utter silence as all eyes turned to the doorway that framed him like a picture. *Evil in black*, Gabbie thought, eying his black clothes and black hair.

She swallowed, then forced a smile. "Of course they are, Barrett. Everyone knows that. Just as everyone knows it's not acceptable to use them in the classroom. Please sit down. Your tardiness has been noted and will be reflected in your quarterly grade."

"Five minutes after the bell," Lynne pointed out.

"Lance," Gabbie said, nodding at the plump, unhappy boy in the second row. "We're ready to hear your essay."

She deliberately turned her head away from Barrett. When she looked at him a minute later, he sat sprawled in the last seat in the row beside the windows, his eyes glued to a distant spot outside.

Lance mumbled his essay as though it were a long, strung-out sentence. The subject was movies he considered to be classics and why he liked to watch them again and again. An interesting subject, but his comments were so vague and repetitive, Gabbie had to cover her mouth to hide a yawn.

"Bor-ing," Heather said as soon as he finished. Then added quickly. "But a good topic, Lance."

"Yes, a very good topic," Gabbie agreed, watching Lance's face turn strawberry red. "Let's help Lance spice up his essay."

"Lots of sexy women," someone called out.

"Torture scenes," Lynne added, cracking her gum. "Sorry," she quickly apologized before Gabbie had a chance to reprimand her.

"All very graphic," Gabbie said, "but think, what makes a movie a classic?"

Dexter raised his hand. Though this was his first participation in class discussion, Gabbie shook her head. "I said think. And after you've thought, write down five distinct, specific elements that make a film a classic. You have five minutes."

She walked through the rows, delighted to see brains in action. The results were creative, too. When she got to Barrett, she saw he was drawing tiny pictures in his spiral notebook. She caught a glimpse of a burning house. Two figures were lying on the ground. She shook her head, recoiling.

"Start working on your list," she said.

"I'm thinking," Barrett answered, and inked in a knife stabbing one of the bodies on the ground.

I must speak to his guidance counselor, Gabbie told herself as she walked back to her desk. The class spent the next ten minutes going over their lists. The kids all wanted to read theirs aloud, and much as she hated to squelch their enthusiasm, it was time to move on. She took a deep breath, let it out slowly.

"We've one more essay to listen to. Barrett, are you prepared?"

Instead of the excuse she'd expected followed by a request for an extension, Barrett surprised her with a broad smile. "Good thing I had a copy of my essay at home. I'm ready when you are."

She disregarded his impudence. "Please begin."

"I've chosen to dispute a slogan from the Bible."

"Slogan?" Gabbie questioned. "A slogan is something we associate with advertising or propaganda."

"Whatever." Barrett shrugged. "My essay is 'The Strong Shall Inherit the Earth.'"

The essay was every bit as horrendous as she'd feared it would be. The writing was amazingly powerful, the language almost beautiful in its simplicity, as Barrett defended his theory that the strong had always ruled because they were entitled to rule. When he started extolling Hitler's virtues, she interrupted.

"Enough, Barrett. What you're saying is offensive."

"I've every right to read my essay aloud just like everyone else."

"Your essay isn't like everyone else's," she retorted. "Please leave it on my desk and take your seat."

"Whatever." He did as she'd requested and returned to his drawing.

After class, Lydia sat down in the English office and read Barrett's paper. The last part was the worst: "The unproductive, the elderly, the sick and insane should abide by the laws of the strong and able. Those unable to add to the society of the strong should be put down out of kindness to themselves."

"Out of kindness to themselves!" She spit out the words as she gathered her belongings and strode off to the guidance office.

This time she was in luck. George Breck was leaning back in his swivel chair, gazing out the window. He was a large man—his navy blazer gaped open to reveal a considerable paunch. She stepped past the secretary, who was on the phone, and knocked on the open door.

"Hi, George, Gabbie Meyerson. I've taken over Lydia Ketchem's classes, and I need to speak to you about a student."

Dark, intelligent eyes assessed her. "Come in, Gabbie. Please close the door and take a seat."

When she was sitting, he asked, "How're things going?"

"Fine except for Barrett Connelly."

A slow smile spread across George's face. "Tell me why I'm not surprised."

Encouraged, Gabbie went on. "He's uncooperative, draws pictures of death and destruction, and he wrote this." She thrust the essay toward him.

George scanned it quickly and handed it back to her.

"Not a democratic thinker, is he?"

Gabbie glared at him. "This is far from a joke. I think Barrett's dangerous. God, have you people forgotten Columbine?"

"Of course not. And we're well aware of Barrett's eccentricities. But we've no indication that he's dangerous."

"That's not what I've heard about him and his pal, Todd Ross."

George picked up a pencil and balanced it between his two index fingers. "Yes, we've all heard the stories. But hearsay and having evidence of criminal behavior are two different things entirely. Without proof to back us up, the school district could be sued for accusing a student of criminal activities."

"What about zero tolerance! Schools are suspending students for making threatening comments."

"We do what we can. If Barrett and Todd wear black trench coats to school, they get in-school suspension. I'm afraid that's all we can do legally without proof of dangerous intent."

Gabbie shook the essay she held in her hand. "What about this? It shows violent tendencies."

"It shows he's taking issue with a Biblical quote. Professing a philosophy that runs contrary to our belief system."

"A philosophy our country considered evil enough to fight against," she said dryly.

"I'll make a copy to keep in his folder," George said, heading for the copy machine in the outer office.

She rose as he reentered his office and handed her the essay. "And that's it?"

"For now. Sorry." He let out a rueful chuckle. "I don't even think I can change his English class this late in the year. Too many teachers have asked me to remove him from their classes."

"I'm not asking you to." She sat down again. "But I'd appreciate your telling me about his background."

George stretched both arms above his head then clasped them behind his head. "Barrett's an only child. Father's a garage mechanic, mother's an RN. Surprisingly enough, both parents are decent, caring people. Which is why, when he got into trouble in Queens, they moved out here, thinking a rural-suburban environment would make a difference. They've tried putting him in therapy a few times, but Barrett wouldn't cooperate."

"What kind of trouble did he get into?"

"Truancy. Caught lifting a few items from a local store." He paused. "His parents told me he'd been suspected of starting a few small fires."

Gabbie's heart began pounding. "Two of the big three," she murmured.

George nodded. "We've no proof of the fires or the dog shaving incident."

She appreciated his honesty. "No proof but you'd think—"

"Sorry to cut you short, but I've an appointment in two minutes. I'll let you know if I hear anything and would appreciate it if you'd do the same."

"Sure," Gabbie said, deciding she liked George Breck. He'd just told her, in his own fashion, that much as he'd like to take action, there was nothing he could do until Barrett did something worse.

CHAPTER TEN

Lunch was a turkey sandwich at the Harbor Diner. Gabbie wondered if Darren would put in an appearance and was both disappointed and relieved when he didn't show up. She drove over to the library, intent on boning up on photography. She found a book so wordy and precise in its details about shutter speed and light, F stops, and digital cameras, she quickly returned it to the shelf. She flipped through books of photographs. Some nature shots were heartbreakingly beautiful. Seeing them gave her an idea.

Instead of focusing on the technical side of photography, she'd work on composition. She knew enough about that from the various art appreciation courses she'd taken over the years. She smiled, planning as she went along.

Gabbie decided she'd bring whatever kids showed up Friday afternoon out to the woods behind the school. She'd select one aspect of nature—say, a tree—and ask them to capture its unique qualities. Each student would pick a tree they found appealing and photograph it, illustrating its shape and color, texture and size. It would be a lesson in keen observation. Viewing an ordinary object from an original and personal perspective. Either set off by itself or as a part of the whole.

Yes! Excited, Gabbie started searching through the books for photographs of trees. She'd take these to the meeting and show them to the kids before they went out and found their own tree to photograph.

She was about to check out the books and leave for home, when she decided to look up the newspaper reports of Cam's death. *Newsday* must have run an article about it, as well as the two or three local papers that covered the news of Chrissom Harbor and the neighboring towns.

Gabbie went over to the reference desk and asked to see the old copies of Long Island papers.

The gray-haired librarian, whose name tag said she was Mrs. Stockwell, nodded. "We've everything for the past year in the newspaper stacks." She pointed to the room behind the glass wall. "Over there, just past the computers. Actually, you can also go to their web sites and bring up articles on the computer. Anything I can help you with?"

"No, no," Gabbie said quickly. Then, afraid that she'd offended the woman, added, "I just wanted to look up some things about the town, now that I'm living here."

Mrs. Stockwell gave her a broad grin. "The articles on Cameron Leeds are in the last two May issues of our local paper, and either the second or third week in June."

"Oh," Gabbie said. Some detective she was. About as subtle as a grizzly bear in a general store. "Well, I thought I'd take a look."

"Don't forget *Newsday*. May nineteenth and twentieth, I believe."

Gabbie saw that Mrs. Stockwell was right on target the moment she spread out the newspapers on one of the tables. The first local paper had it plastered across page one: "Body of Local CH Man Found on Beach."

"The body of 37-year-old Cameron Leeds, a Chrissom Harbor resident, was discovered by two teenaged boys as they walked along the beach."

She gasped as she read the next line: "'Todd and me, we were on the beach around seven-thirty, eight o'clock—just fooling around—when we saw this guy just lying there,' said 16-year-old Barrett Connelly."

Todd and me, she repeated silently. *What the hell were the two of you doing there?*

Did they do it? Could they have killed Cam for the money? And why hadn't anyone mentioned that those two awful boys had discovered the body?

She scanned the rest of the article, then read the follow-ups. The doctor's report appeared weeks later in the local paper.

"'No suspicion of foul play' declared Dr. Bradley, after examining the body of local businessman, Cameron Leeds. 'Poor Cam must have lost his footing at the edge of the bluff and fallen to the beach below. Plenty of contusions and his neck was broken.'"

There were enough gory details to entertain the readers, but the fact that Cam had been drinking had been kept out of the paper.

Something between a squawk and a gasp hit her right ear. Gabbie spun around and found herself nose to nose with Sonia Russell. Before she could speak, Sonia took off at a half-trot in the direction of the circulation desk.

What on earth was Sonia doing peering over her shoulder? The poor woman was obviously distraught about Cam's death. Still, she had no business spying on Gabbie.

Perhaps Sonia was upset because she'd seen something the day Cam had been killed. Gabbie considered chasing after her to find out. Sonia lived next door to the Leverettes. She might have overheard Jill and Cam arguing. Or saw Jill or Fred leaving the house that afternoon and, for some reason, followed her neighbor to the cottage.

Gabbie shook her head. It was too farfetched. But Sonia worked in the library and could have overheard a conversation about Cam, a conversation connected to his death. Gabbie made a mental note to question her about the day Cam died, but she'd have to do it when Sonia was in a calm state of mind.

As she was putting the newspapers in order, a headline in one of the May issues caught her attention:

"Construction of Luxury Homes to Break Ground in June"

Gabbie read on. She'd passed the site on Sunday as she was driving to Chrissom Harbor, though the homes weren't visible from the road. No doubt, this was the property that had belonged to Reese, Jack, Terry and Don. The property Cam had convinced them to sell to him and which he in turn sold to the Coxwell Development Corporation for a tremendous profit.

She refolded the newspapers and stood to return them to their proper place. She smiled as Jill walked toward her. "Are you taking a break between students?"

"Actually, I'm finished for the week. I'm on my way to Reese's office to work on payroll." Jill gave her a rueful smile. "I'll be there 'til after six."

"Theo and Charlie persuaded me to hold a meeting of the Photography Club this Friday. I think I'll have them take pictures in the woods behind the school."

A flicker of fear crossed Jill's face. She shook her head, and it was gone. She gave Gabbie a tremulous smile. "Why don't you come for dinner Friday evening? I've the afternoon free, and time enough to prepare something decent."

Gabbie hesitated. Was it protocol to accept a dinner invitation from the mother of one of her students? But Jill was a neighbor of sorts. And Cam's lover, which put her high on the priority list. She stifled a snort of laughter as she realized that finding his murderer had become the uppermost concern on her mind. "Sure, I'd love to," she said, graciously. "I'll bring a bottle of wine."

"Lovely. Theo will be pleased. She told me she likes you."

"She did?"

Gabbie blinked at the warmth spreading across her face, and Jill laughed in response. "Believe me, my daughter's not one to show her feelings." Her voice went flat. "And you'll meet Fred, of course. How about seven? We live at 24 Greenbriar Lane."

"I'll find it. Thanks a lot."

Fred was the only suspect she hadn't met, and she'd be seeing him in two days. *Good work, Gabbie,* she silently praised herself. *Now, on to Sonia.*

She felt a ping of excitement as she approached the circulation desk. The other clerks were probably out on a break, because Sonia was the only one on duty. She waited until Sonia checked out several children's books for a young mother who had two little ones running wild, then stepped up to the desk. Sonia saw her coming and busied herself with some papers.

"Miss Russell. Sonia," she said, when she got no response, "could I speak to you for a moment?"

Sonia turned to Gabbie with a sigh and an eye roll. "What is it?" she said, not bothering to hide her irritation.

"I couldn't help noticing your reaction to the article I was reading," Gabbie said gently. When she got no response, she continued. "Did you know Cameron Leeds well?"

Sonia ducked her head, but not before Gabbie saw the red rising across her plain face. "As well as anyone, I suppose."

"Then I imagine you were very upset when he died."

Sonia raised her head, her glare sharp and unmistakable. "He's dead and gone, and you'd best let sleeping dogs lie."

"Do you think it's possible someone murdered Cam?"

Sonia's mouth worked. "I–I—" was all she managed to say. To Gabbie's dismay, the woman turned and escaped through the door for Employees Only.

Cam was prepared to swear on a stack of Bibles that Sonia knew nothing about his death. "Are you kidding? She's the meekest person in Chrissom Harbor. As I remember, she never even set foot in this cottage."

"What does that have to do with the price of tea?" Gabbie asked.

Cam shrugged. It was a graceful gesture. Gabbie could imagine how it must have sent women swooning at his feet.

"Nothing, I suppose. But I can tell you Sonia was crazy about me. She loved when I flirted with her."

Gabbie scrunched up her face. "I can't imagine anyone flirting with Sonia. What on earth did you say?"

Cam grinned, clearly pleased with himself. "I always made a big fuss over her when I saw her in town. Sometimes I'd whisper I was mad about her, and we'd tie the knot one day."

Gabbie shook her head in disgust. "How could you?"

"Where was the harm? It was all in good fun. It made Sonia giggle and feel important. Gave her male attention in a safe way."

Gabbie sighed. "I suppose you're right. You've got me suspecting everyone I run into in town of murdering you."

"You're doing great, Gabbie. I have confidence you'll find the one who did it."

She eyed him balefully. "Let's hope he doesn't try to kill me first.

Gabbie ate an early dinner and decided to stop at Logan's for dessert. Cam was right—the restaurant was the heart of CH, and the best place to gather information about what had been going on the day of Cam's death. Her heart raced with anticipation as she outlined her lips then applied lipstick. She was getting obsessed with finding his murderer.

She opened the door to the bar and squinted in the dim light. Terry and Jack were talking avidly at the same table they'd occupied on Monday night. A small, plump woman sat beside Jack. Gabbie saw her pat his arm with great affection.

"*Muy buenas noches, señorita.*" Terry smiled up at her. "Are you joining us tonight?"

"Hello, everyone. I thought I'd stop by for dessert." Gabbie took the empty seat next to Terry.

"Hello there, Gabbie," Jack said. "Meet my wife, Adele. 'Mutt and Jeff' is what they call us."

"Hi, Gabbie." Adele smiled and waved across the table. "Pleased to meet you."

Mike came over to tell her the two pasta dishes that were the specials. When she said she only wanted dessert, he advised her to try the Apple Betty.

"I certainly will. And a cup of decaf please."

Terry, Jack, and Adele went back to their salads and to the conversation they'd left off, filling Gabbie in with relevant bits of information so she'd know what they were discussing. The topic was new sewers, one that didn't interest her, so she said nothing as she sipped her coffee, feeling oddly at home. She appreciated the warm welcome she'd received from everyone she'd met at Logan's and experienced a pang of guilt for scrutinizing them as Cam's possible murderer.

Reese joined them as Mike was serving Terry, Jack, and Adele their main course. "Meatballs with ziti and a Bud," he said to Mike, who left and returned with Reese's beer and a salad.

"Is Don coming too?" Gabbie asked.

"Nope," Reese said, his voice muffled by his mouthful of lettuce. "He only shows up Mondays and Thursdays, which are Tessa's nights out with the girls."

Terry and Jack burst out laughing. Clearly Don didn't trust Tessa. *Not since her affair with Cam*, Gabbie thought. She was wondering how to introduce the subject of Cam, when Reese did it for her.

"Of course, Tessa's been as good as gold since her little escapade with Cam three years ago."

"Don knows better than to upset his apple cart," Adele said dryly. "Tessa's the money maker. All he does is strut around the salon and order supplies... when he isn't playing cashier because the receptionist's busy."

Terry winked. "Now how do you know that, Adele?"

Adele let out a sigh of exasperation. "Jeez Louise! I do have my hair cut once a month."

The subject of Cam had come and gone. Gabbie needed to revive it. "I was reading about Cam's fall in the old newspapers in the library. Didn't the police even consider the possibility that it might not have been an accident?"

Reese grinned. "You mean, did Darren think one of us got irate enough to do him in? Sure, it crossed his mind. Questioned half the town, didn't he?"

Terry nodded. "The four of us, anyway. He let up when the old doc said there was no sign of a struggle—on the body or the terrain."

"What was the cause of death?" Gabbie asked.

"Broken neck, I think," Reese said, chomping down on a bread stick. "Didn't it say so in the newspaper?"

"And the body had contusions from the fall," Terry added.

Adele shuddered. "Please! Must we rehash this? Sorry, Gabbie. I suppose you're curious, living in Cam's house and all, but to us it's old news and not the most appetizing dinner table conversation."

"Sorry," Gabbie murmured. She was eager to change the subject, too, now that she'd gotten what she'd asked for.

Jack, Adele, and Terry ordered coffee and dessert, and Reese dug into his meatballs and ziti. They talked about the new development being built with remarkably little rancor.

"One good thing," Reese said. "Those houses will help lower our taxes, though they put more of a strain on our water supply."

"But not on the school system," Terry commented. "The school population's gone down in the last few years." He turned to Gabbie. "How's the job working out?" He raised an eyebrow. "Anyone give you any trouble?"

"Everything's fine," Gabbie answered with a smile.

She was dying to find out what they might know about Barrett Connelly, but decided it wasn't ethical for a teacher to talk about a student in Logan's. Anything discussed here might as well be aired on the local TV channel. If Barrett found out, he might retaliate by pulling a malicious stunt. At the very least, hearing she'd asked about him was sure to feed his ego and urge him on to more outrageous behavior, something Gabbie certainly didn't want to encourage.

Time to leave, she told herself. She ate the last bite of her Apple Betty and asked for her check. Mike brought it over and slid it across the table like it was top secret. "Pot roast tomorrow night. It's dynamite."

"Sounds great. Good night, guys. Nice to meet you, Adele."

She bent down to pick up her pocketbook. When she straightened up, she found herself face to face with Darren Rollins. She drew in breath, taking in the scent of his now familiar aftershave mixed with the leathery smell of his bomber jacket.

"Hi, everyone," he said. "Gabbie, don't tell me you're leaving."

She nodded, wishing she could think up a plausible excuse for staying. No, it was better that she was going. Darren was a distraction she didn't need in her life. Their eyes locked. He gave her a slow, knowing smile. She quickly turned away with the distinct impression that he knew exactly what was running through her mind.

CHAPTER ELEVEN

Outside was cold and dark. As she drove slowly back to the cottage, she tried not to think about Darren. She unlocked the front door and, feeling desperate for company, headed straight for the den.

Cam appeared immediately. He flopped down on the couch and stretched out his long legs to rest on the coffee table. "Hello, Gabbie. Who was at Logan's?"

"Jack and his wife, Terry, Reese." She felt herself blush. "Darren came in as I was leaving."

"Ah."

To change the subject, she told him about the essay Barrett had written for her class.

"He's a hand grenade, waiting to explode," Cam said.

She let out a snort of exasperation. "And the school won't do anything to stop him."

"That's Tim Jordan's fault. He's been spineless from the beginning."

"When I was in the library this afternoon, I looked up the newspapers from last May. Did you know it was Barrett and Ross who'd found you on the beach?"

"Nope." He walked to the sliding doors and gazed out at the night.

"Do you think they did it?"

He turned and shrugged. "I don't know. They had no reason to kill me. Unless they did it for the money."

"Yes, but they had no way of knowing you kept such a large sum in the house."

"True enough. Only some people who should have known better kept up the buzz that I made millions on every deal. And I rarely locked the cottage, so anyone could have come in."

He shook his head. "It's hopeless, isn't it? There's no way we'll find out who killed me."

Gabbie had the sudden urge to hug him as she would a child. "I ran into Jill at the library," she said brightly. "She invited me to dinner on Friday night."

"Good. You'll meet Fred."

She laughed. "From what you've told me, he doesn't sound like I'm in for a treat. But I can ask him a few questions. Though I tried that tonight at Logan's and came up with zilch. Adele reprimanded me for bringing you into the conversation."

Cam stood before her looking pensive. "I'm beginning to think I was wrong to ask you to play detective. All your snooping around is leading nowhere. Except it might upset my killer and send him after you."

Gabbie fought the tremor of fear that spread through her body. "In which case, we'll know soon enough who's the guilty party."

He reached out both arms as though he meant to shake some sense into her, but let them drop to his side. "Please don't do anything stupid. I couldn't live with myself if he killed you, too."

Gabbie shuddered at his choice of words. "The person I have to convince is Darren. He's so damn certain you died accidentally because he trusts Doc Bradley."

"Then talk to Darren if you like, but to no one else."

"I'll be careful," she said, knowing she wouldn't stop asking questions. So far, she'd learned very little, but the residents of Chrissom Harbor loved to gossip. Sooner or later, someone was bound to let drop a vital piece of information that would reveal the identity of Cam's murderer. "Well, good night, then."

He faded away. Gabbie brewed herself a cup of tea, which she carried into the den along with her school bag. She stretched out on the couch and started reading *The Great Gatsby*, stopping occasionally to make notes regarding lines she felt warranted class discussion.

Her leg cramped up and she changed position.

The phone on the desk rang. She got up to answer it. "Hello?"

Silence. Then—breathing. Slow, steady.

"Yes? Is someone there?" she asked, her grip tightening on the receiver.

"Hello, Gabbie. Are you alone?" The voice sounded muffled, as if a handkerchief were being held over the receiver. The question sent her heart thudding against her ribs. "Who is this?"

"A friend who wants to give you some good advice."

"What do you mean?" Her words came out weaker than she'd intended.

"Leeds' death was an accident. Stop asking questions or you just might fall and break your neck like he did."

Gabbie heard the click of the disconnection but couldn't unclasp her grip on the receiver. Finally, her hand opened, and the phone clattered to the table. She drew in deep breaths to free herself of the paralyzing terror.

Damn, if only she had Caller ID! She tried *69 and got a busy signal. The creep had thought of everything.

Who was it? Whose buttons had she pushed? Her heart pounded against her ribs, and she had trouble breathing. Yet, underneath her nervousness ran a vein of anticipation. The murderer was afraid Gabbie would uncover evidence that he or she had killed Cam.

Gabbie shivered. What helped keep her fear at bay was knowing she wasn't alone. Cam must be within calling distance.

"Cam?" she said softly. "Please come. I really need to talk to you."

She shouted his name a few more times, but he didn't appear. Her shoulders slumped as the memory surfaced—he'd told her about the other place he often inhabited. Clearly, he wasn't always hovering about the den, ready to make an appearance at her beck and call. The realization frightened her. She was alone in the cottage on this desolate road.

She checked to make sure the doors and downstairs windows were securely locked, then she turned on every light in the cottage and went upstairs. She put Darren's card with his phone numbers on her night table. Reassured that she'd done everything she could to make herself safe, she got ready for bed, where, after some tossing and turning, she managed to fall asleep.

Thursday Gabbie gave her sophomores a quiz on *Gatsby* and was pleased to see that most of them understood the point Fitzgerald was making in writing this novel. They saw that Jay

Gatsby was a self-created figure, a one hundred percent American product, invented and spurred on by his love for Daisy.

"Does he really love Daisy," one student had the sense to ask rhetorically, "or is she an illusion created by her class and wealth?"

"There's that bit about her laugh," another pointed out.

Careless Daisy, Gabbie thought, zooming ahead to the end of the novel. *She's ninety percent responsible for his death.*

Barrett walked in late to class, then crossed his arms on his desk and pretended to sleep through the period. Fine with me, Gabbie thought, ignoring him. Let sleeping dogs lie. She was even happier on Friday when she read his name on the absentee list, and he didn't show up. She put him out of her mind as she talked to her seniors about F. Scott Fitzgerald and Hemingway, and the many famous writers and artists who'd lived in Paris in the 1920s.

After her last class, she went into town to buy a bottle of wine to take to the Leverettes that evening. She decided to do a small grocery shopping, have a quick lunch, and be back at school by three-fifteen to meet with the Photography Club. As she wheeled her shopping cart to her car, she heard someone calling her name. She turned and saw Don Terranova, a bag of groceries in each arm.

"Hey, Gabbie, where were you last night? We were all disappointed you didn't show up at Logan's."

She gave a little laugh. "Sorry, but I can't afford to eat out every night." She unlocked her trunk and started stowing the first bag in when he moved in close enough for her to smell his metallic breath.

"I'll help you with that."

"No need," she said firmly, and set the bag inside. Too late she discovered he'd inched even closer. When she stood up her rear bumped into his stomach.

"Excuse me," she said, jabbing back her elbow.

"Ouch!" Don hopped out of arm's reach. "You don't have to get physical!"

"Exactly." She glared at him until he looked away.

She expected him to trot off in a snit, but instead he gave her the wide-eyed smile of an innocent child. "When are you stopping by the shop? Tessa can't wait to meet you."

Gabbie ran her fingers through her hair then glanced at Don, who grimaced as he shifted the heavy bags in his arms. Lover boy was bound to behave around his wife. "I'll call next week and set up an appointment."

"Tuesdays and Wednesdays are slow."

"I'll keep that in mind. Goodbye, Don."

"Nice to have run into you," he said, making a dash for his car.

"He's a pig," Cam said when she'd finished telling him about her encounter with Don in the supermarket parking lot. "You get full marks for the way you handled him."

"The weirdest part was he acted like nothing had happened, then told me Tessa wants to meet me."

"The poor slob expects to be rejected. I think he'd turn tail and run if anyone ever gave him the come on. Even Tessa can't stand him that way, and he knows it."

"Then why does she stay with him?" Gabbie asked.

"She pities the poor guy. She knows he'd fall to pieces if she threw him out. So instead, she has affairs."

"Oh, sure." Gabbie rolled her eyes.

"You think I was the only one? Tessa and Terry had a thing going for a while. Even Jack was in there for a one-night stand."

"Well, well," Gabbie said, grinning. "Chrissom Harbor's beginning to sound like Sin City. Now, I better grab my camera and get back to school. I'm taking the Photography Club shooting outdoors."

"And tonight, you're having dinner at Jill's." He sounded wistful. "I wish you could give her my love."

"And I wish I could tell Darren to reopen the case." She looked over at him, stretched out on the couch. "Are you sure he didn't kill you?"

"As sure as I am of anything. At least tell him about the call you got the other night."

"Why? What can Darren do about it?"

"Stop by occasionally. Keep an eye on you."

It sounded wonderful, which was precisely why she had to keep her distance. She wanted no romantic entanglements.

"Bye, Cam. See you tomorrow."

"Tomorrow? I expect a full report as soon as you get back from dinner."

"We'll see." Gabbie grinned as she dashed upstairs. At times it was most convenient that he couldn't leave the den.

CHAPTER TWELVE

I t was snowing lightly when Gabbie drove back to school. Maybe she should reconsider taking the Photography Club outside this afternoon. Maybe, she thought hopefully, no one will show up.

No such luck. Four students sat waiting for her as she entered her classroom: Theo, Charlie, and two boys, one short and chubby, the other tall and slender with a bad case of acne. The short boy introduced himself as Sean, the taller one Richard. They all had digital cameras and were raring to go.

Gabby gave them a little speech, explaining that though she wasn't a photographer, she was eager to help them, and that she'd planned a project for the afternoon.

Richard gave her a lovely smile. "That's okay, Ms. Meyerson," he said. "I know lots about photography. We just need a sponsor so we can get credit."

"Oh," Gabby said, feeling somewhat deflated. "Well, I thought we might go outside today and take pictures of trees.

I was going to talk to you a bit about composition and focus, but if you've other ideas—"

"That sounds like a great idea," Theo said, staring at each of the boys as though daring them to contradict her. "And the snow's letting up, see?"

Gabbie and the boys turned to the window. Sure enough, the sun shone brightly, reflecting off the freshly fallen snow.

"Hey, let's get going while there's still snow on the branches!" Charlie exclaimed. "They sure look pretty like that."

"I thought you might take photos in the woods behind the playing fields," Gabbie said.

"Great idea," Sean agreed. "We'll get some dynamite shots there."

"You can leave your knapsacks in the classroom," Gabbie said. "I'll lock the door behind us."

Eagerly, they made their way through the empty halls, past the thumping, shouting basketball practice going on in the gym. They stomped across the playing field.

Theo lagged behind to walk with Gabbie. "Mom said you're eating dinner at our house," she said.

"Yes. I'm coming over tonight."

Theo paused, "You won't tell any of the kids, will you? I mean, not Charlie or anyone."

Gabbie held back her smile. "Of course I won't. It's nobody's business. Your mother was kind enough to extend a friendly invitation because I'm new in town, and I appreciate it."

"She's always extending friendly invitations," Theo said sullenly, then dashed ahead toward the boys before Gabbie could respond.

Gabbie discovered there was little she could tell her avid little group. They caught onto her proposed project immediately. Soon they were snapping happily at their chosen tree or bush from every conceivable angle. Charlie even climbed a tree to get an overhead shot of his bush.

"Now let's aim higher," Gabbie suggested. Why don't you capture interesting patterns of branches against the sky?"

Again, the woods sounded with the clicking of four cameras taking several shots.

It was growing dark as they made a mad dash back to the classroom with barely enough time to gather up their things and catch the late bus.

"We'll meet again in two weeks," Gabbie called after them. "Bring four by sixes of what you shot so we can study and critique them."

They shouted their thanks over their shoulders as they ran off, leaving her to lock up.

Gabbie drove home, pleased with the way the afternoon had gone. The kids were enthusiastic, and Richard hadn't been bragging when he said he knew a lot about photography. He answered the other kids' questions and helped them set up many of their shots.

Maybe at their next meeting she'd have them take photos of each other. That was a fun project they were bound to enjoy.

She showered and put on a red silk turtleneck polo, her embroidered vest, and black trousers. After retrieving the wine from the refrigerator, she set out for the Leverettes's house. It was a five-minute ride. Nice and short, she couldn't help noticing, for Cam and Jill to enjoy a quicky in the afternoon.

The Leverettes lived on a block full of ranches and Cape Cod-style homes. Their house was a muddy brown. The front door must have been painted white a good many years ago, judging from its cracks and peelings. The few scrawny bushes and one bare tree added to the aura of neglect.

Gabbie pulled onto the cracked black-topped driveway and rang the bell. Jill opened the door immediately and gave her a peck on the cheek. Gabbie smiled and handed her the wine.

"You shouldn't have!" Jill exclaimed, "though Fred will be pleased. He'll be home in a few minutes."

"Oh, I parked in the driveway," Gabbie said. "I'll move my car."

She turned, but Jill reached out to stop her. "Don't bother. Please. He can leave his old heap in the street."

Gabbie shook her head, insisting. "I'd feel better if I move it." She returned to her car and parked on the street. As she walked back toward the house, she saw a curtain flick in an upstairs window of the house next door. Was that where Sonia lived? Did she spy on the Leverettes because her own life was empty?

Gabbie handed Jill her parka to hang in the hall closet, and followed her into the living room. The room was modest in size as was the adjoining dining room, where the table was set for four. Both were tastefully decorated in contemporary furniture in light blue and beige. Jill gestured to the sofa and the appetizers on the cocktail table.

"Make yourself at home. Have some crackers and cheese while I open the wine."

The aroma of meatloaf wafted into the living room, and Gabbie realized she was starving. She topped a cracker with cheese and stuffed her mouth just as Jill appeared, bearing two wine glasses.

Embarrassed, Gabbie chewed and swallowed too quickly, which made her cough. Jill hurried over to pat her on the back. When Gabbie glanced up, Theo was staring at her.

"Are you okay?" she asked.

"Yes, something just went down the wrong way." The coughing started again.

"Theo, please bring Ms. Meyerson some water."

Theo returned immediately, glass in hand.

Gabbie drank. "Much better, thank you."

"Fred's always doing that," Jill said as she perched on a nubby beige chair.

"No, he's not," Theo contradicted, plopping down in the matching chair. The soda in her glass rose dangerously high. "It only happened at Thanksgiving, and you had to carry on and embarrass everyone to death."

"Theo," Jill said in a warning tone. "Please don't act up in front of your teacher."

"I'm not acting up, just clarifying. We do lots of clarifying in class, don't we, Ms. Meyerson?"

"Some of the time, yes," Gabbie agreed cautiously, not wanting to get caught in a squabble between mother and daughter. To change the subject, she said, "We had a great afternoon out with the Photography Club, didn't we?"

Theo shrugged. "I guess."

Gabbie was piqued. This wasn't the same Theo who had loosened up halfway through the afternoon and enthusiastically called her over to extol the beauty of her tree.

Jill glanced at her watch then smiled at Gabbie. "I'll be back in a moment. Just want to check on dinner."

"Certainly," Gabbie said.

Theo offered no conversation, so it was difficult to pretend she couldn't overhear Jill on the phone. She asked for Fred, then demanded, her voice rising, "When will you get home? You knew we were having company!"

When Jill returned to the living room, her cheeks were flushed with two bright red spots. "I'm afraid Fred's been held up at work. He said to start without him."

"Sure, whatever's best for you," Gabbie said lightly. She picked up her wine glass and followed her hostess to the table.

The meatloaf, mashed potatoes, broccoli, and salad were delicious. Gabbie took great pleasure in the first real home-cooked meal she'd eaten in ages. But her enjoyment was marred by the tension between Jill and Theo, and by Fred's glaring absence. She did her best to be an attentive guest and asked Jill questions about Chrissom Harbor. Theo picked at her food and spoke only to contradict her mother.

"And what does your father do?" Gabbie asked Theo.

"He's a chemist at Forsythe Labs." Her pride rang out like the ping of good crystal.

"I've heard of Forsythe. They're fifteen minutes from here," Gabbie said. "How convenient."

Theo frowned. "Daddy had a more important position when he worked in the city, but Mom made him change jobs."

"Theo, what a thing to say!" Jill protested.

Gabbie turned her gaze, pretending not to notice the color rising in Jill's face. She was beginning to wonder if coming here tonight was a mistake when they all turned at the sound of a key in the door. Fred came in and draped his jacket over the wrought iron divider that separated the narrow hall from the living room. Then he strode purposefully into the dining room, a gleam in his eyes. A far cry from the lethargic man Gabbie had first seen in Logan's Place. Someone or something had perked him up.

"Hi, sweetie." Fred kissed his daughter on the forehead. He turned to Gabbie. "And you must be Mrs. Meyerson."

She didn't correct him but smiled and shook his extended hand.

"Sorry I'm late," Fred said to Jill. "Ralph needed the report for this week's conference, and I couldn't start working on it till four-fifteen."

Jill left her seat and headed for the kitchen. "I'll get your food. I've been keeping it warm."

"Go easy on the portions. I'm not very hungry. I had a sandwich while I was working."

Bastard, Gabbie thought. "I've already eaten" had been one of Paul's ploys when he wanted to get at her. But Jill obviously knew enough to ignore her husband's request. She brought in a plate loaded with food. Gabbie watched Fred gobble down his meatloaf and vegetables. He drank deeply from his wine glass.

"Good wine," he said to Gabbie. He reached for the bottle and read the label. "Mmm, no wonder. That was a good year for Mondavi."

Gabbie, who had chosen the bottle on the say-so of the wine merchant, nodded knowingly. "I've never gone wrong with Mondavi."

Now that she'd caught his attention, Fred regarded her intently. "So, you're Theo's new English teacher. She's pretty impressed with your take on *Gatsby*. Stayed up late last night to finish the book."

"Thanks a lot, Dad!" Theo turned cherry red, as if her father had exposed her for doing something reprehensible instead of reading ahead. But then kids like Theo hated to be suspected of playing up to their teachers, even when they weren't.

Gabbie found it interesting that although her father had embarrassed her, Theo showed him none of the animosity she'd been spewing at Jill. Annoyance, yes, but affection ruled the father-daughter relationship.

"Thing's get nicely tied up at the end, don't you think?" Gabbie said.

Theo missed the irony in her tone. "For Daisy and Tom," she answered scornfully. "They cause all the trouble, then get off scot free."

"We might call them careless," Gabbie offered.

Theo's gray eyes stared at her, then she nodded slowly. "Careless, yes. They don't give a damn about other people. People like that don't deserve to live."

Gabbie shivered. Emotions were flying fast and thick, turning her stomach into knots. She wanted to bolt but couldn't think of a decent exit line at the moment.

"Everyone ready for coffee?" Jill asked brightly. She set a steaming carafe of coffee on a trivet. "Theo, would you please help me clear the table?"

Theo groaned as she pushed herself up from her chair.

Action was better than just sitting there. "Let me help," Gabbie offered, starting to rise.

"I've got it," Theo said, lifting Gabbie's dish and salad plate.

The phone rang in the kitchen. Fred gave a start, then shook his head as his daughter hurried to answer it. "You'd think people would have the decency not to call during dinner hour," he complained.

Liar, Gabbie thought. *You thought it was your little playmate, then decided she wouldn't be that foolish.* Angry at him on Jill's behalf, Gabbie felt the urge to goad him. "People call now because they figure you're home and they can reach you."

Fred looked meaningfully at Jill. "Well, at least we haven't been getting any more of those mysterious hang ups."

A red blush spread from Jill's neck to her forehead. "I'll be right back with the cake and fruit."

Gabbie noticed she hadn't bothered to remove Fred's dishes from the table. Not wanting to remain alone with Fred, Gabbie cleared his setting and carried it into the kitchen.

"Thanks," Jill said as she passed, both hands filled with dessert. "Just leave everything on the counter. Please get the small pitcher of milk from the fridge."

Theo was nowhere in sight. Gabbie took out the milk and was about to close the refrigerator door when she heard Theo's muffled voice coming from the hall.

"Calm down, Charlie. I can't make out a word you're saying. Did they hurt you?"

Gabbie held her breath while Theo listened, hoping the girl wouldn't suddenly turn toward the kitchen and find her eavesdropping. She had no business straining her ears to catch what Charlie was telling Theo. Then she felt a flair of anger. Damn it, Charlie was her student, and she could well imagine who had come after him.

"They took out film cartridge—you told me three times. Is your camera okay?"

Gabbie hoped fervently losing his film cartridge was the worst of it. Obviously, it was.

"I have an extra cartridge you can borrow. You can shoot some more pictures on your own. I'll go out with you, if you like." A pause. "I know the snow probably won't be on the trees, but so what? Ms. Meyerson won't care."

"Gabbie!" Jill called. "Where are you?"

"Coming." She started walking toward the dining room when Theo's voice stopped her cold.

"I'll think of something! Those bastards deserve a bullet right through their heads." There was a pause, then she said. "We're almost done. I'll come over as soon as I can."

After dessert and coffee, Gabbie helped Jill clear the table then prepared to leave. Theo had never reappeared. Fred looked up from his newspaper, which he was reading in a living room chair, and called out, "Nice meeting you, Gabbie. I hope we see you again soon."

Jill walked her to the front door and hugged her. In a low voice, she said, "I'm so glad you came, though it didn't turn out quite as I'd planned, what with Fred coming home late and Theo being... Theo."

"Ssshh." Gabbie put a finger near Jill's lips. "I was glad to be here. You're a wonderful cook and hostess."

Jill frowned. "I should've known it would turn out like this. Theo's been so resentful. Ever since—" She paused, then smiled at Gabbie. "I guess I just thought, since you and I hit it off..."

"In the bathroom," Gabbie put in and grinned to lighten Jill's mood.

Jill smiled back. "—I thought we could be friends."

"Me, too," Gabbie answered. When she pulled the door shut behind her, she realized it was true.

She walked toward her car and looked around before getting into the driver's seat. Her gaze went automatically to the window of the house next door, where someone had been watching when she'd arrived. The upstairs windows were dark, but the downstairs lights were on in the room she now knew was the den.

Pulse racing, Gabbie crossed the lawn and peered into the window. The blinds were closed but not completely.

She saw Charlie, his eyes glued to the TV in the corner of the small room. Gabbie was puzzled. If this was Sonia's house, what was Charlie doing here? She felt conspicuous, playing peeping tom, with no bush or tree to hide her activity. *Why was Charlie here?*

Then it dawned on her. Sonia and Charlie had the same last name. *She must be his aunt!*

As though to prove it, Sonia came into the room and handed Charlie a cup. He put it to his lips and began to drink. *Hot chocolate?* She watched Sonia pat Charlie's shoulder then sit down beside him on the sofa in the dimly lit room.

CHAPTER THIRTEEN

"See anything interesting?"

Gabby jumped a foot in the air. She spun around and gasped when she caught sight of Darren's grinning face. "My God, you scared the living daylights out of me!"

"Sorry," Darren said, not sounding sorry at all.

"I—I was wondering who was watching me before, when I came to visit the Leverettes. It was Sonia Russell."

As they walked across the lawn to Gabbie's car, Darren asked, "Have a tough time getting through dinner with America's most dysfunctional family?"

"Yes—no," she flip-flopped. "How did you know?"

The streetlight backlit Darren's face. He was grinning again, showing teeth white enough for a toothpaste ad. "We've all been there, done that. Jill asks and we go out of kindness." He lowered his voice. "I'm sure you've heard Jill and Cam were involved. Things have gotten worse for the Leverettes since he died."

"God, what an incestuous town! Do you all keep tabs on what's happening in each other's home? When people go to the bathroom? Have sex?"

Darren's tone turned solemn. "Gabbie, I'm the law here. I make it my business to keep abreast of things."

Breast. Her face grew warm as she imagined his hands running down her breasts. She suddenly felt hemmed in. It was time to make tracks. Gabbie unlocked her car then turned to him as an awful idea occurred to her. "Were you spying on me?"

He laughed. "You mean spying on you spying?"

She shrugged. "Before Sonia was spying on me. More important, Charlie's there now. He called Theo during dinner, and I overheard her part of their conversation. He was upset because someone roughed him up… I'd guess Barrett and Todd." Her dread of involvement overcame her. Her hand flew to her mouth.

"I shouldn't have said that. It's really none of my business."

The grin disappeared. "Of course it's your business. Evil is everyone's business."

He pointed his chin toward Sonia Russell's house. "She called the station, but when I tried to talk to Charlie, he wouldn't say a word. Looked scared as a bunny rabbit and fought to hold back his tears. He's worried things will get worse if they find out he snitched."

Gabbie threw her hands into the air. "It's wonderful how fear works to protect the bullies of the world."

"Not always, I hope. Did you get any specifics?"

The compassion in his voice humbled her and urged her to answer. "They took the cartridge from his camera. We—the Photography Club, that is—were out in the woods this afternoon, shooting pictures." She shook her head. "Can't you do anything about those bullies?"

"Believe me, we're working on it. But with kids like Charlie refusing to file a complaint, it's damn near impossible to press charges."

"Interesting how it was Barrett and Ross who found Cam's body on the beach," she said.

He cocked his head and grinned. "Interesting meaning maybe they pushed him over the edge to his death?"

Gabbie shrugged. "Just mentioning what I read in the library." She started to get into her car a second time when she felt his hand on her shoulder. She hoped he didn't hear her breath catch in her throat.

"Want to go out for a cup of coffee?'

She looked up at him. "Aren't you on duty?"

"I fix my own hours. Work a hell of a lot more overtime than I put in for."

Go for it, encouraged her adventurous side. *Get out while the going's good,* commanded her voice of reason. Having had enough excitement for one day, Gabbie opted for the straight and narrow.

"I'm kind of tired," she said. It was true enough, so why did it strike her as a flimsy excuse?

"That's too bad." After a pause, Darren asked, "Would you like to do something tomorrow night?"

"You mean Saturday night?"

"Yes. Is that a problem?"

Gabbie considered. She hadn't been out on a Saturday night in months. Neither the idea of going to a movie alone nor watching TV with a ghost was appealing. This time her sense of caution was overruled. She needed some fun in her life. Besides, she told herself, she'd have Darren's undivided attention and the perfect opportunity to milk him for information about the various suspects.

"Sure. Why not?"

The grin was back. "Great! Let's make it for dinner. And I don't mean Logan's."

"I could use time away from Chrissom Harbor, too," Gabbie admitted. "I thought I'd found a quiet spot where the natives would leave me to myself. Instead, I find myself caught up in various situations."

Darren raised his eyebrows. "What were you escaping from?"

Gabbie shrugged. "Just… things."

She was afraid he'd press her for answers, but he merely nodded and said, "The restaurant I have in mind is some distance from here. I think you'll like it."

"Great. Surprise me." She waved as she drove away and was pleased that Darren waited until she was halfway down the block before he got into his car.

Cam called out to her as she climbed the stairs to her bedroom and much needed sleep.

"Tomorrow, Cam. I'm exhausted."

"Please, Gabbie. I'm desperate for news."

Gabbie trudged down the steps and plopped down on the den couch, where she let out a gigantic yawn. "I pay rent here, you know. I'm entitled to some privacy."

"I know, I'm sorry, but I had to hear all about your dinner at Jill's. Did she mention me?"

"Not once," Gabbie said ungraciously. "She was too busy juggling dinner and playing the good hostess. It wasn't easy, with her family out to undermine her efforts. Fred came home late. I got the definite impression he'd been with a woman. And Theo was insolent and deserved a good swat on her butt."

Cam sighed. "Poor Jill."

Gabbie stood up. "I like her all right, but the evening was too gut-wrenching after my own descent into hell." She bit her lip, shocked at her revelation, but Cam hadn't noticed. He was too wrapped up in self-recriminations.

"It's all my fault," he muttered. "She wanted to go away with me. She told me her life was unbearable, but I was too intent on putting CH far behind me to hear."

"Too selfish, you mean."

"Right." He sank onto the couch and covered his face with his hands.

Gabbie discovered she was suddenly wide-awake. If she went to bed now, she'd only toss and turn. She sat down on the couch again, leaving two feet between them.

"Tell me about the last day."

He looked at her quizzically. "You really want to know?"

"Of course. Besides, telling me might jog your memory. You might remember the identity of the murderer."

"Let's see. I spent the morning packing and doing last minute things—stopping the mail and the newspapers. I called the rental office to cajole Mary Hanley to put real effort into renting the place."

"Mary Hanley," Gabbie said, "Tell me more about her."

Cam's eyes widened in astonishment. "You don't seriously imagine she bumped me off?"

Gabbie shook her head. "Why is it every time I mention a name to you or to Darren, you both assure me the person is innocent?"

Cam grinned. "Somewhere, somehow, you saw Darren tonight!"

Damn! She wished she hadn't mentioned Darren's name. Still, she wasn't about to lie. "He caught me peeking into Sonia's window. She was comforting her nephew after his run-in with some kids, probably Barrett Connelly and Todd Ross."

She fidgeted as Cam's grin grew wider. "Darren's a good guy. I'm surprised he hasn't asked you out by now."

She opened her mouth to answer, then thought better of it. Not that it mattered. Either she was as transparent as glass, or Cam had the knack of reading people.

He laughed, an eerie, hollow sound. "So, you guys are getting together! Great. I knew you were his type."

"I am not his type. He is not my type. This is about you. Remember, you asked me to find your murderer. Besides, Darren's my best source of information, which is why I agreed to have dinner with him tomorrow night."

Cam winked. "Still, I get these vibrations about the two of you."

"Cam," she said firmly, "don't say another word on this subject, even as a joke, or I'll never set foot in this room again. I may even pack up and leave town ASAP."

Something in her voice made him realize she meant what she'd said, because he went quiet and nodded. "Sorry."

"That last day—what time did Jill come over?"

"About four o'clock. She knew a limo was coming at six-thirty to take me to the airport. Her eyes were all puffy and I knew she'd been crying. We'd said our good-byes the night before.

"She told me she'd tried to keep away but felt she had to give our relationship one last shot." He swallowed, remembering. "She insisted we belonged together and my leaving her behind was criminal." His voice went soft. "She said she didn't know if she could live without me."

"I'm pleased to see that she can," Gabbie snapped. "What time did she leave here?"

"I've no idea, but she didn't stay long. When I told her this was the best way and I'd send for her when I was settled, she gave me a cynical smile. 'Sure you will,' she said, and walked out before I could answer."

"So," Gabbie said, "if Jill didn't throttle you as you deserved, that means someone else came along and did the job."

"And stole the money. Don't forget the money."

"I did for a minute," she admitted. "Where did you get all that cash? You never said."

"A business deal."

"You mean the land you bought from your four friends and sold to the developers?"

"Of course not. That happened several months earlier."

"Did Jill see the cash?"

"Probably. A courier delivered it just before she arrived, and I was stashing it in the bottom drawer of the desk." He peered at her. "Five hundred thousand in hundred-dollar bills take up a lot of room."

"I wouldn't know," Gabbie said dryly.

"I started drinking after she'd gone. Not martinis, which I preferred, but gin straight from the bottle." He gave a little laugh. "I only did that once before in my life, at a fraternity party."

"Was it because you knew you'd made a mistake, sending her away?"

"Could be, but I wasn't about to change my plans, either."

A huge yawn escaped, and she quickly covered her mouth.

"Sorry if I'm boring you," Cam said, hurt.

The fragile male ego. Gabbie laughed. "It's nothing to do with you. I've had a grueling week, and my fatigue has caught up with me. Right now, I'm much too tired to think. We'll talk about this tomorrow." She stood. "Good night, Cam."

Gabbie woke up refreshed. She hummed as she leaped out of bed and danced her way to the bathroom. She recoiled when she realized what she'd been humming, an old song entitled "Taking a Chance on Love."

"I sincerely hope this good mood is not because of Darren Rollins," she announced to her reflection.

She put on an old sweat suit and sneakers, intending to take a brisk walk after breakfast. She made herself a bowl of hot cereal and was sipping her second cup of coffee when the phone rang.

"Morning, Gabbie. It's Darren."

She glanced at the clock. It was only eight-thirty. "How did you know I'd be up?"

"And I hope you slept well, too." he answered.

He's an ignorer, Gabbie decided. He won't hear what he chooses not to hear.

"I slept just fine. I'm going walking, then I plan to run some errands."

"This afternoon I'll be directing traffic and keep an eye on things over at the high school till about six. They're holding the indoor Olympics, which is a big deal around here. I asked my deputy, Lionel Daggett, to take the late shift for me."

"Oh." She was touched that he'd called in a favor for the sake of their date.

"There's this terrific restaurant in Southhold I think you'll like. How's about I pick you up at seven?"

"Seven's fine," she said, and felt a foolish smile spread over her face as she hung up the receiver.

She shivered when she stepped outside the front door. The cold nipped at her cheeks and nose. Though the sun gave off meager heat this early in the morning, it brightened the sky, giving the day overtones of cheer. Gabbie took care as she made her way down the wobbly wooden steps to the beach. She could break her neck on these steps. She shuddered, thinking of Cam.

Someone had broken his neck, perhaps stood with him at the edge of the bluff and pushed him down. No, that couldn't be. Cam was murdered in the den, then someone tossed him over the cliff. Someone strong enough to carry him, or Darren would have seen drag marks. And if he'd seen drag marks, he would have known that Cam had been killed.

Unless... Gabbie shook her head so hard she almost lost her footing. She refused to consider Darren a suspect. Darren was the police chief of Chrissom Harbor and Cam's best friend. What's more, he struck her as an ethical person. To think anything else meant she'd allowed her disillusionment with Paul turn her cynical and suspicious of every man she met. She needed Darren's help to find Cam's killer.

The sand was firm beneath her sneakers as she began her stretches. Several feet away, the water appeared dark, almost opaque, as it lapped gently against the shore. Gabbie looked around, surprised at how many people made use of the beach in the dead of winter. A runner whizzed by, waving as he passed. She smiled at a gangly boy dragging his stick along the sand while his black Lab wandered down to the water. The boy ignored her, but his dog came over to lick her hand.

She preferred race walking to jogging and started off at a comfortable pace. She felt someone coming up on the left and she moved to let him pass.

"Morning, Gabbie."

It was Terry Lopez, looking damn sexy in black spandex pants and a matching jacket.

"Hi, Terry." She flashed him a smile and watched him run past, just as he'd intended. He moved along in a nice, easy stride totally in sync with his compact, well-built body. Not that she was interested in his body, except as an aesthetic attraction.

A minute later he disappeared around the curve and from her thoughts. Gabbie built up her speed until she was breathing deeply. She race-walked for twenty minutes, then turned around, hoping to recognize the stairway that led up to her cottage. She should have made a mental note to remember a landmark.

"Hi, again," Terry called out on his return. He jogged beside her, slowing down to her pace. He pulled a large handkerchief from his pocket and wiped the sweat from his face.

"Do you do this every Saturday?" she asked.

"Run the beach? Occasionally, when the weather's decent. It's a nice change from the gym."

Gabby nodded. "I see lots of people have the same idea."

"Why not? May as well take advantage of what the town has to offer." He gave a little laugh. "Which isn't much, at least not during the winter."

They slowed down to a walk. "Then why do you stay here?"

Terry shrugged. "Habit. I like my house and, believe it or not, the job. Our dealership is one of the busiest in Suffolk County."

"Then you must really be a great salesman."

He grinned. "I won't say no, but our manager knows what he's doing. We fill many orders from outside the tri-state area." His keen eyes met hers. "And how do you like our little town?"

Gabbie turned from him to gaze out at the Sound. "It suits me fine till I decide what to do with the rest of my life."

"Ah."

The one syllable expressed enough sympathy and under-standing to open the floodgate of the dam. Gabbie hovered on the verge of spilling out the whole sorry story of her sour marriage and the ugly divorce. Just in time, she gathered her resources and drew a deep breath.

"I enjoy teaching the kids," she said instead. "And trying to solve the mystery is taking up the slack."

Terry wrinkled his brow. "Mystery? Oh, right. You think that maybe Cam was pushed to his death."

Gabbie stopped walking and eyed him intently. If she expected to solve the murder, she had to stop pussyfooting around and start asking the difficult questions. "That's right. Drunk or sober, I find it hard to believe he fell from a place he'd known all his life."

Terry blinked, then gave a little laugh. "So what? Nobody gives a damn, except for Darren Rollins and a bunch of pathetic love-starved women."

"That's a strange thing to say. I thought you guys were friends."

Terry shrugged. "Cam was a great drinking buddy, but he wouldn't think twice about stabbing you in the back."

"You mean the land deal?"

"For one thing. While the four of us made fifty thou each, Cam got a million and a half easy."

For one thing? "From what I've heard, Cam got more because he put the deal together."

"So what? Anyone could have done it—anyone whose cousin works for the county and gets wind of construction companies checking out land to buy and develop."

Terry bent down to tie his sneaker. He was about to take off.

Gabbie racked her brain to drum up more questions that would give her more information. "What kind of business was Cam in anyway?"

Terry stood and raised his eyebrows. "Nothing nine to five, if that's what you mean. He was always on about some hot deal. Always coaxing us to put money in a new stock or some dot com business while they were hot."

"Did you invest?"

"Sometimes," Terry admitted. "I made a few thou, lost a few. Came out about even." He pointed a finger at her. "But Reese, Don, Jack, and I figured it out one night. Good deal or bad deal, Cam always came out ahead."

"But he continued to live in the cottage," she said. "If he was making so much money, where did it all go?"

"Most of it went into bank accounts in his brother's name. We found that out after he died. You see, it wasn't the money Cam was after, but the game."

Gabbie wasn't so sure, but now wasn't the time to discuss what made Cameron Leeds run. Instead, she asked, "Is that how he saw women—as a game?"

Terry froze. *Yes!* Gabbie cheered silently. She'd hit the mother lode.

Finally, he said, "All women were game to him, especially married women."

"Your wife?" she asked softly.

The nod was barely perceptible. "She practically had a breakdown when he dropped her. We split. She took our kids and moved back to New Mexico. I hardly ever get to see them anymore."

"I'm sorry," Gabbie said. A rage like a brush fire flared up inside her breast. *Poor Terry. No wonder he was glad that Cam was dead.*

Terry waved as he moved away. "Gotta go. See you at Logan's Place."

"See you," Gabbie answered, watching him start up a wooden staircase. She headed for home.

Cam, she scolded silently, *you've been careless with people—just like Daisy Buchanan.*

CHAPTER FOURTEEN

S he dashed past the den, glad that Cam wasn't around. Upstairs, she showered and dressed then drove into town to run errands. On impulse, she made her first stop Don's wife's beauty salon.

The place was bright and cheerful, the walls and stations done up in purple and silver. Four operators, all women, were busy at their chairs, cutting or blow-drying hair while other customers sat in plastic capes, their hair covered in gook, waiting for their coloring process to take. The harried receptionist hung up the phone and asked Gabbie how she could help her.

Gabbie tucked a wayward curl behind her ear. "I'm long overdue for a haircut."

The receptionist pressed her lips together. "Sorry, there's no way I can fit you in today. Marnie's out sick, and the other operators are on overload doing her customers and their own."

A short, dark-haired woman approached the desk. Her plump, curvaceous body exuded energy, sex appeal and abundant self-confidence. "Nancy, have Dilly shampoo Mrs. Havens. Then she can pull through the color on Sonia's hair."

Gabbie turned to leave but halted when a fuchsia-taloned hand touched her arm. "You must be the new schoolteacher."

"Yes, I'm Gabriela Meyerson."

The dark brown eyes twinkled with mischief. "Don described you to a tee. I'm Tessa, by the way, and you're in dire need of a good haircut."

"I know, but since you're completely booked, I suppose I can live like this another few days."

"Not if I have anything to say about it," Tessa said. "Nancy, see who's free to wash Ms. Meyerson's hair. I'll be cutting it myself, soon as I blow out Deena Tibley and her mother."

"But Tessa," Nancy protested. "You have Marnie's two perms and—"

Tessa didn't bother to answer. She winked at Gabbie. "See you in a little."

Minutes later Gabbie was wrapped in a plastic cape and tilted backwards as nimble fingers massaged her scalp then rinsed the shampoo from her hair. She almost moaned with pleasure. This was the closest she'd come to heaven in the longest time.

"You can sit up now." The slight, pretty young woman had a lilting Spanish accent. "Tessa will be with you soon." She patted Gabbie's hair dry and placed a fresh towel around her shoulders. Then she directed her to a chair next to Tessa's station.

Tessa was in deep conversation with the woman whose hair she was blow drying. "I say enough is enough! Go to the police. Get your brother to sue the school! That will force wimpy Tim Jordan to do something."

"I can't," the woman said softly.

Gabbie's eyes widened when she saw it was Sonia. "Charlie won't say one word against those boys. They told him—" Her voice dropped to a whisper and Tessa leaned forward to catch the rest of the sentence.

Tessa sighed. "Pacifying them won't help the poor kid. They'll only come down on him worse."

Gabbie nodded as though in agreement. The movement caught Sonia's attention. She stared at Gabbie and gasped. In one jerky motion she stood and pulled off the plastic cape, then ran toward the coat room.

"Come back, Sonia," Tessa called after her. "I still have to spray you."

She slapped her hands against her thighs and gave Gabbie a sheepish grin. "Me and my big mouth. Now I won't see her for at least six months."

"I know about the latest incident," Gabbie said. Tessa's easy manner encouraged her to add, "I was having dinner at Jill's, when Charlie called Theo. I couldn't help overhearing what had happened."

"And no one stops those bullies!" Tessa's voice rose in anger. "Things are going to escalate. Mark my words, someone's going to get hurt real bad."

Gabbie shuddered.

"Come and sit here. Let's see what I can do for you."

Gabbie moved to Tessa's chair. Tessa stood behind her and studied her face in the large mirror. "Hmm, you've a perfectly oval face. Have you ever considered the close-cropped look?"

Gabbie swallowed. "You mean, cutting most of it off?"

Tessa lifted a lock of Gabbie's hair. "Keep it full at the crown, tapered in the back. You'll look smashing."

Gabbie giggled. "Let's go for it. I could use a change of hair style."

"To go with the changes in your life?"

Gabbie stiffened, then she relaxed. "New place, new job, new haircut," she said airily. "Why not?"

Tessa didn't seem to hear. She was still studying Gabbie's face in the mirror. A slow smile spread across her face as she clipped back all but one section of Gabbie's hair. Holding it taut between two fingers, Tessa snipped – short, fast motions. Deftly, she completed the section and moved on to another.

"So, you met Jill and Fred," Tessa said as she worked.

"Uh huh."

"A bore, isn't he? Can't imagine why she doesn't pick up and leave him." Tessa let out a chuckle. "Though folks around here must be wondering why I don't do the same."

Gabbie wasn't about to so much as clear her throat at that. But the mirror must have given her away, because Tessa said, "For all his faults, Don loves me. I need that to start me going in the morning."

"I hear he's very devoted to you," Gabbie said politely.

That got her a big guffaw. "And no doubt you heard about my fling with Mr. Sexy Bones, your former landlord."

"Well—" Gabbie began, not certain what to say next. Tessa's blunt revelations rendered her speechless, a feat no one else had managed to accomplish as far back as she could remember.

Tessa lowered her head so that her lips were a hair's breadth from Gabbie's ear. "Cameron Leeds was the sexiest, most romantic male ever put on this earth. I don't regret it for one single minute. Pity it was only four times, total."

"I heard he was quite a Romeo."

"And then some," Tessa agreed. "No problem if you heeded what he said about just having fun and not getting involved. Of course, sometimes he didn't take his own advice."

"Jill?" Gabbie asked.

"Uh huh. But the fool couldn't see it. I bet he went to his grave never realizing how much he loved her."

Gabbie let the words hang in the air as she turned to the mirror. She reached up, fingers brushing the skin where her hair used to fall. Her neck felt bare, almost unfamiliar—but striking. She looked great. She looked exotic—French.

"Wow, I like it!"

"Wait till I'm done," Tessa said with a grin. "The men will be after you like flies."

"Oh, great. Just what I want." Gabbie made a face. They both laughed.

"What about Terry's wife?" Gabbie asked. "I heard she had an affair with Cam."

"So Terry gripes every time he gets a chance. Pilar and Cam? Now that's a twosome I'd swear never got off the ground. I think he played big brother and listened to her moan about Terry." Tessa lowered her voice. "Did you know he beat her?"

"No!"

"Hold still! I almost turned you into Van Gogh. Here's a towel."

Gabbie pressed the cloth to her stinging ear. "But Terry's so nice. I was just talking to him down at the beach."

"I know and we all love him, but sometimes he flies off the handle. Besides, Pilar was homesick for the Southwest. She's happier living there. She's dating someone now, and the kids like him, too."

"God, you know everything that's happening!" she said, amazed.

Tessa waved her hand. "What I just told you, you could read in the local paper. It's nothing like some of the stories people tell me in confidence—stuff they know I'll take with me to the grave."

She grabbed her hand dryer and directed the air flow all over Gabbie's head, using her small brush to set the hair in place. When she was finished, she handed Gabbie a mirror. "Now look!" She spun her around.

Gabbie stared in awe at the back of her head. The short wavy hair tapered to her neck, giving her a sexy, playful look.

"Great, huh? Shows off your fabulous features. I'd kill for those cheekbones, not to mention your shapely little nose. Next time how about going for some highlights?"

"I don't think so, Tessa."

Tessa shook her finger. "Don't be closed-minded," she admonished. "Just consider it. And have a great time tonight with Darren."

Unbelievable! Gabbie mused as she walked around the corner to pick up a few things at the drugstore. *You'd think they read each other's diaries from the way they know the intimate details of each other's lives: wife beating and affairs, and my date with Darren. But, with the exception of Jill, no one even speculated that Cam might have been murdered.*

A disturbing idea flashed through her mind, bringing her to a dead stop so that an elderly man bumped into her. "Sorry," she apologized, oblivious to his admonitions that she look where she was going. What if everyone in Chrissom Harbor had taken part in Cam's death, kind of like what happened in *Murder on the Orient Express*? No, she decided. Cam was never cruel or malevolent.

Unless he'd done something really awful, something that everyone—including Cam—was keeping mum about.

She bought a jar of moisturizing cream and a box of Band-Aids, then dropped her boots off at the shoemaker for new soles and heels. Back at the cottage, she opened the country-style metal mailbox and was about to reach for her mail, when she let out a yelp and jerked back. The bloody remains of a field mouse lay on a piece of white cardboard.

Gabbie fumbled in her pocketbook for a tissue, which she used to cover her glove as she removed the cardboard from the mailbox. She dropped the mouse in the woods at the side of the cottage. She would have tossed the cardboard as well, but there was a message written in block letters with a green magic marker:

"Animals live, animals die. So do nosy people. Let the dead rest in peace."

"Only the dead man isn't resting in peace," she murmured above her pounding heart.

After putting the cardboard, with its ominous warning in a plastic bag, she washed her hands, then went into the den.

"Cam," she called, placing the bag on top of the bookcase. "I need to talk to you."

To her relief, he materialized immediately. "Don't you look snazzy! Wait till Darren catches sight of the new you."

"I found a dead mouse and a threatening note in the mailbox. Someone wants me to stop asking questions."

"Precisely what I asked you to do, remember?

She grimaced. "But I can't. I won't. Besides, it proves I'm getting the murderer nervous."

Cam strode past her and gazed out the window. "Nervous people are dangerous." He turned back to Gabbie. "I'm beginning to think it's time you brought Darren here. After all, he is the police chief. It's his job to find out who murdered me."

Gabbie shook the paperweight and watched the snow fall. "I don't know. I'll think about it."

Cam burst out laughing. "You want to find the murderer all by your lonesome."

She slammed the paperweight down on the desk. "I do not! That's the stupidest thing I've ever heard." But his words had struck home, and they both knew it.

Cam's voice turned gentle. "I appreciate the gesture, but I don't want anything to happen to you, Gabbie."

"Thanks," she said begrudgingly. There was the nice Cam again, the one that melted women's hearts and lured them into his bed. Had Cam been a decent person or a devious betrayer of trust? She'd heard so many conflicting reports, it was difficult to know.

She looked up at him. "Tell me about Pilar Lopez."

"Ah, Pilar. A sad and beautiful girl who made the mistake of leaving New Mexico and marrying Terry."

"Did you sleep with her?"

Cam looked offended. "Of course not! Just gave her some fatherly advice, and enough money to help her leave her overbearing husband."

"Did Terry beat her?"

"She wouldn't say, just kept rubbing the bruise on her arm. She cried and said she'd kill herself and the kids if she didn't get away."

Gabbie gulped. This was more complicated than she'd expected. "Do you know that Terry thinks you two had an affair? He's jealous and he hates you."

"Probably, but I doubt that he's the one who offed me."

"Why?"

"Because I once saved his ass. Did he bother to tell you about that?"

She shook her head.

"I didn't think so. The guy's screwed up, but basically, he's a man of honor. He'd never go after me like that."

Gabbie clenched her hands in frustration. "Why is it everyone I mention has a good reason not to kill you, according to you?"

"I gave you a lead. Fred Leverette."

"What about the various deals you brought your friends in on? Some of them took heavy losses."

"Hey, any opportunity I offered had the potential for making big money. But there were always risks. They all knew it."

"Who put money into your schemes?'

"Reese, Terry, Jack, Andy Russell, Mike Logan, Tim Jordan."

"Tim? The high school principal?"

"Sure. Why are you surprised? Half the town treated me as their investment manager."

Gabbie rolled her eyes. "I'm hungry. I'm going to make myself a sandwich."

"Hearty appetite. Don't forget to tell Darren about the note and the dead mouse."

She ate lunch, took a leisurely bath, did her nails, and worked on lesson plans. The afternoon passed pleasantly. It was dark outside when she put on her best sweater set and pants.

Darren arrived precisely at seven. He kissed her cheek as though they were old friends and helped her on with her jacket. Outside, he opened the passenger's door of his silver Camry.

A gentleman, she thought, as he walked around to the driver's side.

"And we're off!" he said, suiting action to words.

It was toasty warm inside the car. A Beethoven piano sonata sounded softly in the background. "The *Appassionata*," she murmured. "One of my favorites."

He glanced over at her. "Surprised?"

"Yes," she admitted. "Very."

He smiled. "I like surprising people."

"Oh?"

"It's a great way to get someone to reveal information he didn't mean to reveal."

"Like asking someone when he least expects it where he was when Cam was murdered."

Darren groaned. "You're a pit bull on that topic. Just won't let go."

Gabbie had a sudden idea. She flashed him a vivid smile. "What if I offered you proof that Cam was murdered, proof you couldn't dispute?"

"I'd reopen the investigation. But this is pure speculation, right?"

"Mmm." It was speculation. Her only evidence was a ghost, a note, and a dead mouse—if they could find it. All together they didn't add up to proof that murder had been committed. But she was revved up enough to ask, "What would you do for me?"

His eyes lit up with a devilish gleam. "Make love to you like mad for an entire night."

"Thanks, but I was hoping for something more practical. Like arranging to have the body exhumed and an autopsy performed by a reputable medical examiner."

She held her breath while Darren considered this. "First, I'd have to bring the new evidence to the D.A. And if he agreed the case should be opened, he'd present the matter to a judge for consideration."

"So be it," she said.

He stopped at a red light and turned to her. "Hey, you're serious about this, aren't you?"

"I have something I want to show you later."

"Sure. I'd like that."

Gabbie felt her cheeks burn and wished she'd stop coming out with expressions that made her sound like a flirt when her main concern was finding Cam's murderer.

His eyes narrowed as he studied her face. "Have I told you how great you look tonight?" he asked.

"No."

"Well, you do. I love your new haircut."

She stroked the back of her head, which felt naked without her mop of curls. "Thanks. Tessa's artwork."

"A masterpiece." The light changed, and he drove on.

The word "love" bounced around in Gabbie's head, tripping the panic button in her brain. *The word's abused and overused,* she reminded herself. *And he used it about your hair, for God's sake. Now calm down and act normal.*

She was relieved when Darren changed gears from sexy date to friendly neighbor and listened avidly while he talked about Chrissom Harbor's residents. She learned that Mike and Monica Logan's daughter was a powerful international attorney in Washington, Tim Jordan, the high school principal was disputing his third divorce, and Darren's ex-wife and little girl, Cindy, lived in Seattle.

"Sorry about that. You must miss her."

"I sure do. But she's coming to spend two months with me this summer," he said proudly. "We'll do the whole daddy-daughter thing. What about you? Have any children?"

"No, thank God." She drew in breath as she realized how heartless her comment must have sounded. "I mean, I like kids, but I'm glad I haven't had any so far."

Darren patted her hand. "Whatever pleases you, Ms. Meyerson."

She flared up, feeling misunderstood. Obviously, he saw her as a self-centered, plastic woman of the twenty-first century. "You don't understand. I've just been through a bad time."

"Want to talk about it?"

"Not really."

"Suit yourself," he said agreeably, and began to whistle.

Finally, to end the silence, Gabbie asked, "What's the story on Jack and Adele McMahon?"

"What about them?"

Gabbie shrugged. "I don't know. I seem to know something about everyone else I've met. I've no idea what Jack does for a living, though he made a comment about moving furniture."

Darren chuckled. "Jack takes whatever odd job comes his way. Sometimes he makes deliveries for the local furniture store, sometimes he works for Reese. He started up his own business a couple of times over the years but never could keep anything going. Racked up some big debts." Darren tapped his head with two fingers. "The poor guy has no business sense whatsoever."

"Owing money doesn't stop Jack and Adele from eating at Logan's."

"Adele earns a good salary as a legal secretary. And an uncle died and left her money a year or two ago. I guess they used it to pay off their debts."

Gabbie remembered Adele's coyness when the subject of Cam had come up.

"Was Adele one of Cam's conquests?"

Darren started laughing so hard, tears came to his eyes. As he wiped them away, he said, "Keep on saying things like that, and we'll have an accident. Cam liked women, but he had discriminating taste. Believe me, Adele McMahon wasn't his type."

"From her comments the other night, I thought she had a soft spot for Cam."

"Maybe so. Lots of women did, but that doesn't mean he slept with half of them."

"I see." And she was beginning to see. Cam wasn't quite the skirt chaser she'd been led to believe.

She looked around the room, admiring the lavender napery, the oil paintings adorning the walls. She was pleased that the tables were well spaced, and she didn't have to hear her neighbors' conversations.

"This is a nice place. Great food. Elegant yet cozy."

"It's family owned," Darren said. "They used to live in Chrissom Harbor."

The tasteful, candle-lit restaurant was crowded, with several parties waiting to be seated. Gabbie was pleasantly surprised when the hostess immediately led them to a corner table. "Enjoy," she told them, with a wink, placing the menus on the table.

"I see you've greased the right palms," Gabbie joked.

"They know me. I come here from time to time."

I'm one of a string of dates, she thought. Her good mood suddenly deflated. Then she pulled back her shoulders and sat up tall. So what? She'd come out with Darren to glean information and have good time, and that's exactly what she'd do.

Darren asked for a bottle of chardonnay. Gabbie leaned back in the well-padded chair and sipped while their waiter took their orders.

When their main courses arrived, Gabbie offered Darren part of her fish, and he gave her a lamb chop.

"Mmm, they're both good," Darren declared. "I trust your choice of dishes. Next time, let's share our entrees. You have to try their special shrimp dish. It's outrageous."

"Sure, why not?" Gabbie agreed, smiling at his reference to a "next time" and what it might mean.

It means nothing, she reminded herself. *Come July, you'll be living somewhere else and everyone from Chrissom Harbor will be memories.*

He beckoned her closer and leaned across the table until their faces were inches apart. "Don't stare," he whispered, "Isn't that Fred Leverette over there, making eyes at some woman who's definitely not Jill?"

Discretely, Gabbie followed his gaze. Along the back wall, at a table considerably smaller than theirs, Fred Leverette was deep in conversation with his dining companion, his expression warm, his attention undivided. She was on the young side of thirty and as drab as her brown dress. Her granny glasses and long, mousy brown hair reminded Gabbie of the flower children of the Sixties. But her small, plain face glowed with vitality as she nodded in agreement with whatever Fred was saying.

Darren grinned. "Sly dog! Who would have thought—?"

"That louse! I bet she's the reason he stayed late at the lab last night."

Darren gave her an amused smile. "I say good for Fred. He and Jill should have split years ago. They both think they're doing Theo a favor by staying together, but they're not."

The words escaped her. "Oh, Cam, what a fool you were."

Darren gripped her arm. "What did you say?"

"Ouch!" Gabbie shook herself free. "I was merely thinking it's too bad she and Cam never got married," she improvised as she went along. "I heard they were involved. Chrissom Harbor's not the sleepy town I thought it was. It's a hotbed of sex and adultery."

"Well, I wasn't fooling around. Allison couldn't take my hours. Soon we were arguing over stupid things, like whose turn it was to go grocery shopping."

"I'm sorry," she said.

"You were married, weren't you?"

She paused, then said, "For six years: three good, one bad, two awful."

Darren laughed. "Mine went two good, two bad, one awful." When she said nothing, he continued, "And I've no intention of going that route again. I'm one of those cops who's better off single. I don't have the time to devote to the institution of marriage."

"Institution, that it is," she babbled, ignoring the sinking feeling in her stomach. Determined to prove that his decision to remain single was one she supported, Gabbie raised her wine glass. He clicked it with his glass and drank deeply.

CHAPTER FIFTEEN

They lingered over dessert and coffee then headed for home. Darren drove fast, but she felt safe, trusting his quick reflexes as he followed the curves in the road. She let her head fall back against the headrest.

"Tired?" he asked.

"A little."

His hand found hers on her lap and he squeezed. "I want us to be good friends," he said.

"Sure." She tried to pull her hand from his grasp, but he held fast.

"Scared?"

"Yes," she admitted. "I've been through an emotional battering, and I need my space."

"I can understand that. It takes guts not only to divorce a rotten husband but help put him away by testifying against him."

Gabbie jerked her hand free and turned on him. "You bastard! You used your police connections to spy on me!"

"It wasn't spying. I merely made some inquires," he said calmly. "I knew something major was bugging you. I had to know if I had a murderess on my hands."

Her laugh held no humor. "Thanks a lot! Admit it—you were being plain nosy."

"Interested," he conceded.

"It isn't fair!" she retorted, though most of her anger had evaporated. "You can access information about me, but I can't about you."

"I'll tell you anything you want to know," he said softly.

"It's not the same thing," she protested, refusing to let him see how moved she was by his offer.

"Besides, as police chief of CH, I'd think you'd want to have me as your good friend."

Her racing heart pumped even faster. Half of her wanted to scream 'Let me out of this car,' but the other half wanted him to kiss her. "I think I do too," she agreed. "But I'm not sure what it means."

"It means this."

He eased the car onto the shoulder of the road and turned off the motor. He put his arms around her and pressed his lips to hers. He started slowly, giving her time to become familiar with his feel and his touch. She breathed in his taste and his tangy aftershave, stirred yet completely at ease.

"Mmm," he murmured. "This feels nice."

"Yes, it does," she agreed, pleased he was a talker and not one of those men who remained silent when they made love, as though what his body did had nothing to do with him.

Darren shifted, putting one arm around her shoulders as he pressed closer. She snuggled into his embrace, shivered when his fingers stroked the nape of her neck. It felt delicious. Exciting yet familiar. So much time had gone by since she'd been with a man, she'd forgotten the glory of it all.

Slowly, he released her, a broad grin lighting up his face. "I knew it would be like this for us."

"Like what?" she asked, teasing.

"Like wonderful."

"Is that why you stopped?"

He turned on the ignition, looked carefully before edging back on the road. "Absolutely. Think I want to frighten you away?"

"You can't frighten me," she said automatically.

"Oh, yes, I can." And then he was whistling. She could have smacked his face for being so pleased with himself.

She felt comfortable in the silence as they drove the rest of the way. Gabbie liked the way their fingers intertwined, their hands rested on his right thigh, which felt as solid and sturdy as an oak tree. This time the Waldstein sonata filled the air. At the cottage, he pulled onto the rutted driveway and stopped behind her car. He made no move to turn off the motor.

"Come on in," she invited.

He hesitated, and when he turned questioningly to her, Gabbie realized he was every bit as nervous as she was. But right now, intimacy was the last thing on her mind.

"I want to show you something." She tugged at his arm. "I promise not to jump your bones."

He smiled. "Okay. I could use your john."

"Great! I mean, good." That would give her enough time to put her plan into action.

She unlocked the front door. As Darren went upstairs, Gabbie flew into the den and switched on the lamp. "Cam," she said softly. "Are you here?"

Silence.

"Cam, please come."

Nothing.

"Dammit! You're never around when I need you."

She felt the cold air before he materialized before her, a knowing smile on his handsome face. "And here I was trying to be tactful. I figured you and Darren might want some after dinner personal time on the couch."

Gabbie glared at him. "Leave my personal life out of this and get serious. When Darren comes in here, I want you to tell him what happened the day you were murdered."

Cam shook his head as he dropped into his old desk chair. "You should have told him, gently and gradually. Darren won't believe his eyes when he sees me. He'll think someone put hash in his mashed potatoes."

Startled, she asked, "How did you know he ordered mashed potatoes tonight?"

Cam grinned. "Because they're his comfort food. He eats them most nights. Now I think I'll leave."

"Cam, don't be a coward. Please stay so he knows I'm not a madwoman talking to the air. Damn, where's that note I found this afternoon?"

"You put it on top of the bookcase."

"Oh yes. Right!" She heard Darren's footsteps on the stairs. "Now don't go disappearing, you hear!"

She turned off the light and met Darren in the hall.

"Were you talking to someone?" he asked. "I thought I heard voices."

"Just to myself." She walked into the kitchen. "Want a cup of coffee?"

"Water will be fine."

He sat down at the table. Gabbie filled a glass at the sink and handed it to him. "Let's sit in the den. It's more comfortable in there."

He grinned. "Decided to seduce me, after all?"

She smiled as she led the way. "I'm considering it."

"In Cam's den of iniquity? I'd like something more romantic for you and me."

Her heart thundered as she tossed back, "I promise you'll never forget what happens tonight."

She sat down on the couch and motioned for him to sit beside her. Stirred as she was by his nearness, she focused on Cam. *Come on, Cam*, she called to him silently. *What are you waiting for?*

To her gratification, he materialized and faced them from across the room.

Darren turned pale. He started to hyperventilate, and moments passed before he could speak. "My God. Am I drunk or stoned or out of my skull?"

"Hi there, old pal. Long time, no see." Cam turned to Gabbie. "How's that for an opening line? Worthy of Peter Lorre, don't you think?"

"It'll do." She put an arm around Darren's shoulder, felt him sink momentarily against her before he sat erect, his hand to his forehead. "That's not Cam. It can't be."

"Wrong, Darren, old pal. It's as close to me in the flesh as I can get. I'm still on this plane because I have to know who killed me. Believe me, it was no accident."

Darren gazed down at the carpet, shaking his head. "This isn't happening. It can't be happening."

Cam moved closer and snapped his fingers. "Come on, pal, I need your help. I'll start fading in a couple of minutes."

Gabbie glared at Cam. "Give him a chance to get used to you like this. It's a shock to his nervous system."

"You weren't this shocked the first time you saw me," Cam complained.

"Of course I was, and I didn't even know you. You weren't my best friend suddenly making a comeback as a ghost."

Darren swallowed the last of his water too fast and launched into a coughing fit. Gabbie pounded his back.

"There's no such thing as ghosts." His eyes narrowed. "Unless this is some kind of a trick. Cam was the master of practical jokes."

"Well, I'm not," Gabbie said. "Believe me, Cam's here." When he didn't answer, she slipped her hand in his. "Please, Darren, try to relax. Listen to what he has to say."

Darren shrugged, his eyes fixed again on the carpet. He flinched when Cam stepped closer and stood in front of him.

"It's me, Dar, or what's left of me on this plane. I can only appear in this room, and not for long, so trust your eyes and your ears."

Darren opened his mouth to protest, then shut it. "All right. I'm listening."

"I was drinking that afternoon as I packed my bags. Jill came, we had words, and I drank some more."

For the first time, Darren spoke directly to Cam. "How much liquor did you consume?"

"I don't know. A lot. More than I've had in years."

Darren nodded. "Then what happened?"

Cam pointed. "I was sitting at my desk, trying to take care of last-minute business. Had a Ray Charles CD going pretty loud. Suddenly I felt this blinding pain at the back of my head. Then nothing. I must have passed out."

"A Ray Charles CD was in the player," Darren murmured, as though Cam had finally presented him with proof he could believe. He met Cam's eyes. "And there was a contusion at the back of your head." He shook his head. "Christ, this is weird."

Cam grimaced. "Not half as weird as it is for me."

"Did you see who struck you?" Darren asked.

"Nope. That's the problem."

"Smell a whiff of perfume? Aftershave lotion? Remember hearing a sound?"

Cam shook his head. "The CD was blasting, and I had trouble concentrating. Even using a calculator, the numbers kept running off the page." He laughed. "It wasn't easy with all the gin I was putting away."

"What time was this?" Gabbie asked.

"I've no idea," Cam answered. "Jill left around four-fifteen, four-twenty, so it was some time after that."

"Still light out?" Darren asked.

"Yep. I'm pretty sure it was."

Darren nodded. "That tallies. The two boys found the – er – you at seven-thirty." He swallowed. "Doc Bradley said death occurred two to three hours earlier."

"Between four-thirty and five-thirty," Gabbie mused. "What time was your flight, Cam?"

"Ten after nine. A car service was picking me up at six-thirty to drive me to MacArthur Airport."

Gabbie turned to Darren. "What did the driver do when his passenger didn't appear?"

"He says he knocked a few times. No one answered, so he went around to the back, found the sliding doors unlocked, and he went inside. He says he shouted up the stairs but didn't go upstairs. Figured no one was home, so he called the dispatcher, who told him to go on to his next pick up. Barrett and Ross found you an hour or so later on the beach."

"Any chance they did it?" Cam asked.

Darren shook his head. "There was no sign of a struggle. You were drunk, Cam. It was dark. You fell and died of a broken neck."

"So you say."

"So Doc Bradley says."

Cam snorted. "That old quack is growing senile and should have retired years ago. Trouble is, you're pig-headed. You decided it was death by misadventure and won't listen to what really happened."

Darren stood up. "Oh, yeah? Dead or alive, you're not giving me much help to prove otherwise."

Gabbie cleared her throat. "I'd better show you the note."

"Don't forget the phone call," Cam said.

Darren threw Gabbie a look of disbelief. "What phone call? What note? You never mentioned either one."

Gabbie walked over to the bookcase and retrieved the note. "I found this in my mailbox today, along with a dead mouse."

Darren read the note, then stared at her. "You waited until now to show me this?"

She sat down and faced him. "I told you I had something I wanted you to see. Besides, I didn't want to ruin our evening."

"Didn't you?" His face drained of all expression. Suddenly he was all cop. "At least you had the good sense to put it in a plastic bag. I'll take it to the lab. Check it for fingerprints. Where's the mouse?"

"I threw it into the woods."

He let out a snort of exasperation. "What about the telephone call?"

"Someone called Wednesday night and said in a disguised voice that Cam's death was an accident. I should stop asking questions or I might fall and break my neck, too."

He gripped her arms tight. "Wednesday night? Why didn't you call and tell me about it then?"

"I—well, so many things have been happening, I didn't get a chance."

"For God's sake, Gabbie, he's given you two warnings! I want you to take this seriously. Stop talking about Cam to every jerk in town."

"That's exactly what I told her," Cam said smugly.

Gabbie glared from one to the other, ready to let loose a retort, but Darren's pained expression stopped her. The poor guy had just gotten the shock of a lifetime, and now he was worried she might get bumped off next.

He managed to offer her a thin smile. "Come down to the station tomorrow, and I'll take your prints. Maybe we'll be lucky and lift the prints of whoever sent the note."

"Do you agree it was murder?" she asked.

"I agree there's a strong possibility. I can start questioning everyone connected to Cam again, but there's no way I can get an order to exhume the body without some solid piece of evidence pointing to murder."

"Too bad there's no way to link the murderer to the missing money," Gabbie said.

Darren looked balefully at Cam. "What missing money? How much?"

Cam shrugged. "Half a mil."

Darren stared, open-mouthed. "In cash?"

"Of course, in cash."

"From what crooked deal? You swore up and down you wouldn't pull anything stupid again."

Cam turned up his palms. "It was nothing... a piece of cake that fell into my lap. I'd have been crazy to have said no. The cash was the extra cushion I needed to start over again. Start it right, wherever I decided to go. Besides—"

"Besides what?" Darren demanded.

"Nothing," Cam said.

"What was it this time? A pyramid scheme? Fake stocks? Bogus investments?"

"What does it matter? The money's gone." He gave a mirthless laugh. "Not that I need it now."

"Where were you keeping it?"

Cam pointed to the desk. "In the bottom drawer." He smiled "Neat piles of brand-new hundred-dollar bills."

Darren whistled. "How were you planning to get it out of the country?"

Cam grinned. "Hey, only some of it was mine. All right, most of it. You saw my plane tickets. I was flying down to Atlanta. Even though Roland's away half the time, I preferred to bank down there. The next day I was leaving for Nice."

"You still haven't told me the nature of your little enterprise. Or who was in on it with you."

Cam sighed heavily. "Some guy I knew asked me to move a load of cigarettes. No taxes. Hey, don't give me that look. Everyone comes out ahead except Uncle Sam. No big deal. It happens every day of the week."

"The big deal is that someone murdered you, probably for the money. Who were your little helpers this time?"

Cam turned to gaze out the window. "No one you know."

"Oh, yeah?" Darren laughed. "You never could lie to me."

"I'm no informer, Darren. The guys involved had no reason to bump me off. They were coming here around five-thirty to be paid off."

"Who, Cam? I want names."

Cam squirmed. "I'll tell you, but only if you promise not to go after them."

CHAPTER SIXTEEN

"Go after them!" Darren slammed his hand against his forehead. "Are you nuts? One or any combination of your partners in crime might have killed you for the money. Are you so stupid you can't see what's obvious?"

"I don't believe it. They were my pals, every one of them."

Gabbie let out a sigh of exasperation. "Tell him, Cam, or we're leaving right now." She turned to Darren. "He pulls this every time I suggest someone as a possible suspect. Of course the guilty person's someone he knew. You'd think he really doesn't want to find out."

Darren ran his knuckles up and down her arm. "Weird as it sounds, I understand what he's going through. I would hate like hell to learn that someone I thought was a friend did me in."

He turned to Cam. "All right. Start naming names."

Cam grimaced. "Reese, Don, Jack, and Terry."

Darren burst out laughing. "How about that? The gang of four. I thought they were furious with you because of the land sale."

"That's why I brought them in on this—to show good faith. I wanted to make up for what they considered their big loss. It was an easy forty thousand to throw their way."

"Forty thousand each?"

Cam laughed. "Are you kidding? Ten for each of them. A bit more for Jack since we used his truck."

Darren calculated, then shook his head. "Leaving over four hundred fifty thousand bucks for you! You devil, Cam!"

"So, you see why it can't be any one of them."

Gabbie glared at him. "Don't be stupid! Of course it could. Forgetting the money angle for a minute, Don hates you because you slept with Tessa, and Terry thinks you broke up his marriage."

"And Reese resents you because of the way you treated Jill," Darren added. "He's really fond of that woman."

"So am I," Cam said mournfully. "What a fool I was not to take her with me. If I'd said yes, I never would have gotten drunk and careless."

For the first time, Gabbie realized how angry he was for having let himself become an easy victim. He was used to running the show, not being someone else's dupe. Cam had been a flawed, amoral human being. He'd used people and pulled all sorts of illegal stunts. Despite all that, she was more determined than ever to find his murderer and let him go to his rest. "We'll find out who it was," she said softly. "I promise."

Darren was too deep in thought to comment. Finally, he said, "No one's gone on a spending spree, at least that I've noticed. Nothing obvious like buying a home in Florida or taking a trip to the Far East."

"You could check their safely deposit boxes," Gabbie suggested.

"Thanks for the lead," Darren said. When he saw her ears redden, he took her hand. "Sorry, I didn't mean to come off sarcastic."

Gabbie recoiled. "I forgot I was talking to the police chief who has every technical device at his disposal."

Though the reference to his checking out her husband made Darren twinge with guilt, he stood his ground. "Gabbie, I don't want to come off like some Neanderthal Man, but this isn't a joint enterprise. You did your part—bringing me here so I could talk to Cam. Leave the rest to me and my deputy."

Cam roared with laughter. "Lionel Daggett? That nincompoop couldn't find his shoes if they weren't on his feet. And you still need to show good cause to have the D. A. reopen my case."

Darren's keen eyes surveyed the den. "The murder took place in this room. Since someone struck the back of your head, there's a good chance the weapon's still here." He turned to Gabbie. "Please bring me some plastic bags, the largest you have."

"But the room's been cleaned," she protested. "I've been using it, touching things."

"She's right," Cam agreed. "Any evidence you gather will be considered tainted."

"But if the lab finds traces of your blood or hairs on a possible weapon, the D.A. will be more willing to open up the case."

Cam nodded. "True."

Darren's eyes shone with excitement. "And Roland's been back in the country three weeks now. Maybe he'll squawk and insist that they treat your death as a murder."

Cam pointed to the phone. "Call him. Tell him anything you like, and he'll back you to the hilt."

Darren grinned. "I know he will."

"His cell phone number's on a Post-it sticking to the side of the top drawer."

Darren opened the desk drawer and whistled. "Damned if it isn't." He picked up the telephone and dialed.

Gabbie awoke early the next morning. She caught a glimpse of the overcast sky and snuggled under her quilt. After breakfast, she'd go to the police station and let Darren's deputy, Lionel, take her fingerprints. Then she intended to relish her day of solitude. Sleet or snow was in the forecast, perfect weather to stay at home and read and do some schoolwork. For dinner, she'd order in a pizza and finish off the entire pie by herself.

She envisioned herself reposing languidly in the den lounge chair and sighed. Technically, it was her den, and she had every right to her privacy, but the reality was that Cam might appear at any moment. Gabbie gritted her teeth. After the tumultuous events of last night, she needed a day of peace and quiet. As much as she wanted to help Cam, he and his murder were taking over her life.

Last night, Darren had bagged various items, among them the statue of the Roman soldier and the wall barometer. He was about to seal off the den to avoid further contamination but postponed doing so when Cam insisted it was the only room where he could manifest, and he might have to communicate with Gabbie.

Darren and Cam had remained deeply engrossed in conversation, and when Gabbie announced she was going to bed, they barely responded to her "Good night." *Some date that turned out to be!*

She chided herself for being silly and admitted that Darren's new priority to solve Cam's murder was a blessing in disguise. It would keep them both too busy to spare more than an occasional thought for each other. That kiss at the side of the road was proof positive of their strong mutual attraction, an attraction that could lead to a hot and heavy romance. And she was determined not to get involved with anyone, including Darren Rollins.

In the morning light, Cam's presence struck her as a different sort of problem. As much as he had her sympathy and she was willing to help him, his constant presence was becoming an intrusion. She needed long stretches of solitude to recuperate from her divorce and the horrendous days in court.

She was indulging in a second cup of coffee, when he called to her. Reluctantly, she went into the living room and faced him across the hall.

"Good morning, Gabbie," he said cheerily. "What I wouldn't give to taste a cup of java."

She groaned. "Not now, Cam."

"If you'll come in the den for ten minutes, I promise to disappear for the rest of the day."

"Oh, all right." There was no point in refusing. He'd only keep after her until she gave in.

She perched on the edge of the desk while Cam sat in the lounger. She curbed her impatience when she realized he was troubled.

"Darren's going to start questioning people today. I'm just wondering, do you think there's a chance he'll find out anything new? I doubt if anyone will remember what he or she was doing eight months ago."

"He'll learn plenty," she said, with more optimism than she felt. "Now Darren knows you were expecting Reese, Terry, Jack, and Don that afternoon. They have plenty of explaining to do."

He sighed. "I can't believe any of those guys offed me."

"That last day when you were going to pay them their share, did you expect all four to show up here together?"

He gave a bark of laughter. "Are you kidding? I didn't set up appointments, just told them to stop by for their money between five-thirty and six-fifteen. No one came, as far as I know."

"So, it's possible the four of them attacked you, or one came early and grabbed all the booty."

"Or it was someone else entirely," Cam said. "You and Darren will find out what happened."

Gabbie grinned. "Thanks for not throwing me off the case like your pal tried to do last night."

"Darren's just looking after you. He likes you, Gabbie. I can tell."

She turned her head so he couldn't see her blush. "Time's up. I have to go to the police station."

"No problem. See you later," he said and disappeared.

After putting the kitchen in order, Gabbie got dressed and headed for the police station. The small building was empty, except for Lionel Daggett, who was waiting for her at the desk. He was a tall, gangly young man who looked eighteen, but Gabbie knew was twenty-seven. His lank brown hair fell over blue eyes that moved constantly yet never seemed to focus on anything. She had to agree with Cam that he didn't appear too bright. But he knew how to go about taking fingerprints.

"That's real exciting news, that Cameron Leeds was murdered," he said as he worked.

"Yes," Gabbie said.

"Darren's not here."

"I can see that."

He didn't seem to notice her sarcasm. "He's going to find Cam's murderer, Ms. Meyerson. First thing this morning, he brought those items over to the lab. Now he's out interrogating witnesses."

"And suspects, too, I hope."

Lionel winked. "Well, sure, but we don't tell them they're suspects right off the bat."

Gabbie drove home through empty streets washed clean by a cold, stinging rain. She made herself comfortable in the den, surrounded by schoolbooks and the latest Elizabeth George she'd tucked into her suitcase before she left for Long Island. Cam was true to his word and stayed away. Soon she was mid-deep in her copy of *The Great Gatsby*, jotting down ideas for discussion in her plan book as quickly as they presented themselves. Hunger pains assailed her. Gabbie glanced at her watch and was surprised to see it was almost two in the afternoon.

"Time for lunch," she said out loud, and went into the kitchen. She opened a can of tuna and had a pot of tomato and rice soup simmering on the range, when the doorbell rang.

Darren! she told herself, her pulse racing. He's come to tell me what he's found out so far. She flung open the door and faced Jill, dressed in a sheepskin jacket and wool hat. Jill must have read the disappointment in her face because her greeting quickly turned into an apology.

"I'm sorry, Gabbie. I didn't mean to disturb you, but I had to stop by before I left town. I'm going away for a bit, and I need to talk to you about Theo and—" A flood of tears put an end to her explanation.

Gabbie feared the biting wind would freeze them as they ran down her face. She took Jill's arm. "Come inside."

In the kitchen, she asked, "Want some soup? I've plenty for both of us."

Instead of answering, Jill dropped into a chair and wept into her hands. "He has someone and he's dating her like he's a single man. And all these months I've been trying to-trying to—" Gasping and wailing prevented her from pouring out the rest of her anguish.

Gabbie removed the pot of soup from the burner as it was about to boil over. She filled two bowls and brought them to the table. "Eat," she ordered, and put bread in the toaster.

Jill wiped her face and blew her nose. "I'm worried about Theo, but she'll be okay with her father. You and I hardly know each other, but I want—I need to ask you to keep an eye on her. You don't have to call her or anything, but since you'll see her every day, just–just give her a kind word or a shoulder to lean on if she feels like talking."

Gabbie grit her teeth. Playing godmother to a hostile teenager she hardly knew was not a responsibility she welcomed right now. But Theo was burdened with more problems than her mother knew about, and Gabbie had always made herself available to her students. "Of course I will, Jill. Though surely you have a few good friends in town who'll be happy to look in on Theo on a regular basis."

Jill met her gaze. "Not really. My best friends from high school moved away, and working two jobs hasn't left me much time to socialize." Tears streamed down her face. "I didn't need anyone else when I had Cam. Damn that man! He was the only one who understood what I was going through.

"And then—" The sobs came, rasping, awful sounds that tugged at Gabbie's heart. Jill struggled to control herself and give voice to what she'd been harboring in silence all these months. "And then it turned out he didn't even want me in the end. What a fool I was. What a fool I am for still loving him and missing him, when I meant nothing to him. That bastard used me like he used everyone else in this town."

Gabbie folded her arms around Jill as a blazing anger toward Cam ripped through her like a bolt of lightning. "Jill, please don't upset yourself. Where are you going now?"

"To my parents. They live in New Jersey. I'll stay with them till I decide what I'm going to do with the rest of my life."

Suddenly Gabbie remembered the investigation of Cam's death had been reopened. Darren would want to talk to Jill again.

"Jill, the police now think Cam was murdered, and—"

Jill nodded. "I know. Darren came by this morning to ask me about the last time I saw Cam. Then he questioned Fred. When he left, Fred was furious."

Gabbie's heart quickened. "Does Darren consider Fred a suspect?"

Jill shrugged. "I don't know. Fred wasn't worried about that. He said since Darren saw him out last night with this Anne from his lab, he figured he might as well break the news to me himself. You were there, too," she added accusingly.

"Yes, I was," Gabbie admitted.

"And you wouldn't have told me either. I bet he looked happy."

Gabbie didn't answer. Jill covered her face with her hands. Gabbie feared another outburst of tears, but Jill pulled herself together.

"After Cam rejected me and—and died, I tried to make the best of things. You can't imagine how I tried. Candlelit dinners, slinky nightgowns." She let out a mirthless laugh. "So hypocritical. Neither of us was interested. But I tried, for Theo's sake."

She shook her head. "And now Darren's saying Cam was murdered. I'm still reeling from that piece of news. What made him change his mind, after all this time?"

"Could be the threatening letter I got made him start to wonder."

Jill cocked her head and gave her a shrewd look. "Are you two a couple?"

"No!" *Damn Fred! Those we see, see us.* Gabbie felt the heat rise to her face. "We're just friends," she added quickly. "Probably because he was Cam's best friend and the police chief, and

I'm living here in the cottage and got to wondering if Cam's death was an accident."

"Oh." Jill nodded thoughtfully. "Though maybe it was an accident, after all. I can't imagine anyone wanting to kill Cam."

"Come on, Jill. I met the guys: Reese and Jack, Terry and Don. They all hated him."

Jill waved her hand and gave a little laugh. "Oh, they were furious with him because of that land deal he pulled over them. Believe me, I know all about it—from Reese and from Cam, himself. But Cam wasn't like anyone you've ever met." She smiled her lovely smile. "The guys were furious with him but trust me, they all loved him. I know for a fact he sat each of them down, one at a time, and wooed and cajoled, apologized and made all kinds of promises till he was back in their good graces. Cam was always forgiven."

"Don and Terry didn't sound forgiving to me," Gabbie said. "And what about Fred?"

Jill waved her hand. "Fred wouldn't kill anyone over me. As for Don and Terry, I saw them having a heart-to-heart with Cam in the diner the day before he died."

Gabbie cast her a speculative glance. "Do you think a woman might have killed him? Maybe someone all torn up about his love 'em and leave 'em ways?"

"I doubt it. When he refused to take me with him, I nearly killed myself that night." She gave a humorless laugh. "Dumb me. I bet even poor, naive Sonia—who Cam used to flirt with to make her feel good—knew he was all talk. Something I should have kept in mind."

They finished their soup in silence. "That was good," Jill said. "I didn't realize how hungry I was."

Gabbie stood. "Let me make you a tuna fish sandwich. You can eat it on the way."

Jill gave her a lopsided grin. "Well, I won't say no to that. Could I use your facilities?"

"Sure. You know the way."

Jill went upstairs. Gabbie raced into the den. "Cam," she called, keeping her voice low, "come here! I need you."

She called twice more and was about to give up when Cam appeared. "What is it?" He sounded annoyed. "I did precisely as you asked and kept away."

"I know, thanks." She put her finger to her lips and spoke softly. "But Jill's here now. It's your last chance to tell her that you love her."

Cam started to fade. "Why did you bring her? I can't do this. I can't—"

"Yes, you can, and you will!"

"No, really Gabbie —"

"For once in your life you're going to do the right thing," she snapped. "Be a man!"

"Gabbie, where are you?" Jill called from the kitchen.

"In the den. Would you mind coming in here?"

"Sure, but I really must get going."

Gabbie grinned. "I won't keep you, I promise."

Jill came into the room. She staggered and fell back against the couch when she saw Cam. "Is it you or am I dreaming?"

"No dream, I promise you," Cam crooned in a voice Gabbie had never heard him use before. "It's me, Jilly, and I've so much to tell you."

Gabbie left them and returned to the kitchen. When Jill appeared half an hour later, she was tearful again.

"Gabbie, I've just had the strangest half hour of my life!"

Gabbie gave her a wry smile. "I can imagine."

"Cam loved me, he really did! He says he loves me now."

"I know. He's told me often enough."

They hugged. Jill put on her jacket, and Gabbie walked her into the hall.

"Take care and try not to dwell on the past. I'll keep a special eye out for Theo."

"Thanks, Gabbie, I know you will."

The door closed behind her. Gabbie heard the car motor start up, then fade away. It was a bittersweet sound, and for a moment Gabbie felt a pang of envy. Jill had left home just as she had, only Jill was fortunate to have the support of a new friend and the reassurance of her former lover to see her off.

"No self-pity and no comparisons," she scolded herself. "You chose your new life. Now get on with it."

CHAPTER SEVENTEEN

G abbie had just finished her schoolwork and was gathering up her books, when the phone rang.

"Hi, how are you today?" Darren asked.

Gabbie grinned. "Fine. I hear you've been busy talking to suspects."

He laughed. "Can't keep a secret in this town."

"Except for the big one of who killed Cam. But we'll find out soon enough."

"We?" She loved the way his voice jumped up an octave when she got under his skin.

"Gabbie, I told you last night, it's my job to find his murderer. I don't want you getting any more threatening notes or worse."

"I doubt that I will, now that it's official Cam's death was no accident."

"I spoke to the D.A.'s office. They told me if something shows up on the statue or the barometer, they'll present it to a judge ASAP, and the body will be exhumed pronto." She heard him swallow. "Trouble is, I ought to be there when the Suffolk ME examines the remains."

"I'm glad I can skip that part."

"It's the least I can do for Cam. Poor guy. Getting killed was bad enough, but having his best friend write it off as an accident must have hurt like hell."

His self-reproach came through loud and clear. She couldn't think of words to soothe away the sting, then realized he wasn't fishing for sympathy. Instead, she said, "Feel like eating a home-cooked dinner tomorrow night?"

"Sure would." He chuckled. "I thought you'd never ask."

The news that Cam's death was being treated as a probable murder spread through CH like wildfire. It was all the kids could talk about on Monday morning. Several of them swarmed around Gabbie's desk at the start of third period, as if she'd been their teacher since September.

"Hey, Ms. Meyerson. Aren't you scared, living in a house where a guy was offed?" Jeff asked.

She knew the best way to calm them was to use this as a jumping-off point for a short discussion and a writing assignment.

"Death is a part of the life cycle," she said. "It excites us and fascinates us. At the same time, it frightens the daylights out of us because we all die. Nobody likes to think about that. Not that you should," she added quickly, gazing into the faces of her captivated audience. "You're young and have your lives ahead of you."

"Unless someone gets hit by a car or catches an awful disease," one of the girls said.

"Yes," Gabbie agreed. "Anything can happen. In fact, there's a death coming up in *The Great Gatsby*. It's a pivotal event in the novel. I want you to be aware of the incidents of cause and effect that lead up to this death, and how the death impacts the rest of the story. Now, let's discuss the chapter you read for homework."

She was in the middle of a similar spiel in her fourth period class when the fire drill bell rang.

"Everyone out! Form a double line and turn right. We follow Mrs. Bolton's class outside."

"We can't go outside like this!" one of the girls complained.

"Hey, I'll freeze my ass off," Ryan Marco said.

"Not your ass, your—"

Gabbie could well imagine what Jed Lancaster whispered, as the group of boys around him burst into laughter.

"No talking! Keep on moving."

Gabbie herded her students into the crowded hall, where they joined the throng moving toward the stairwell. They were descending the steps to the first floor, when the loudspeaker boomed throughout the building.

"This is Dr. Jordan speaking. Students, you are to leave the building immediately. Bus riders, go to the bus area and wait for your bus. Buses will depart in ten minutes. Those seniors who drove to school are to get in their cars and drive home. Everyone must vacate the building! Teachers, see to it that all students leave the building, then go directly to the shop building."

Instead of obeying, many students turned to ask each other what was going on. The anxious buzz filled Gabbie's ears. "Everyone, keep moving!" she ordered, raising her voice above the din.

Someone at the top of the stairs started pushing and kids came rushing into her students. A girl stumbled. Gabbie helped her to her feet. Fearing a stampede, Gabbie threw up her arms and faced the oncoming crowd. "Keep to the right! Keep to the right! No pushing. No shoving." She sighed with relief when they obeyed and moved down the stairs in an orderly manner.

"Hey, Ms. Meyerson, what's going on?" Ryan asked as he pushed past her.

"I don't know."

"I bet it's a bomb scare," Lizzie Terranova said. "Why else would they send us home?" She looked terrified, Gabbie thought. "I hate to leave my good jacket in my locker."

Someone knocked into Lizzie, and Gabbie prevented her from falling just in time.

"I'm sure it will be safe there," Gabbie reassured her.

Lizzie grimaced. "Right. If the school doesn't blow up."

Gabbie hustled students to the exit, then walked to the small shop building behind the main building. Some teachers were there already.

"Is it a bomb scare?" she asked Suzanne Lindstrom, the head of the foreign language department.

"So I've been told." Suzanne pursed her bow-shaped lips. "Tim said the caller's voice was muffled but he sounded like a kid. He told Tim not to worry because he had half an hour to empty the building before it blew. Then he started to laugh." Suzanne lowered her voice. "Tim thought he recognized the voice."

Gabbie's hand flew to her mouth. "Oh, no! Not those two."

Suzanne's expression was wry. "Barrett and Todd. Who else would do something like this? Hopefully, this time they'll nail them and put them away."

"They're a menace to society," Cindy West, another English teacher, snapped.

Gabbie sensed her colleagues' growing agitation as the minutes passed and they were left to their speculations. Finally, Tim Jordan strode into the room. He stood before the faculty, a grave expression fixed on his handsome face as he waited for the clamor to die down.

Gabbie observed his glittering eyes, the chiseled lips that barely contained his pent-up excitement. *He's getting off on this*, she realized. *The school might be in danger of blowing up, but Tim Jordan is glowing in the limelight.* She almost laughed aloud when he nodded, as though he were thanking an unseen pre-senter.

"Hello. Sorry for the delay. I commend you all for shepherding the students to safety."

"Shepherding the students?" echoed George Breck, the guidance counselor. "Give me a break."

Gabbie half-listened as Tim Jordan prattled on about how proud he was of the faculty's masterful handling of a potentially dangerous situation. At this very moment all students were safely out of the building. The police were on the premises, doing everything in their power to get the problem under control.

Andy Gorsky, the short, pear-shaped science and math chairman, finally said. "Tim, since time is of the essence, we'd appreciate hearing about the call you received."

The principal's jaw tightened, the only indication of his displeasure at having his flowery speech cut short.

"It came at eleven minutes past ten to my private number. I was informed a bomb would explode in the high school in one hour. Police Chief Rollins called in the county police. They traced the call to the bagel shop one block from here. As we speak, officers are searching the building for incendiary devices."

"Tim, we understand you recognized the caller's voice," Suzanne Lindstrom said. "Are you going to tell us who it is?"

Several teachers leaned forward, voices overlapping: "Yes, tell us!"

The facial expressions of various faculty members reflected disgust, derision, and anger. *They neither like him nor respect him*, Gabbie decided.

Tim Jordan run his finger along the inside of his collar. Finally, he said, "I can't say for certain, especially since the voice was muffled."

"May we assume this is the work of Barrett Connelly and Todd Ross?" Andy asked in a reasonable tone. "They're our worst troublemakers, and both were absent from their fourth period classes."

Tim blinked, seemingly surprised by this bit of news. "We can't assume anything at this time," he said quickly. "A false accusation could lead to a lawsuit."

"Did anyone see Barrett and Ross near the bagel shop?" Gabbie said without thinking.

Tim lowered his gaze, but not before she noticed his eyes darting frantically from side to side above the crowd. "Yes, Mr. Garcia, the owner, saw them there this morning, but neither he nor his wife can say for certain that they were still on the premises at the time of the call."

One of the social studies teachers chuckled. "Translation, until they're caught red-handed, those two are free to pull this again anytime they like."

Tim Jordan glared at him. "Don't be a fool, Phil. They've been taken to the police station for questioning. That is, they'll be questioned as soon as their lawyers arrive. You of all people should have faith in our legal system and our honorable police department."

Phil nodded. "Maybe I would if they weren't exhuming a murder victim they claimed earlier was an accidental death."

A murmur rose, grew to a loud din, as teachers asked each other what the hell was Phil Tarkleton talking about. Gabbie felt her cheeks burn on Darren's behalf. It was an oversight, not stupidity, that he'd declared Cam's death an accident. And besides, how had Phil found out about the exhumation so quickly?

"Quiet, please! Quiet!" Tim shouted.

He sounded desperate. He was in a tough spot, eager to give the impression he was on top of the situation, yet reluctant to name names and risk a lawsuit. But his egotistical arrogance prevented Gabbie from feeling any sympathy.

"You're free to go home now," Tim concluded. "If you learn anything about the bomb scare—and I don't mean hearsay or speculation—please contact the police. I'll see you all tomorrow morning." He made a hasty exit before anyone could ask him further questions.

Wet flakes floated from a dim gray sky, melting as they reached the ground. Gabbie pulled up the hood of her parka and hurried toward her car. She slipped the Volvo into reverse and zipped out of the parking lot, eager to put distance between herself and the high school. She was filled with impotent rage: toward the two juvenile delinquents who had the power to shut down a high school, and at Tim Jordan, who didn't have the balls to take a stand and mete out the punishment they deserved. *The idiot! Didn't he realize his passivity only encouraged Todd and Barrett to pull more dangerous stunts as they thumbed their noses at school authorities and the law?*

A traffic light turned red, and Gabbie screeched to a halt. While she had faith in Darren's interrogating skills, Barrett would be a tough nut to crack. Todd was younger and more vulnerable, but his wealthy parents would see to it he had a lawyer skilled at damage control. At best the boys would be fined or receive a suspended sentence. Gabbie shook her head. At least it would be something.

As she approached the Long Island Expressway, she made a sudden decision to drive to the mall fifteen miles away. She turned onto the ramp and joined the westbound traffic. The snow still wasn't sticking, and mindless window shopping was guaranteed to erase all thoughts of bullies and bomb scares from her mind.

Gabbie's first stop was Barnes & Noble. She indulged in one of her favorite pastimes, skimming through novels in hopes of adding titles to her must-read list. She flipped through large coffee-table photography books, which inspired her with ideas for future Photography Club projects. One day she'd have them photograph old houses in Chrissom Harbor. Another afternoon they'd go down to the beach and take shots of the sand, the water, and the sky.

She suddenly remembered that Barrett and Ross had accosted Charlie and had taken the film cartridge from his camera. The thought led her back to the bomb scare and to Cam's murder. Gabbie shivered. Chrissom Harbor was a dangerous place.

Oh, right, she mocked herself. *It's a jungle out there! Get a grip and cut out the melodrama and negative thoughts.* Determined to put action to thought, she marched into the first department store she came to and lost herself amidst the cosmetics and perfumes she used so sparingly.

An hour later, as her fingers stroked a cashmere turtleneck she couldn't afford, Gabbie's stomach began to growl. No wonder she was famished. It was close to three o'clock. At a cafe-style restaurant open to the mall, she bought a turkey sandwich and a cup of coffee. She ate quickly, oblivious of the light stream of shoppers passing her in both directions.

"Hey, Ms. Meyerson! How's it going?"

Startled, Gabbie looked up, into Barrett's grinning face. Todd, his sidekick, had a malevolent gleam in his eye, as though he were waiting for something nasty to happen. *I won't give them the satisfaction of uttering one word*, she silently vowed. Though she'd lost all appetite, she raised her coffee cup to her lips and was furious to see her hand was trembling.

Barrett nudged Todd. "We heard there were big doings at school today, didn't we, Todd?"

The smaller boy giggled, his body quivering with pent up energy. "Right-o. Too bad we were absent and missed all the excitement."

When she made no reply, Barrett nodded, an arrogant smirk on his lips. "At least you got some shopping done," he said. "Looks like the bomb threat was a gift to everyone, wasn't it?"

Gabbie's nostrils quivered with fury. They were high on their victory! Darren must have questioned them and had to let them go. Now they were taunting her about it in a public mall in broad daylight.

Still, they were children, she told herself. Teenagers who were out of control partly because their wimp of a principal allowed them to ride roughshod over poor kids like Charlie Russell. On the other hand, Barrett was her student. If she backed down now, she'd never be able to discipline him unless she sent him to the office every day.

She met Barrett's mocking blue eyes. "A bomb threat's no joke, Barrett. I'm surprised the police released you so quickly."

"They had to since we didn't do anything," Todd said. "Right, Barrett?" They slapped their thighs and laughed. The sound grated on her nerves. Impotent rage made her blurt out the first lie that came to mind.

"I suppose they had to let you go for now." She forced her lips into a knowing smile as she slowly panned from one to the other. "But they'll bring you in again, soon as they hear all the facts from their secret witness."

The antics stopped. Todd's face went white. "What witness? Who?"

Gabbie hid her delight with a shrug. "I've no idea. It's something we heard at school before we left for the day."

She nibbled at her sandwich, pretending not to notice that Barrett's face had turned grim. His hands closed into fists. "Then somebody's lying."

"Lots of kids go to the bagel shop," she said as she chewed. "It's only logical that someone would have seen who made the call."

Barrett's eyes rolled up as if he were trying to remember who'd been at the bagel shop that morning. He grabbed Todd's arm. "Come on. We gotta go." His eyes, now devoid of all expression, turned on Gabbie. "See you tomorrow, Ms. Meyerson."

It sounded like a threat.

CHAPTER EIGHTEEN

As soon as they disappeared from sight, Gabbie disposed of the rest of her lunch and headed for her car, berating herself every step of the way. She was the adult, a member of the high school faculty. Regardless of the provocation, she should have remained calm and collected. Inventing an eyewitness to their crime had to be the most pathetic thing she'd done in weeks! Surely Barrett and Todd had checked to see they were alone when they called in the bomb scare.

Still, they'd gotten upset when she'd mentioned her fictitious witness, which made her wonder if some kid had been in the vicinity when they made the call. Darren and his dim-witted deputy couldn't possibly question every student, one at a time, to find out if anyone had seen them. And a general appeal wouldn't work. Too many kids were frightened of Barrett and Todd.

Discovering three inches of wet snow had fallen while inside the mall, Gabbie drove cautiously along the slushy road that led to the Expressway. She spotted a large supermarket and decided to stop to buy groceries for tonight's dinner.

The place was mobbed with shoppers, obviously panicked by the snow. Gabbie put a package of chicken breasts in her wagon for the one decent chicken dish she knew how to prepare, then went up and down the aisles in search of eggs, breadcrumbs, lemons, salad, and couscous.

Even the express checkout line was long. Dusk was falling by the time she placed the grocery bags in the trunk of her car. On impulse, she walked over to the bakery two doors down from the supermarket and bought a small chocolate cake. Back in the Volvo, Gabbie turned on the radio and heard the Expressway was at a standstill. She opted to take local roads home and was glad that she had.

An hour later she was back in Chrissom Harbor. The plow had cleared the main streets, but her road had been ignored, she discovered, when her car skidded into the turn. She inched her way home, wishing she'd remembered to buy some kitty litter to sprinkle along the icy, rutted driveway.

A loud scraping noise coming from the vicinity of the cottage startled her so, she almost swerved into one of the pine trees fronting the property. She straightened the wheel and drove past the driveway entrance. A pickup truck equipped with a snowplow was clearing her driveway. Gabbie backed up, leaving plenty of room for the driver to maneuver onto the road in case he hadn't seen her. A minute later, the driver reversed the truck so that it faced the direction of town.

When the pickup finished its task, the driver pulled up beside her Volvo. She saw it was Jack McMahon. He opened his window and motioned to her to do the same.

"Hey, Gabbie. Mary Hanley called, said to be sure to do you first. Looks like I finished just in time." He grinned, showing the space between his two front teeth.

Gabbie smiled. "Thanks, Jack. I sure appreciate it."

"I was surprised to find you out this afternoon. I guess a little bit of snow doesn't scare you like it does some folks."

"The driveway scares me more than the snow," she joked. "It's so rutted and icy, I worry I'll skid right into the cottage."

Jack rubbed his head under the woolen hat. "It sure is in awful condition. Come the spring, Roland ought to have it black-topped. Be sure to tell him so if you run into him."

Gabbie stared at him in astonishment. "I thought Roland lived in Atlanta, when he's not off excavating in Africa."

Jack nodded. "He does, but he's coming home to CH, now that Darren's all fired up that Cam's death was no accident." His inky blue eyes seemed to bore into hers. "I wonder who stirred him up with that notion."

Gabbie discovered her hands were trembling. She clenched them tight in her lap. "I've no idea. Maybe Roland found something among Cam's things that made him think someone hated Cam enough to kill him."

"Like what?" Jack demanded.

Gabbie shrugged. "I wouldn't know."

He snorted. "Darren didn't say Roland found anything like that."

"Oh? When did you talk to Darren?"

"This afternoon, soon as he finished giving those rotten kids the third degree." He shook his head in wonder. "I watched them leave the station whooping with joy. Boy, I hope they get what they deserve and real soon."

"Why did Darren have you come to the station?" Gabbie asked, trying to sound as innocent as she could.

"Same old, same old. Went over where I was the day Cam died. If I'd seen him, which I didn't. A few other things. Told me they're going to exhume the body on Friday." Jack gave a mirthless laugh. "What's left of it."

Gabbie shuddered. Poor Cam. He must be waiting to speak to her this very minute. "Well, thanks for clearing the driveway, Jack. What do I owe you?"

"Not one cent. Roland pays. See ya around."

He drove off. Gabbie pulled into the driveway and gathered up the cake and two bags of groceries. The phone was ringing as she unlocked the front door. She dashed into the kitchen and picked up the receiver, smiling when she heard Darren on the other end.

"I've been trying you all afternoon," he said by way of a greeting. "Where have you been?"

"And hello to you, too," she said.

"You really have to get a cell phone," he said.

"I will. When I get my first paycheck."

"I'll lend you the money. Hell, I'll treat you to a cell phone. There's a murderer on the loose."

Gabbie felt her irritation rising. "Darren, please! I'll be careful. I promise."

"Sorry," he said, picking up on her tone. "I know you don't want me to play bodyguard. It used to drive my wife crazy. But I get this way when I'm stressed out. It's been that kind of day."

She set everything down on the counter. "I can imagine, dealing with a bomb threat and investigating a murder."

He gave a mirthless chuckle. "And getting nowhere fast."

"Jack was clearing off my driveway when I came home. He said you'd been asking him questions."

"Along with several other people. A waste of time. But the autopsy will give us definitive answers. And maybe we'll get lucky and one of the items I brought to the lab will turn out to be the murder weapon."

"Things are moving along, Darren."

"Are we still on for dinner?"

"We certainly are. Seven o'clock all right?"

"Fine. I'll bring the wine. Red or white?"

"White," she said, and hung up.

She put away the groceries, then dashed upstairs for a quick shower. When she came downstairs, Cam called to her from the den.

"I can only talk for a minute," she said, leaning against the door jamb.

"What's happening with the investigation?"

"Nothing yet, though your brother's coming here, and—" She stopped.

"And?" Cam prodded her.

They're, um... they're exhuming the—er, your—your body. To, uh, examine it. For cause of death."

"Oh." Cam looked squeamish, as if he'd just eaten a mouse.

"Gotta go and start cooking," Gabbie said. "Darren's coming for dinner. I'll let you know if he has any news."

"Don't worry, I'm fading fast. I have enough smarts to know when I'm not wanted."

When Darren arrived at five after seven, the table was set, the salad and couscous were ready, and the chicken breasts were warming in the oven. He planted a kiss on her cheek and followed her into the kitchen.

"Roses!" she exclaimed with delight when she saw what he'd been hiding behind his back.

"White wine, red roses." He handed both to her.

"I'll take care of them. Go on into the den. I've put out some appetizers."

Darren's eyebrows shot up. "Will I be having company?"

"Nope. Cam promised to keep away."

"That's good." He lowered his voice. "I hate to say it, but it feels creepy talking to him. I mean, I know he's dead, then suddenly he's there in ghost form, acting the same as always. I can't decide if I should tell Roland."

"When's he arriving?"

"Early Thursday morning. He has meetings tomorrow and Wednesday he can't miss. I told him Thursday's soon enough. He's damn glad I'm reopening the case. He claims the thought of Cam falling to his death stuck in his craw from day one. But since I'd done the investigating, and old Doc Bradley checked it out, he let it go."

"Don't be hard on yourself." She gave him a little push. "Go on. I'll join you in two minutes."

Gabbie found a vase for the flowers and opened the wine. She filled two wine glasses and brought them into the den. Darren was standing before the bookcase, riffling through pages of a book.

"I hope you don't mind, but a team of county investigators are coming out tomorrow to examine the cottage," he said. "I'll seal off this room when I leave, more for appearance's sake than any practical purpose."

"Sure." She handed him a glass and moved to the couch. "I'll give you a key."

He sat down beside her. "I doubt they'll find anything, after so many people have trampled through this place. And the ground out back is covered over with snow."

"Don't be negative," she chided. "You're doing everything you can."

"Eight months too late," he grumbled. "I could kick myself every time I remember how I should have given the murder angle more consideration."

"You saw no sign of a struggle. No drag marks. And Cam was drunk."

He nodded. "Pissed to the gills. Still, he'd riled lots of people in town. I should have insisted that the ME do an autopsy. I hate to think I was negligent because I didn't want Cam to have been murdered."

"Is that what you thought at the time?" Gabbie asked.

"No. From the looks of things, I really thought he'd fallen to his death."

"Then stop second guessing and find out who murdered him."

They clinked glasses and sipped. Gabbie spread crabmeat dip on a cracker and offered it to him. He downed the hors d'oeuvres and grinned.

"Mmm, delicious."

"Have another," she said, handing it to him. She smiled as he polished that one off, too. "What's Roland like?"

"Well, growing up, we always called him Rolly because he's round, with the chubbiest cheeks you've ever seen. When he turned eighteen, he asked us—no, ordered us—to call him by his proper name, Roland."

"And you did?"

Darren chewed on his lower lip as he considered her question. "The interesting thing is, Cam and I called him Roland after that, can't tell you exactly why. He looks like a pushover, but underneath his padding, Roland's tough as nails. The complete opposite of Cam. He goes excavating in Africa, then comes back and handles himself like a political pro at the press conferences that always follow."

"Oh," Gabbie said. "I'm impressed."

"You should be. Roland's experienced in raising funds for his trips and dealing with the public. Today he raised holy hell with the powers-that-be and got them to agree to have the body exhumed ASAP."

"Has he found anything among Cam's papers?"

"Not a clue."

"And you got nothing from Jack, Reese, Terry, and Don?"

"They all denied being in on a deal with Cam and swore they hadn't seen him the day he died." He shook his head. "They stuck to their stories, even when I spouted details about the cigarette deal and when they were supposed to pick up their money."

He shook his head in admiration. "Dammit, they're good liars, every one of them."

"Did they account for where they were that afternoon?"

"Terry and Reese were at work, but neither has a witness to attest that he stayed at work past five o'clock. Don and Jack were out and about. Don says he drove to a warehouse in Riverhead for beauty salon supplies. Jack was making deliveries for the furniture store where he occasionally works." Darren let out a snort of dissatisfaction. "None of them has what you'd call an air-tight alibi."

"So," Gabbie said slowly, "any one or combination of the four could have done it. That would account for your not seeing drag marks on the lawn."

"And I have nothing concrete that proves they all had a reason to come here that day." He slapped his thigh in disgust. "I can't very well bring a ghost's sworn statement into a court of law."

They stared glumly at each other. Gabbie regretted having brought up the subject.

She touched Darren's arm, felt the muscle respond to her. It gave her an amazing sense of power. "Let's go and eat. Everything's ready."

Darren smiled. "It's the best offer I've had all day."

Gabbie served their dinner and was pleased that everything had turned out well. It was almost a year since she'd taken the trouble to prepare a meal for anyone beside herself.

"You're a great cook," Darren said, eating his last forkful of chicken."

"It's coming back to me," Gabbie quipped. "But I suppose cooking's something you never forget how to do. Like riding a bicycle."

"And making love," Darren added.

Gabbie bowed her head so he wouldn't see the blush coloring her face and ears. But he obviously knew she felt uncomfortable, because he changed the subject.

"How did you spend the afternoon?"

Gabbie frowned. "I went to the mall and had the misfortune of running into Barrett Connelly and Todd Ross. They were cocky enough to taunt me by alluding to the bomb scare."

Darren pursed his lips. "They were gloating for getting off scot free. We questioned each of them separately in the presence of his lawyer. They had their story down pat. Yes, they'd been to the bagel shop earlier, but then they went to Ross's house. No, they couldn't prove it since no one was home then."

Gabbie sighed. "There must have been someone at the bagel shop who saw them. What about the owners?"

"Business was slow just then, so the husband went into the back room while the wife ran an errand. The public phone's in the vestibule entrance, not visible from the back room."

Gabbie was about to tell him of the boys' reaction to her lie that someone had seen them, when Darren's cell phone rang. He gave her an apologetic smile and answered it.

"Oh, no! Christ, is he all right?"

He listened another minute. "Okay. Smart thinking. Did you call Pete?"

Gabbie's eyes widened as the sound of hysteria came through the phone.

"Okay, Lionel, calm down. She'd have found out sooner or later. Sooner's better. Sonia would turn on you like a tiger if you hadn't called her. Just keep on trying Pete and that bar he goes to. I'm leaving for the hospital now." He looked down at his watch. "Be there in fifteen minutes."

Gabbie stared at him. "What happened? Don't tell me—"

He cut her off. "Charlie Russell's been beaten up real bad. He's in the emergency room at MidSuffolk Hospital with two broken ribs. They're watching him for a concussion."

"Who did it?"

"Charlie's not saying, but we can guess, can't we?"

Gabbie's hands flew to her mouth. "My God! It's all my fault! I said something stupid to those monsters, and they went after Charlie."

Darren eyed her curiously. "What did you say, Gabbie?"

Her breath came in gasps. "I told them someone saw them calling from the bagel shop. I know it was dumb, but they were acting so damn cocky and arrogant. I couldn't bear to let them think they could keep on getting away with what they've been doing. I made it up, only I saw immediately I'd touched a raw nerve."

He was on the verge of asking her another question, when he stopped himself. "We'll talk tomorrow. I gotta go. Sonia's carrying on at the hospital, yelling it's unsafe for her nephew to live in this town. And you know what? I don't blame her."

His lips brushed hers. "Don't let anyone in, and I mean anyone. There's a murderer out there."

"And two loose cannons."

Darren grimaced. "Right, but now we have ourselves a witness."

CHAPTER NINETEEN

G abbie cleared the table and put away the leftover food in record time. The news about Charlie had left her much too agitated to settle down. She went into the den and threw herself onto the couch. "Cam!" she called. "Can you hear me?"

No answer. She tried a few more times, then gave up. The poor fellow was proving true to his word and had left for the night. On impulse, she sat down at the desk and opened drawers. Hired workers had packed up Cam's papers and other possessions and sent them to Roland, but surely something must have been left behind. Some clue that could lead them to the murderer.

She found it disturbing that Reese, Don, Jack, and Terry had all lied to Darren about their involvement in the cigarette deal. They each had a reason for being at the cottage that afternoon. Gabbie found it hard to believe that none of them had come by to pick up his share of the money. Unless the man who killed Cam came first, and by the time the others put in an appearance, both Cam and the money were nowhere to be found.

Maybe the night she'd met them at Logan's they were really grumbling about Cam's cheating them a second time. Only they couldn't say so in public, so they pretended they were angry about the land deal. And, of course, the murderer or murderers joined in, pretending to be angry, too.

The various complications and possibilities spun around in her head as she examined each drawer with care. As far as she could tell, the desk had no secrets to reveal. Best to leave that type of detective work to the investigative team that was coming tomorrow. Too fidgety to sit home alone, she decided to go to Logan's.

Despite the snow, the parking lot was full of cars as usual. Gabbie opened the door to the bar and was hit by a blast of beery warm air and the buzz of conversation. A suspenseful excitement pulsated as sentence fragments and names swirled around in the dim light.

"Hey, Gabbie!" Don called out to her. "Come join your friends."

My friends, she thought sarcastically, then brightened when she saw Tessa at the table, along with Terry, Reese, Jack, and Adele. She smiled when Terry got up to get her a chair, and the others moved closer to one another to make room for her. *These are my friends—or rather my acquaintances—even though one of them is probably a murderer.*

"Stella Artois?" Mike called to her.

"Sure," she called back.

"Hello, Gabbie," Tessa greeted her. "What must you think of us, with these awful incidents happening in Chrissom Harbor?"

Terry nodded. "They keep on coming, one after another."

"Ever since Gabbie came to town," Jack drawled.

"Now that's not true, and you know it," Reese said. "Cam was killed last spring, and those two hoodlums have been growing worse each day."

Adele made a clucking sound. "My heart's breaking for poor Charlie Russell. Beat up and in the ER. Someone should put those two in jail and throw away the key."

Gabbie turned to the plump, motherly woman. "How did you hear about Charlie?"

Jack answered for his wife. "Lionel called here looking for Pete. Pete came by, not ten minutes ago, and Mike told him to go to the hospital."

Sick as she was about Charlie, Gabbie was determined to redirect the conversation to Cam. "Jack tells me Roland's coming to Chrissom Harbor."

Reese nudged Terry. "I wonder if they'll let him watch the autopsy. Rolly's used to looking at old bones."

Terry grinned. "Except these bones still have some meat on them."

Tessa glared from one to the other. "Enough already! Show some respect for the dead."

Her husband wore a pained expression. "Honey, except for you, no one at this table gives two hoots that Cam is gone. Our lives are nice and peaceful since he died."

"And boring," Adele added, her round, plain face turning a beet red.

No question about it, Gabbie thought. *Adele had been a Cam admirer.*

Jack frowned at his wife then turned to the others. "The way I see it, they're digging him up for nothing. Darren doesn't have one lousy clue that points to murder. That's why he's questioning us all over again." He shrugged his hefty shoulders. "It's a waste of time and effort. If it was murder—and I'm not saying it was—the trail's gone cold."

Terry nodded. "I'm surprised he let Jill skip town."

Tessa chuckled. "Surely you don't imagine she pushed Cam off the bluff."

"No, I don't," Terry answered. "But she might know something." He lowered his voice. "If we were betting on who did it, I'd put my money on hubby, Fred."

Gabbie's pulse quickened. "Why? Do you think he killed Cam?"

Terry shrugged. "I wouldn't be surprised. That guy has one hell of a temper. I saw him yelling at Jill in the diner parking lot two days before Cam died. He shoved her into a parked car and off he went, not bothering to see if she was okay."

"Do you think he knew about Cam and Jill?" Gabbie asked.

Don let out a loud guffaw. "He'd have to have been blind not to see what everyone in town knew was going on."

Reese frowned. "Sometimes Cam picked her up from work at my place. I told Jill it wasn't smart, that people would talk, but she paid me no mind."

Tessa looked pointedly at Terry. "Fred's not a wife beater like someone I could name. Mostly his mind's on his work, so I think there's a good chance he didn't know about Jill and Cam. Could be he was so riled up that time you saw him because he'd just found out."

"Maybe you're right, hon," Don agreed. "Since that was two days before Cam was killed, it's more reason to say it was Fred who did Cam in. Darren must think so, too. He questioned the Leverettes on Sunday, before he got to any of us."

Reese gave a snort. "I wonder if he questioned those rotten kids while he had them in the station. After all, they found Cam's body on the beach."

Jack let out a sharp breath through his nose. "They're bad ones, all right. Too bad we can't ship them off to the army. The sergeant would drill them into shape."

"Right," Adele said in a teasing voice. "Just like they did you, Jack honey. And trained you to keep yourself nice and neat."

Everyone but Gabbie burst out laughing. She looked over at Jack, noticed that the second button down on his plaid flannel shirt was missing.

Tessa waved her hand. "Those two boys are skunks, all right, but they're not murderers. Not yet anyhow."

Gabbie felt compelled to say something. Anything. "The police have to find cold, hard evidence before they can arrest anyone."

"Right!" Don agreed. "And so far, Darren doesn't have one lead, one shred of proof that points to a murderer."

"That you know about," Reese said scornfully. "He must have something, or the DA wouldn't have agreed to an exhumation."

Don shrugged, clearly embarrassed. "I guess you're right. It makes sense when you think about it. And there's the mystery of who took—" He stopped dead and looked at Gabbie. "Well," he finished off lamely, "Cam knew how to piss everyone off."

Terry smiled at Gabbie. "Don't be surprised if Darren comes to search the cottage. He must be desperate for clues."

"He's looked around," Gabbie said in what she hoped passed for an off-hand manner.

"What's left there for him to find?" Reese demanded. "The cleaners went through it months ago. Believe me, they're damn thorough. I recommended them to Mary. And whatever they missed would have been picked up by that packing company that sent Cam's things to Rolly."

"Still," Terry said, half mocking, "could be the murderer lost something like a cufflink, and it rolled under the radiator."

Don laughed. "Oh, sure. Right. Just like in the movies. Besides, who wears cufflinks these days?"

Tessa yawned and tapped her hand to her mouth. "Time for this working girl to go beddy-bye." She winked at Gabbie as she rose to her feet. "Your hair's looking great. Stop in soon for some highlights."

Suddenly the men were figuring out the bill. Gabbie tossed in a few singles and followed the others out the door. She chimed in her good-byes, hoping they now regarded her as a "regular" and hadn't the slightest inkling she'd come for information. She chuckled. Tonight had been a total washout. The only thing she'd learned was that Adele McMahon must have had a crush on Cam, like Sonia and half the women in town.

The frigid air made her teeth chatter. Gabbie ran to the Volvo and turned up the heater. She drove slowly, admiring the white-edged trees standing out against the clear sky. Fresh snow made everything look new and clean. But not safe. She parked close, looked around quickly, then dashed to the front door and double-locked it behind her. Upstairs, she undressed quickly and slipped under her quilt. She fell asleep almost immediately.

The sense of an alien presence in the cottage jerked her awake. Gabbie sat up, totally alert. She heard a cabinet door being opened, then another. Something fell to the floor. A muffled curse. Gabbie reached for the telephone to call 911. Damn! She couldn't see to dial, and putting on a light was out of the question. She slipped into her robe and felt along the top of her dresser for her scissors. Glad she'd worn socks to bed, she slowly descended the stairs.

The intruder was in the den. She saw the long, narrow ray of his flashlight as he moved about. Terror pierced her heart like a dagger. *Cam!* she called to him silently. *Please come, I need you.* But Cam had promised to stay away. He wouldn't return until the morning.

Damn! Too late, she remembered the squeaky step, third from the bottom. She froze, hoping whoever was there would assume the noise was merely one of the many nocturnal creaks of the old cottage. She held her breath in the sudden darkness, sensing he was holding his breath as well. She heard movement, blinked as a light flashed into her eyes.

A sharp pain pierced her left temple as whatever had been thrown hit its target.

Gabbie came to, heart thudding against ribs. Where was she? Why couldn't she see? Slowly, she made out objects in the dim light and realized she was lying beside the bottom step in the hall. The throbbing pain started at her temple and continued to the back of her head. She shivered as cool air swept over her legs. Was that the sound of a car driving away? Or was she remembering a sound she'd heard minutes ago?

Tentatively, Gabbie stretched out her hand, felt the round form of her paperweight beside her. Her fear turned to fury. How dare someone turn her favorite possession against her! She half-crawled, half-walked to the den and fell onto the couch.

"Cam," she moaned. "Where are you? Please come! I need you." She closed her eyes, longing for a pill that would make her pain go away.

"Gabbie! My God, what happened?"

She felt a wave of relief at the sight of his pale, concerned face hovering over her. It wavered in and out of her vision.

"Someone broke in and threw my paperweight at me. I think I blacked out for a few minutes."

"Dammit! We should have expected something like this to happen!"

Gabbie blinked. "Why?"

"Because," he said in exasperation, "once word got out that I was murdered, the perp was bound to come back for the murder weapon or something he may have dropped."

She groaned. "Dropped? After all this time? Everything's been taken out or cleaned by now."

He cursed under his breath. "I should have been on guard. I could have scared him off."

"Must call Darren," she mumbled. "Have to find his cell number."

But she had no time to look for it because Cam was rattling it off. She staggered to the phone on the desk. But when she pushed buttons, her fingers faltered, and she had to start over again. Darren answered on the first ring.

"Police Chief Rollins," he said thickly. She'd woken him up.

"It's me, Gabbie." Her voice quivered from the cold seeping into the room. Of course! The sliding door was open.

"My God, Gabbie, what's wrong?"

"Someone broke in and struck me on the temple with my paperweight."

"Should I send an ambulance?"

"No, just come right over. As fast as you can."

"I was planning to," he said, and broke the connection.

He arrived in record time. She unlocked the front door and fell against his warm, hard body. "We need light," he said. She winced when he switched on the hall light to examine her wound.

"Sorry, I'll turn it off in a second." His gentle ministrations were a balm to her sore body and soul. "Doesn't look too bad, but I'm taking you over to the ER. What happened?"

Gabbie told him as he helped her to the den couch. When she was finished, Darren turned to Cam.

"Did you see who did this?"

"Dammit, no. I came because Gabbie called out to me."

"It's the murderer, isn't it?' Gabbie said. "He's after something he left behind."

Darren grimaced. "I should have spread the word I'd checked out the cottage and hadn't found a thing." He walked over to the wall unit, observed the open cabinet drawers beneath the

TV, the books tumbled to the floor. He stood there gnawing at his lower lip as he thought.

"Interesting that he focused on this part of the room."

"There's nothing to find," Cam said. "I haven't come across anything, and Roland would have let you know if he'd found anything by now."

"I'll call and ask him to go through your things again." Darren pointed to a shelf. "Isn't that where you kept your statue of a Roman soldier?"

"Of course!" Gabbie said. "That must be the murder weapon! He's probably worried about fingerprints." She grinned at Darren. "Good thing you took it over to the lab."

"Hmm," Darren said. He turned on the outdoor floodlight and opened the sliding door. Gabbie pulled her robe tight against the night air.

"He came in this way, but the snow's too deep for footprints." Darren slid the door closed. "Doesn't seem to be forced."

"A charge card could have opened one lock," Cam offered, "but not the deadbolt."

"That was in place the last time I checked," Gabbie said.

"When was that?" Darren asked.

"Two, maybe three days ago. I haven't opened the sliding door since the day I came to see the cottage with Mary Hanley."

Darren shot the deadbolt in place. "Tomorrow, we get a locksmith from another town to change all the locks."

She shivered. "You don't think someone who has the key to the cottage—"

"We'll figure that out later. Now, let's get you to the hospital."

He helped her into her parka. She leaned on him as they made their way to his Camry. "How's Charlie?" she asked.

"Coming along. The doctor told him to stay home from school for a day or two. Sonia insisted on keeping him in her house, and Pete didn't argue."

The roads were deserted as Darren drove to the nearest hospital. He parked at the emergency entrance and opened the car door for Gabbie. He held a firm arm around her waist and escorted her into the waiting room. Though her head still throbbed and hurt like the devil, she felt strangely at peace. *Darren's here*, she thought, *and no one can harm me.*

The small waiting room was empty. The nurse on duty greeted Darren with a jaundiced eye. "You again!" She gave Gabbie a once over, then said the doctor would see her just as soon as she filled out some forms.

Gabbie fumbled for her wallet inside her purse. "Here's my insurance card. I doubt that I can fill out forms. I have a blinding headache."

The nurse was about to give her a starched reply, when Darren grinned and said, "Come on, Abigail. Don't be hard-assed. She's sustained a blow to the temple and can't even see straight."

Abigail appeared neither surprised nor impressed by this bit of news. She pointed to the forms on the clipboard. "In that case, you fill them out for her."

Darren sighed and started writing. The nurse handed Gabbie an ice pack. She returned five minutes later. "You can go in now."

The young Indian doctor examined Gabbie's temple. He said she could expect a nice lump since she hadn't applied ice immediately. His warm brown eyes settled on Gabbie then on Darren.

"You might have a concussion. I'll feel better knowing that someone will be monitoring you tonight."

"I live alone," Gabbie said. She giggled as she thought of Cam. "Though I sort of have a roommate."

Darren shot her a warning glance. "I'll stay over," he said quickly, before she could mention that she lived with a ghost.

Gabbie caught the doctor's knowing smile but was too befuddled to give him a piece of her mind and set things straight. She and Chief Rollins were not involved that way. The moment passed, and Gabbie listened to his instructions to rest at home for a day or two before returning to work. She drifted off in the car and woke up because someone was stroking the back of her hand.

"Gabbie, we're home," Darren said.

She blinked her eyes a few times. "Oh." She turned her head. He meant the cottage. She shivered, not wanting to go inside.

"Where did you go before?"

"Before?" she repeated stupidly.

"After dinner, when I left to see about Charlie. I called an hour later and got no answer."

"Oh. You didn't leave a message on the tape."

"No, I didn't." He made no move to open his door.

His disapproval filled her with dismay. "I went to Logan's. I guess to talk to people."

"About Cam's murder, I suppose."

"Yes."

She flinched when Darren punched the steering wheel. "Dammit, Gabbie, you have to stop playing Miss Marple. Who was there? What did you say?"

"I can't remember. Don and Jack were there with their wives. And Terry and Reese." She tried for levity. "You know, the gang of four."

"What about Fred Leverette? Was he there?"

"I didn't see him. Why?" She did her best to gather her wits together. "Do you think he's the one who broke in? Terry said he has a rotten temper. He saw Fred shove Jill against a parked car two days before Cam was killed."

"Gabbie, honey, anyone's capable of violence. Which is why, until I find who murdered Cam, I'm asking you—no, begging—you to stop going to Logan's to sniff out information like Sherlock Holmes."

She gave him a weak smile. "I thought I was Miss Marple."

"Gabriela!" He pressed his lips against hers and kissed her soundly for what seemed like minutes. When they moved apart, he punched the wheel again.

"I had no intention of doing that, at least not tonight. I'll stretch out in the lounge chair and check on you every few hours."

She grinned, happy to know he'd be staying. "You don't have to."

"Oh, yes, I do. Besides, I want to."

She felt sleepy again and was barely aware of his helping her into the house and up the stairs to her bedroom. She suddenly remembered. "I have to let Mrs. Green know I won't be in school tomorrow."

"I'll call and tell them you were injured in an accident and had to be taken to the ER."

"Okay," she agreed, and promptly closed her eyes.

CHAPTER TWENTY

G abbie awoke the next morning with a blinding headache. For one awful moment she feared she'd overslept and was late for school. The events of the previous night rolled into her mind, and she groaned. She needed a strong cup of tea.

Her legs trembled as she crept down the stairs.

"How are you feeling?" Cam called from the den.

"Lousy. My head hurts."

She felt a pang of disappointment as she read Darren's note. He'd arranged for a locksmith to come some time in the afternoon to change all the locks. He'd be at the police station all morning and she was to call if she needed anything.

Of course he'd gone to work. She scolded herself for expecting to find Darren in the kitchen, eager to prepare her breakfast the moment she woke up. The need for company drove her into the den. She seated herself gingerly on the couch while Cam scrutinized her from the lounger.

He clucked his tongue. "You look like hell. Take two aspirins and get back into bed."

"Gee, thanks. Just what I need—a sympathetic friend."

Cam grinned. "I am sympathetic. I'm telling you to rest up as the doctor ordered."

"Darren's instructions, I suppose." Gabbie turned to glare at him, and an excruciating pain shot through her head. She closed her eyes and lay down slowly. "Did anyone try to break in while I was sleeping?"

"Not a soul."

"Good, but please stick around. I'm afraid he might come back."

"I'm your bodyguard for the next few days. It's the least I can do."

When the pain subsided, she had toast and marmalade with her tea and downed two aspirins. Preparing and eating her small breakfast exhausted her. She went upstairs to nap.

As she was drifting off the phone rang. A man's voice she didn't recognize came through the phone. "Detective Wolfert," he said. He wanted to know if he and his team could come now to examine the cottage or, as Chief Rollins suggested, do this another day.

She was on the verge of telling them to come another time, then thought she'd feel safer having a crime scene unit about. Their presence would definitely ward off intruders. "Today's fine," she said. "Let yourself in and leave the key in the kitchen when you leave. I'll be resting upstairs."

"We heard what happened last night, Ms. Meyerson." The detective's tone was grim. "Sorry. We'll be quiet and work as quickly as we can."

She slept soundly until one-thirty and was pleased to discover the investigating team had come and gone. She wasn't at all pleased to see they'd left black powder on the sliding door and all over the bookcase. She showered, dressed, and was about to make herself a tomato and cheese sandwich when the phone rang.

"Gabbie, dear girl, are you all right?" Tessa asked. "We just heard about your midnight visitor and the nasty bop on your head. Maybe you shouldn't stay there all by your lonesome."

"I'm okay," she said automatically, then realized she was feeling much improved. The pain in her head had receded to a dull ache. "How did you find out?" she demanded, thinking murderous thoughts about Darren. How dare he tell anyone what had happened?

"Cindy Patel came in for a manicure. You know, her boyfriend's Vikram."

"Vikram?" Gabbie echoed. She'd never met a Vikram in her life.

Tessa laughed. "Dr. Vikram Mehta. He's the doctor who took care of you last night. In the ER."

"Oh," was all she could muster. As much as she liked Tessa, she was in no mood to socialize.

"I hope they find Cam's killer real soon, before he hurts someone else." The curiosity in Tessa's voice was palpable. "I wonder what he was after."

"I've no idea," Gabbie said. Then, just in case Don had been the intruder, she added, "An investigating team just left, so I'm sure there's not a trace here of anything suspicious or of any value to anyone."

"Did they find any clues? Any evidence?"

"I really don't know and I'm not up to chatting. Good-bye, Tessa."

The moment she hung up, the phone rang again. She smiled when she recognized Darren's voice.

"Hi, Gabbie. Feeling better today?"

"Much, thank you." She heard him stifle a yawn. "And thanks for watching over me. You must be exhausted."

"I'll survive."

"Detective Wolfert and his men finished here while I was napping. Did they find anything?"

"Nothing conclusive. They took fingerprints off the sliding doors in case the intruder wasn't wearing gloves." He paused. "I'm sure they were thorough, but I'd like to take a look around myself."

"Sure," Gabbie said, eager for his company.

"In that case, Lionel and I will be over shortly. Oh, one more thing."

She heard the excitement in his voice. "What is it?"

"Looks like he was after the statuette, after all! The lab found traces of blood and a hair on the back of it. They'll check for a match when the body's exhumed on Friday."

"Any fingerprints?"

"Just a partial too smeared to be of any use."

"Damn," she said. "How disappointing."

"Don't you worry, we'll get him!" Darren crowed. "Now that we're investigating, pieces are starting to fall into place."

Five minutes later the locksmith showed up, a tall, rangy older man with a full head of white hair and a handlebar mustache. Gabbie told him to change the locks on the front and back doors. He worked quickly and efficiently. By the time Darren and Lionel arrived, as he was finishing the job.

"Good to see you, Rex," Darren greeted him. "I'm glad you came yourself to change the locks."

The locksmith grinned at Darren, eyes twinkling as he looked at Gabbie. "Once you told me this was a special case, I made it my business to take care of it."

Gabbie, who had been worrying because there wasn't enough money in her checking account to pay for the new locks, was relieved when Darren told Rex to make the bill out to Roland. "He'll be here in a few days. I'll make sure he gets it."

"No problem."

Darren and Lionel left to inspect the den. When the locksmith was satisfied that the new key fit in the lock he'd just installed, he called to Gabbie. "You're all set now," he said, handing her two new keys. He asked her to sign a work order and left.

A short while later, Darren and Lionel came into the stuffy living room where she'd been reading. Darren shook his head.

"Nothing. Whoever broke in must have come back for the Roman statuette—either to take it or wipe it clean." He grinned. "I'll spread the word we found the murder weapon, then order everyone I questioned to be fingerprinted. That'll shake up the murderer and, at the same time, steer him away from here."

Gabbie smiled up at him. "Shrewd thinking, Chief, and much appreciated. How about a cup of coffee?" She rose cautiously from her chair.

Lionel's eyes lit up. "Hey, that sure sounds like a super idea, Ms. Meyerson."

Darren glared at his deputy. "Ms. Meyerson is just being polite, Lionel. She's not up to playing hostess, remember?"

"I'm feeling much better, Darren, and I've even some cake to go with the coffee." *The cake we never got to last night*, she thought as she went into the kitchen to fill the coffee pot.

When they'd finished all the coffee and most of the cake, Darren told Lionel to wait in the car while he had a few words in private with Ms. Meyerson.

Lionel winked. "Take your time, Chief, take your time."

"Daggett!" Darren thundered after his fast-departing deputy.

Darren double-locked the door. Very gently, he put his arms around Gabbie. She nestled against his chest and sighed. "I'm glad you came to check out the den," she murmured.

"Me, too." He slipped her earlobe between his lips. Darts of pleasure shot through her body.

"Mmm, that's nice."

He whispered into her ear, "I'm glad you think so, because it's your quota for today."

"My head hardly hurts anymore," Gabbie said. "I'll be glad to get back to school tomorrow."

"How about I stop by tomorrow night to see how you're doing? I'll bring dinner."

A warning bell went off in her brain, and she drew back from his embrace. "I don't know, Darren. This is getting to be a habit."

"A nice habit, don't you think?"

"I suppose," she agreed, and told herself they had to work together until they found Cam's murderer. "Did you speak to any of the suspects today?"

"I talked to Terry and Jack by phone. They still claim they know nothing about any cigarette deal. And they both denied coming here last night. I checked out their financial affairs. Last June Terry became a silent partner of that gym he's always going to."

"That's interesting."

"Interesting but far from conclusive. I couldn't find out if he'd paid in cash. Besides, Terry was named best salesman last year, which means he made plenty of dough."

"And Jack?" she prompted.

"No big purchases in addition to what I've already told you—he paid off a substantial loan he'd accrued from two failed businesses. But the loan was paid off a year ago, probably with money Adele inherited from her uncle."

She sighed. "So, we're back to square one."

"Far from it, and I've only just begun."

She was surprised at how good it felt to be back in school, hearing the kids chattering as they changed classes, some of them greeting her as if she'd always been part of their scenery. No one mentioned Monday's bomb scare. After all, today was Wednesday. Monday was long gone. History.

Her first two classes flew by. Gabbie took pleasure in imparting information, as well as in coaxing answers from students, answers they knew as long as they'd done their reading assignments, but lacked the facility to put into words.

Both Charlie and Theo were absent. She made a mental note to find out how Charlie was getting along. And she'd call Theo. She'd promised to keep an eye on her, and she'd do so at the first opportunity.

When she passed Todd in the hall, he gave her a goofy grin edged with malice. *Where was Barrett?* she wondered, and hoped he was absent. When sixth period began and he didn't show up, she sighed with relief. Then she berated herself. She had no intention of expending energy worrying each day whether or not he would make an appearance.

The sun was high overhead when she left the building. The temperature was mild enough to have melted some of the snow, and the streets and sidewalks were slushy and wet. Gabbie drove to the library. She waited until she was alone with Sonia at the circulation desk to ask how Charlie was feeling.

Sonia frowned. "He has a bump the size of a peach on the back of his head and two broken ribs. But he's up and about, no thanks to those hooligans. Someone ought to give them the punishment they deserve."

Gabbie lowered her voice. "Did Charlie say who beat him up?"

Sonia let out a mirthless laugh. "He doesn't have to. Everyone in town knows who's responsible, including Darren Rollins. He questioned those two animals and let them go. I'll have you know, our police chief's not half the man he used to be."

Gabbie swallowed, all too aware that she was referring to Cam and Darren beating up the boys who had raped her all those years ago.

"I'm sorry, Miss Russell. Please give Charlie my best wishes and tell him we missed him in school."

"Oh, I will." Sonia barked the humorless laugh again. "Sorry to hear they attacked you as well."

"I don't think—"

Sonia waved a finger at her.

"Take care, Ms. Meyerson. Chrissom Harbor's a dangerous place, and that cottage has seen one murder already. Maybe you should find yourself somewhere else to live."

After a stop at the supermarket, Gabbie went home and made herself a tuna fish sandwich for lunch. She took two aspirins because her head was aching, both from her injury and from her encounter with Sonia. The woman was definitely unpleasant and possibly deranged. But what if she knew something? After all, she lived next door to the Leverettes and might have seen Fred and Cam arguing.

She went into the den and leaned back carefully in the lounger.

Cam appeared almost immediately. "You look all done in," he commented from his perch on the edge of the desk.

"I'll be all right after I rest up a bit. But I've been wondering, and I'd appreciate your input."

Cam grinned. "Shoot."

"Sonia thinks Barrett and Todd broke in the other night and threw the paperweight at me."

"I doubt it. Seems to me they caused enough mischief with their bomb scare that day to need the thrill of breaking in here, too. And why would they? Unless you think they murdered me and were looking for the statuette?"

"No, I don't. Besides, I had the definite feeling one person broke in that night. And Darren saw one set of footprints in the snow." She thought a minute. "Did you and Fred ever argue because of your relationship with Jill?"

"Nope. We made a point of avoiding one another. Why do you ask?"

"Just wondering." She gave a nervous laugh. "I'm trying to figure out what prompted Sonia to suggest that I move out of the cottage. It sounded ominous."

"Don't waste your time and brain power. Sonia Russell doesn't need a reason to act weird. Half the things she says don't make sense."

Relieved, Gabbie sighed. Her thoughts returned to Todd and Barrett. "I just realized Todd was in school today and Barrett wasn't. It could mean absolutely nothing, but as a rule, either they're both in school or both are absent."

Cam didn't comment. His expression was thoughtful, as if he was busy working something out. "Does Barrett play sports?"

"Not that I know of," she said. "I can't see him as a team player. He needs a stooge like Todd, not peers on his level. Why do you ask?"

"Whoever threw that paperweight has good aim and a strong arm. Did you know Fred Leverette used to pitch for his high school baseball team?"

"Hmm. Maybe I could talk to him and sound him out."

"Leave that to Darren," he said sharply. "As far as I'm concerned, he's our man." When she didn't answer, he went on. "Fred had both motive and opportunity that day. He makes his own hours at the lab."

"Do you think he's a thief as well? Would Fred have taken the five hundred thousand dollars?"

Cam let out a snort of laughter. "Why not? He's the type to rationalize the money was coming to him. Recompense for my relationship with Jill. Even though I'd bet he's had his little playmate all along."

Gabbie grimaced. "I hate to think of Theo living alone with him."

Cam waved his hand. "Don't worry about that. Fred adores Theo. Believe me, he'd never harm his daughter."

His words did nothing to ease her sudden sense of foreboding. "I wonder why Theo didn't come to school today," Gabbie said. "I think I'll take a ride over there. After all, Jill asked me to keep an eye on her."

She was putting on her parka when Cam called after her. "Gabbie, don't go there! I know you're really after Fred. He's not someone you want to tangle with. Besides, he's probably at the lab."

So Cam sensed something, too. Gabbie turned and gave him a sweet smile. "If he's at the lab, I'll be safe and sound."

At the Leverettes' house she was almost relieved that Fred's old Ford wasn't parked in the driveway. She pressed the bell and listened. Silence. Disappointed, she rang again but got no response. She tried the door. Locked.

On impulse, she walked across the lawn to Sonia's house. The front door stood ajar. She opened it a little wider and was assailed by the noise of young voices arguing. She stepped inside the hallway. Theo and Charlie were going at it in the kitchen.

"—the stupidest thing I've ever heard!" Theo shouted. "Where is it? Where'd you put that damn gun?"

"Why would I tell you anything after the way you turned on me?"

Gabbie heard the slap of hands hitting thighs in exasperation. "I'm not turning on you! I'm trying to keep you from ruining your life."

"Mind your own business, okay!"

"Okay, I'll mind my own business. Then what? You shoot Barrett. They find you and throw you in jail. Charlie, don't ruin your life for that creep. He's not worth it."

"It would be worth it, Theo, to wipe him off the face of the Earth!"

"Then tell Chief Rollins about the things he did to you."

Charlie's cynical laughter chilled Gabbie to the core.

"Oh, right. You're so naive, if you expect the law to help me. Everyone knows he and Todd called in that bomb threat, but they got away scot free."

"They wouldn't have if you'd told the police you saw them."

"Yeah, like they'd believe me. And even if they did, I have no proof. It's my word against theirs."

Theo's tone was scornful. "You kept your mouth shut and they went after you anyway."

"That won't happen again."

"I knocked but I guess you didn't hear me," Gabbie lied as she strode into the kitchen.

Theo and Charlie turned to stare at her, surprise, guilt and resentment apparent on their faces.

"Theo, I came by because your mother—" She stopped as Charlie crumpled to the floor.

CHAPTER TWENTY-ONE

"Oh, no!" Theo's hands flew to her face. "He was supposed to stay in bed and rest. I told Sonia I'd come over and make sure he's okay. Only—only—" She was on the verge of tears.

"Let's help him back to bed," Gabbie said calmly, though her heart was pounding. "Where is he sleeping?"

"In the den."

They placed Charlie's limp arms around their shoulders and half-dragged him into the den. For a little fellow he was surprisingly heavy. They were both panting when they set him down on the made-up sofa bed.

"Do you think we should call the doctor?" Theo asked.

"Don't call anyone," Charlie said, his eyes blinking madly. "Please."

"God, Charlie, you scared the daylights out of me!" Theo said.

The color seemed to be returning to his pale face. "Do you feel okay?"

He attempted a grin, but it didn't quite land. "Are you kidding? My head's killing me and my ribs ache like the devil, but I'm better than I was last night."

"He took his medicine a few minutes ago," Theo said. "Sonia said the pills could make him woozy."

Gabbie straightened out the bedding. Charlie was wearing jeans and a red polo shirt. She was about to suggest he put on pajamas and get some sleep when he stumbled to his feet.

"Thank you, ladies. I can take it from here."

He stood up. Theo put a hand on his arm to stop him. "Where are you going?"

"To the bathroom, if you don't mind." His steps were wobbly as he walked out of the room.

"Promise me you won't do anything stupid," Theo called after him.

He turned and gave her a half-smile. "Of course not. It must have been the meds speaking. Anyway, I'm dead tired. I'm going to sleep, so you both can leave."

Gabbie and Theo ignored his dismissal. They watched him close the bathroom door behind him, then Gabbie followed Theo back into the kitchen. Even with the lights on, the room looked dreary. The appliances were Harvest Gold, the popular color from decades past. The wallpaper, a pattern of large gold and rust-colored flowers against a white background, was peeling along the seams.

They sat down at the narrow kitchen table. Theo was as pale as Charlie had been when he'd fainted. Her eyes glanced down at her lap, but Gabbie saw the tears streaming down her face.

"Everything's gone wrong. Everything!" Theo moaned. She began to sob, softly at first, then in deep, gulping gasps that wrenched at Gabbie's heart. She moved to hold Theo. The girl went rigid. After a long minute, she allowed herself to be comforted, and wrapped her arms around Gabbie and held on tight.

Gabbie let her cry. When the storm subsided, she patted Theo's shoulder and gently removed herself from her grip. "I think we could both use a cup of tea."

Theo nodded. Gabbie handed her the box of tissues she'd found on the counter, then filled the kettle with water and set it on the range. She grinned at the honking sound of Theo blowing her nose.

"I stopped by your house because your mother asked me to look in on you occasionally and make sure you're okay."

"It's all my fault she's gone." Theo rubbed her fists in her eyes. "I drove her away."

Her trembling voice made Gabbie fear another flood of tears. To head it off, she decided a shot of tough love was in order. "This isn't about you, Theo, so go easy on the drama. It distorts the reality of the situation. Your mother was unhappy living with your father. When she found out he was involved with another woman, she decided to leave. She'd have taken you along, but she didn't want to disrupt your life, especially since you get along well with your father."

Theo turned her mournful brown eyes on Gabbie. "I did drive her away. I was obnoxious because I was angry. She was in love with Cameron Leeds, and I despised her for not loving my father."

Her eyes grew shiny as tears welled up. "And all the time he had his own re-la-tion-ship." She dragged out the word, ridiculing it. "I heard more than I wanted to know about that when they quarreled Sunday morning."

"It's not your fault," Gabbie said as she opened cupboards in search of tea bags and cups. "Parents are human. And we humans do a wonderful job of screwing up our lives."

"Well, they should have thought of me!" Theo blurted. She gave Gabbie a baleful look. "Or is that being a drama queen?"

"Certainly not. You're their daughter. Their only child. They were selfish not to consider the impact all this would have on you."

Gabbie watched Theo's hunched up shoulders relax.

She put tea bags in the two mugs she'd found, then poured in boiling water. "Any chance Sonia has some cookies to munch on?"

Theo pointed to the narrow pantry. "In there."

Gabbie found an opened package of chocolate chip cookies and brought it to the table. Theo reached eagerly for one and took a huge bite.

"I hardly know your parents," Gabbie said, "but I had the definite impression they weren't getting along."

"They couldn't stand each other," Theo said, stuffing the rest of the cookie in her mouth. "I always blamed Mom. She used to pester Dad because he kept long hours at the lab, and then didn't talk to her when he got home. But he always talked to me, so I figured it was her fault."

Hateful memories of her own marriage rose unbidden to her mind. "It's always the woman's fault," Gabbie murmured.

"You're being sarcastic," Theo said.

"Absolutely and completely."

Theo's lips turned up. Then she was laughing, making Gabbie laugh, too. The tension their conversation had created evaporated into thin air.

"I think your mother's been unhappy for a long time," Gabbie said. "She felt guilty about her relationship with Cam. When he died, she tried to make things work with your father and got nowhere. Finding out about his affair gave her permission to leave."

Theo had a faraway look. "I hope she's happy now. She was so sad after Cam died, though she tried to hide it."

"Did you like Cam?"

Theo gave her a wry smile. "I tried not to, but he was totally irresistible when he wanted to win you over."

Don't I know it, Gabbie thought. "Handsome and charming?"

"Uh huh. And funny. Two summers ago, he took Mom and me sailing, along with a few other people: Charlie and his dad, Reese and his wife." The memory softened Theo's expression. "We sailed out into the bay, then dropped anchor so Charlie and I could swim off the side of the boat. And later we had a clam bake on the beach. We all laughed a lot and sang songs. It was one of my best days ever."

"Did you know they were involved then?"

Theo looked sheepish as she shook her head. "Naive, aren't I? I thought they were just old friends, and Cam felt sorry for Mom because Dad's always working. I found out about it that fall. Caught them in a clinch."

"And you've been mad at her ever since," Gabbie murmured.

"Not anymore! Now I'm furious with my father. What a hypocrite, pretending it was all mom's fault when all this time he was screwing around with someone from the lab. I don't want to live in that house with him one more day!"

Gabbie shook her head. "Theo, you have to stop being angry at your parents because they don't behave the way you want them to."

"But they're the adults! They're supposed set an example and give me a home, instead of running off and screwing around!"

"It's time to grow up, Theo."

Theo stared at her open-mouthed, too shocked to answer.

"I know you're only sixteen, and it doesn't seem fair to ask you to act maturely when your parents don't, but you've no choice. You're an intelligent girl. You've got to look after your-self, study and get good grades, so you can make the most of your life."

They both gave a start at the sound of a door closing. Theo ran to the den with Gabbie at her heels.

"Oh, no! He's gone!" Theo wailed. "He faked that fainting bit so we'd leave him alone, and I fell for it. I can't believe I fell for it!"

Gabbie peered out the front door. She caught a flash of movement down the street, just before it disappeared around the corner. She pointed. "There he goes. Where's he heading?"

"To the woods. We have to stop him!" Theo raced out the door.

Gabbie caught up with her halfway down the walk. She grabbed hold of her arm. "Think, Theo. You're wearing clogs, and the ground's covered with snow and ice. You can't go run-ning into the woods like this."

Theo wriggled free. She was panting now, hyperventilating with fear. "Charlie has a gun, Ms. Meyerson! We have to stop him before he kills Barrett Connelly!"

"A gun?" Gabbie's heart pounded like a jackhammer as she remembered the conversation she'd overheard earlier. "Where did he get hold of a gun? From his father?"

"His Aunt Sonia. He said it's a family heirloom."

"In that case, maybe it's old and won't fire. Is it loaded?"

"I don't know. He didn't say." Theo whimpered as she stared down at her clogs. She tugged at Gabbie's sleeve. "Please, Ms. Meyerson, help me find him! If we drive toward the beach, we can stop him."

"You said he was heading for the woods."

Theo nodded, exasperated. "He is! And the woods slope down to the beach. Everyone knows that."

Gabbie bit back the reprimand Theo deserved. "Okay, we'll drive around and look for him. But first we're going back in the house so I can call Chief Rollins."

"Then it will be too late," Theo wailed. "Let's call him from the car."

"I don't have a cell phone," Gabbie admitted.

Theo threw up her arms in despair. "Oh, God! I left mine at home." She rolled her eyes at Gabbie. "You have to be the only person on Long Island who doesn't have a cell phone."

Duly chastened, Gabbie said, "I'm buying one this weekend."

Gabbie called the police station from Theo's house. She told the dispatcher it was an emergency and was connected with Darren immediately. When she finished explaining what had happened, he said he'd be there as soon as possible.

Back in the car, she followed Theo's directions. She drove to the end of the street, then made a sharp right onto a narrow road that ran through woods. On their left, beyond the woods, was the Sound.

"Keep going," Theo instructed.

"How do you know he came here?" Gabbie asked. She figured they were driving northeast and were about half a mile from her cottage.

"Because this is where Barrett and Todd hang out. They fixed up an old shed. Put on a new roof to make it waterproof, strung up electricity for sound equipment. Mostly they play music and get high."

"Where'd they get the money?"

Theo threw her a withering glance. "The Rosses are loaded. Todd's father owns this land, as a matter of fact. Stop!" she shrieked.

She flew out the car before Gabbie came to a full stop. She cupped her hands into a megaphone and shouted, "Charlie! Charlie, come back here!" then took off like a madwoman down the path.

Gabbie started to follow her but spun around when she heard a car motor. The approaching police car came to a halt. Darren and Lionel ran toward her.

"We just got here," Gabbie said. "Theo's gone into the woods looking for Charlie. She's frantic."

"I'll catch up with her," Darren said. He turned to his deputy. "Lionel, check out the shed."

"You know about it?" Gabbie asked.

"Of course," Darren called over his shoulder as he strode past her.

She felt superfluous. *I'm not waiting around like a dummy,* she decided, and followed after them.

The terrain sloped downhill toward the Sound. Though trees grew all around her, she realized she was walking along a narrow footpath. The snow was barely an inch deep, and she could make out various sets of footprints – she had no idea how many.

About a hundred feet ahead of her, Darren and Lionel had stopped next to Theo, who was shouting and banging on the door to a shed half-hidden by overgrown bushes. Gabbie watched Darren put a hand on the girl's shoulders, who shrugged it away. He appeared to be asking her a question, to which she shook her head no.

The girl stood hugging herself while Darren and Lionel walked around to the side of the shed and peered through a small window. Obviously, Charlie wasn't inside, because the three continued along the path toward the Sound.

Gabbie was about to call after them, when she noticed a second footpath veering off to the left and down to the beach. She followed it, realizing too late the path must have been abandoned years ago. She soldiered on, pushing aside branches and stumbling over stones as she continued down the slope. The path ended suddenly at a rickety staircase that led down to the beach. Gabbie looked at the splintery steps half buried in snow and wondered if she should take a chance or if she'd end up twisting her ankle or worse. She saw the flash of red below as a figure ran out of sight.

"Darren! Theo! Charlie's down on the beach! He's running away from town!"

She climbed back up the footpath and shouted twice again before they heard her. Minutes later, they were at her side. Darren grabbed Theo's arm to keep her from dashing after Charlie. Gabbie couldn't hear what he told her, but she saw Theo stamp her foot then follow Lionel up the road to the parked cars.

Darren gestured to Gabbie to walk beside him as they trailed behind. "I alerted the county, and they're sending along a few men to help us search for Charlie." He whistled. "I hope we find him before it gets dark."

"I hope he doesn't catch pneumonia. He's not even wearing a jacket."

Darren gestured toward Theo. "Do me a favor and take her home. I don't want her going after Charlie on her own, especially since he's armed."

Theo's head whipped around. She let out a snort of contempt. "Right. He's really going to shoot me, the only friend he has in the world. For a cop, you know beans about kids!"

Gabbie bit back her retort. Now wasn't the time to lecture Theo on keeping a civil tongue. Besides, Darren's instructions took precedence. "We're on our way," she said, as much to Theo as to Darren.

She strode over to her car and opened the passenger door. The girl got in, her sullen expression proclaiming her displeasure.

Gabbie turned on the motor, then glared at Theo. She was about to give her a lecture on attitude and respecting her elders, when she saw Theo was shivering. She retrieved an old army blanket from the trunk and wrapped it around Theo, who sat stiffly as tears streamed down her cheeks.

Theo sniffed. "Charlie needs this more than I do."

"Hopefully, Chief Rollins will find him and bring him home real soon."

Theo took the tissue Gabbie offered and blew her nose. "I should have made him tell me where he hid that gun instead of blubbering on about my pathetic family." Her voice curled with self-contempt. "I let him fool me when I should have been looking out for him."

"Theo, don't be so hard on yourself. You're not responsible for Charlie."

Theo turned the full force of her fury on Gabbie, and for a moment Gabbie feared she would strike her.

"Yes, I am responsible for Charlie. I'm his friend. No one else gives a damn about him. No one stops those creepy bullies from tormenting him all the time, in and out of school."

"I'm sorry," Gabbie said softly. "He should have told his father what was going on."

"He did. And for once Mr. Russell put down his bottle and took action. He went up to school and told Dr. Jordan that Barrett and Ross were teasing Charlie, taking away his books and things."

Gabbie pressed her lips together, dismayed by what she knew would follow.

"'Sure,' Dr. Jordan said. 'I'll handle the situation.'" Outraged, Theo whipped her long hair from side to side. "And as usual, he did squat. Gave those creeps a talking to. And you know what?" Her eyes blazed into Gabbie's. "They were worse to Charlie than before."

"I hope they both die, only I don't want Charlie to be the one responsible."

The car filled with the sound of wracking sobs. This time, Gabbie made no attempt to comfort her. *Let her get it out of her system*, she thought. *All the frustration and pain she's suffering because bad things are happening, things no one can control or make better.* She put the car in gear and drove slowly toward Theo's house.

By the time she pulled into the Leverettes' driveway, Theo had herself under control. She offered Gabbie a half-smile. Even tear-stained, her face revealed a sweetness that Gabbie knew was a forecast of the beauty she was destined to become.

"Two crying jags in one day," Theo said ruefully. "I hope you don't get the impression I'm a hysterical wimp 'cause I'm not."

Gabbie held back the hug she wanted to offer. Instead, she said, "I think you're a caring person who's on overload."

Theo cocked her head and asked shyly, "Do you think I'll make a good writer?"

"Is that what you want to be—a writer?"

Theo nodded. "More than anything in the world."

"I don't see why not," Gabbie told her. "You're smart, articulate, and disciplined. Keep a journal of what's been going on around you. God knows you have enough material for at least three novels."

Theo leaned over to give Gabbie a quick hug. "Thanks, Ms. Meyerson. I'm glad you stopped by, and we got to talk."

Gabbie smiled. "Will you be all right on your own?"

"Sure. I'm used to taking care of myself."

"I'll phone if I hear anything about Charlie," Gabbie called after her, and watched till Theo was safely inside.

Darkness was falling. Gabbie felt too heartsick to go to Logan's for company or information. She drove to the cottage and made herself a sandwich. After eating it, she sat reading on the musty living room couch because she didn't feel like talking to Cam, either. The phone rang at eleven o'clock, startling her out of a half-sleep.

"Ms. Meyerson. It's Theo. They found Charlie."

"Oh, thank God," Gabbie said. "Where was he? Is he all right?"

"I guess. Chief Rollins brought him over to Sonia's about ten minutes ago. I ran over there, soon as I saw the police car. She got him into a hot bath and asked me to heat up some soup, then she chased me home."

Gabbie's heart was pounding as she asked, "Did he meet up with Barrett and Todd?"

"I don't know." Theo's voice went dead. "Charlie wouldn't say, but I could hear him crying. Sonia must have asked him about the gun, because he shouted, 'I don't have it! I don't have it anymore!'"

"Oh, God!" Gabbie murmured. After a pause, she said, "Well, thanks for telling me, Theo. I'll see you in school tomorrow."

She was hanging up when Theo shouted, "Ms. Meyerson, wait!"

"Yes?"

"I was wondering... my dad's staying with his girlfriend tonight, and I feel creepy here all by myself."

Gabbie suppressed the anger she felt toward Fred Leverette as best she could. Still, her voice had an edge when she asked, "Does he know what happened with Charlie?"

"Mmm, I didn't go into it when he called. Dad doesn't like it when I get involved with Charlie's problems. He thinks he should fight his own battles."

"I see."

Theo's words came in a rush. "Do you think I could spend the night with you? I won't be a bother, I promise. I'll sleep on a couch. I just can't stand to stay here another minute by myself."

"Of course you can, Theo. Gather up your books and clothes for tomorrow, and leave your dad a note. I'll come by for you in just a few minutes."

CHAPTER TWENTY-TWO

She went into the den and called out to Cam. He didn't appear. *Dammit, where was he? He always showed up when she wanted her privacy, and now—*

"What's the urgency this time?"

She heard his question before he materialized.

"Cam, Theo's coming to spend the night, and I'm putting her in the den, so please—"

"How did this come about" he asked, tilting his head, his grin widening with interest. "Are you taking up the role of substitute mother?"

"Don't be absurd!" she snapped. "She was out of her mind worrying about Charlie because he ran off with a gun. Darren found him minus the gun. He seems to be okay, but the whole ordeal's left her feeling spooky—er, nervous, about staying alone."

"Alone? Don't tell me Fred's gone away and left her too."

"He might as well have. He's staying with his girlfriend."

"The bastard," Cam said, without heat. "I'll watch over Theo all through the night."

"Cam, that's precisely the point! I don't want you around."

"And I don't want anyone breaking in while Theo's asleep in this cottage. I promise she won't even sense my presence."

Gabbie threw up her arms. "I haven't the time to argue, but, for God's sake, don't upset the poor child. She's had enough to contend with, without seeing you, too."

"Always a woman of tact, Gabriela," Cam chided as she fled the room.

Theo looked like a forlorn waif as she waited for Gabbie outside her front door.

"Did you leave your dad a note?" Gabbie asked as Theo tossed her knapsack into the back seat of the Volvo. "We don't want him to worry if he should come home and not find you here."

Theo got into the passenger seat and closed the door. "Sure, though he'll probably go straight to the lab tomorrow morning with his girlfriend."

Gabbie didn't like Theo's pallor. She wished she had some hot chocolate at the cottage, but tea would have to do. But when they got back, Theo refused her offer. She followed Gabbie into the den and curled up on the couch.

"Bathroom's upstairs. I'll go get some linens," Gabbie said.

When she came down again, Theo was fast asleep. Gabbie tucked a blanket around her and retired to her bedroom. She read a few pages, before she turned out the light. Hours later, two sharp sounds interrupted her sleep. She sat up, terrified, but realized the noise had come from a distance away. *Must be a car backfiring*, she thought groggily, and snuggled deeper under her quilt.

She'd set the alarm at seven-thirty. When it went off, Gabbie sprang out of bed, intent on preparing Theo a healthy breakfast before she drove her to school.

"A cup of black coffee will be fine," Theo told her. "I can't eat early in the morning. It makes me nauseous."

"No cereal?" Gabbie asked, disappointed. "I could scramble you some eggs."

Theo flashed one of her rare smiles. "I wouldn't mind a piece of toast."

"A piece of toast it will be."

Gabbie dropped her off at school and came right home. She considered stopping by Sonia's house to see how Charlie was feeling, but his aunt would probably resent her appearance and think she was intruding.

I am intruding. She chuckled, realizing how far afield she'd wandered from her original plan. Her intention to lead a quiet, solitary life had gone up in smoke now that she was involved in her neighbors' lives, deaths, and love affairs.

She straightened up after her overnight visitor, musing that she was growing fond of Theo Leverette. Beneath her sarcastic, explosive veneer was a warm-hearted, loyal young woman. Gabbie was glad she'd been able to offer her shelter and comfort.

The phone rang as she was carrying a pile of soiled clothes and linens to the tiny laundry room off the kitchen.

"I can talk for five minutes," Darren told her by way of a greeting. "I'm driving Roland over to the ME where they're performing the autopsy."

Her stomach lurched. "Don't tell me you're going to watch."

"No, we won't, but we want to be there. Gabbie—"

"Theo spent the night here. She told me you found Charlie and took him to Sonia's. What on earth happened?"

"Barrett's dead."

"What!" Gabbie sank into a kitchen chair. The dirty laundry tumbled to the floor.

"Terry discovered the body early this morning while he was jogging down at the beach."

"The beach. You mean, where you found Charlie last night?"

"Actually, closer to your cottage. The body was half hidden by bushes. Terry claims he saw a boot sticking out, so he went to take a look. Poor guy was still awfully shaken when I got there. Nearly tossed his breakfast."

"How was he killed?" she asked, having to know yet dreading to hear his answer.

"Two shots to the chest. No sign of the weapon."

The dread turned to terror. Her heart thumped against her ribs.

"Is it the gun Charlie took from Sonia's house?"

"It's possible, though Charlie swears up and down he didn't shoot Barrett. He claims Barrett took the gun away from him and told him to scram."

"Charlie said?" Then it dawned on her. "You've been questioning him. Don't tell me you dragged him down to the station to give him the third degree."

"You've seen too many bad movies, Gabbie. I secured the scene with Lionel on guard and called the Suffolk County police—again." He laughed, but without humor. "They must think Chrissom Harbor's turned into a war zone. Then I stopped at Sonia's. Had a devil of a time convincing her to wake up Charlie, but he must have heard us, because he came into the kitchen to see what was going on."

Gabbie struggled to shake off the apprehension pressing down on her shoulders. "Charlie's not your suspect!" she shouted. "He'd no more kill Barrett than set the school on fire!"

"My sentiments exactly. Trouble is he has motive, opportunity, and possibly the weapon."

Darren's logic was like an ice cube sliding down the back of her shirt. "I know he threatened Barrett, but he'd never act on it. I bet someone killed Barrett while Charlie was sleeping soundly in his aunt's house. Can't you tell by rigor mortis?"

Darren laughed. "It takes four hours after death for rigor mortis to set in, Miss Marple, so there's a good chance you're right. Unless Charlie has the stamina of Superman and snuck out of Sonia's house, which she claims he didn't. When we found him last night, he was all tuckered in. And he didn't look much better this morning."

She suddenly remembered the sharp noises that had interrupted her sleep.

"Darren, I may have heard the shots! There were two of them."

"There were two bullet holes," he said grimly. "What time was this?"

"I've no idea," she admitted, "since I went right back to sleep." She thought a moment. "But it must have been near dawn because I remember seeing a glimmer of light along the side of the shade."

"Just a second."

She heard voices in the background, then Darren was back on the line. "I have to go. Stop by the station later, if you can. I should be back around two."

"I will. And thanks for letting me know about Barrett. I didn't mean to yell at you before."

"Forget it." She heard the smile in his voice. "I'm used to getting flak from friends because I'm the law-and-order man. Couple of times, Cam came close to throwing me a punch."

"I can believe that," she remarked dryly. "Don't worry. I won't get physical."

"Hmm, that might not be a bad idea."

She smiled as she hung up the phone. It was a good thing Darren had a sense of humor. The poor guy, she'd gone and spilled her anxieties all over him when he was only doing his job. Playing the role of policeman to his friends and neighbors had to be sticky at times.

Her smile disappeared when she remembered why Darren had called her. Barrett was dead. Someone had shot him. Her eyes stung with unshed tears. She hadn't liked the boy. In truth, she'd feared him. Still, the death of someone so young, so full of potential was terribly sad.

Barrett had hassled a number of people in CH. Gabbie couldn't keep track of all the comments she'd heard that 'he had to be stopped, he had to be punished.' No doubt, someone finally decided he'd gone too far and killed him.

But it wasn't Charlie. Charlie had insisted Barrett and Todd had taken the gun from him and ordered him to move on. Maybe they got into an argument, and the gun went off. Darren hadn't mentioned Todd. Surely, he intended to question Barrett's sidekick. Todd held several pieces of the jigsaw puzzle, and he was bound to be more talkative, now that Barrett wasn't around to lead him into trouble.

Gabbie turned on the washing machine and glanced down at her watch. She'd better get moving or she'd be late for her first class. She combed her hair and put on some lipstick, then reached for her school bag.

The doorbell rang. Without thinking, she flung the door open and gave a start when she saw Fred Leverette. Gabbie had never noticed his resemblance to a grizzly bear before—the large, shambling physique, the broad shoulders hunched up beneath his brown parka.

"Ms. Meyerson–Gabbie. I'm so glad to find you in."

"Er–good morning."

His closeness made her uneasy. She stepped back. He moved forward and entered the cottage.

"I'm just on my way out," she said quickly. "I have to go, or I'll be late for my first class."

"I stopped by to thank you for looking after Theo last night. This business with Charlie Russell has gotten her rattled."

Then why weren't you there for her? Gabbie considered asking. Instead, she merely nodded.

"I saw the police were at Sonia's, no doubt to question Charlie about that Connelly kid's murder. Jeez, I don't know what this town is turning into."

She marveled how, even though Fred had spent the night with his girlfriend a few towns away, he'd managed to get the latest CH news flash.

"Excuse me, but I have to leave now."

Fred was oblivious to both her dismissal and her frosty tone. "Poor Charlie's afraid of his own shadow. He hasn't the guts to kill anyone. If you ask me, I'd put my money on his aunt Sonia."

"Sonia?" Gabbie's curiosity was aroused.

Fred gave her a smug smile. "Yessiree. I know she looks fragile, but the woman's crazy. And fierce as a lioness when it comes to that nephew of hers. I wouldn't put it past her if she decided to stop his tormenter once and for all."

Gabbie suddenly realized she'd followed Fred into the den. His eyes darted about the room. "Nice and cozy here. I bet this was their little love nest."

Her anxiety, which had disappeared when the subject changed to Sonia, returned. She drew back her shoulders, refusing to be intimidated. "Mr. Leverette, Fred, I need to leave now."

He shook his head as though waking from a dream. "Oh, sorry. I didn't mean to keep you. Thanks again for letting Theo spend the night." He lumbered out the front door and backed his old jalopy down the driveway before Gabbie finished locking the front door.

What was that all about? she wondered as she drove to school. *A sincere gesture of appreciation? A chance to see where his wife had cheated on him?* Or—her pulse raced—was Fred Leverette the intruder who had struck her, and was still after whatever he'd been searching for the other night?

CHAPTER TWENTY-THREE

G abbie signed in at the Main Office and headed for the faculty lounge for a quick cup of coffee. Suzanne called out her name and pointed to the vacant seat beside her on the couch. Gabbie poured herself half a mug and sat down.

"Did you hear the news about Barrett Connelly?" Suzanne asked in a half whisper.

Gabbie nodded and caught the tail-end of a story Andy Gorsky was relating to five of his colleagues at the far end of the room.

"And no one's going to tell me he didn't put sugar in my experiment, screwing up two weeks of work," he declared.

"Tsk, tsk," Suzanne chided, a twinkle in her eye. "Speaking ill of the dead, Andrew?"

Andy Gorsky scowled at her.

"My sympathies are with Charlie Russell." Barbara Chin, the beautiful art teacher, cast down her eyes in sadness. "The poor kid was driven to an act of desperation."

Gabbie nearly overturned her mug of coffee. Was there a spy system running through Chrissom Harbor? How on earth did they connect Charlie to Barrett's murder?

"Charlie would never kill anyone, and that includes Barrett Connelly!" she declared.

George Breck, the guidance counselor, chortled. "Do you need a photograph of what happened? Get real, Gabbie. We all like Charlie, but you have to face facts. He grabbed his aunt's gun and went after Connelly. I heard he admitted all that when they found him last night."

"He was angry, yes. But if you know so much, you also know Barrett and Todd took the gun away from him!"

Bald, skinny Oscar Tweeney, who the kids called Ichabod Crane, laughed. "Well, sure, that's what he told the police. That's what anyone would say."

Gabbie glared at the math teacher. "Interesting, how you pick and choose your facts. I wouldn't want you on my jury."

"Now, now," Suzanne murmured. "Let's not go to battle over this."

Before either Gabbie or Oscar could respond, Mac Debrowski, the assistant principal, strode into the room.

"Todd Ross is missing. He didn't come to school, which is no big surprise. But when Donna called his house, his mother was frantic. She said his bed hadn't been slept in."

Gabbie shuddered. She wondered if Darren had known Todd was missing when he called her. At any rate, she was glad he'd brought the Suffolk Police in on the case. The situation was growing more ominous by the minute.

Mac looked around the room and grimaced. "Two minutes to assembly time."

Suzanne met his gaze. "Is it really necessary to have an assembly in honor of Barrett Connelly?"

The assistant principal gave her a wry smile. "Tim's position is any student who dies while attending Chrissom Harbor High School deserves a school-wide tribute."

"Then Tim better be prepared to make a speech full of platitudes," Andy Gorsky said tartly. "Everyone I spoke to—and that includes the presidents of the school council and the senior class—refuses to stand up and say anything good about Barrett Connelly."

Mac cleared his throat. "I'll be saying a few words. We'll shorten the assembly if things get too awkward." The bell rang. "And remember, you're all expected to show up and help maintain appropriate behavior."

Suzanne stood close to Gabbie as they rinsed out their mugs. "Even Tim, who loves to make speeches, has to find this one a toughie."

Gabbie nodded. As they headed down the hall toward the auditorium, she said, "I bet plenty of kids are relieved their tormentor won't ever bother them again."

Suzanne opened her eyes wide in mock amazement. "*Zut alors.* One might dare say we're all better off, now that he's dead."

"Obviously, someone felt strongly enough to act. Could be Barrett went too far."

Suzanne pursed her lips. "Oh yes, Barrett did many bad things, pushed too many people's buttons. He was bound to come to a bad end, sooner or later."

Clearly, she had a specific incident in mind. Gabbie was about to ask what it was, but they were approaching the auditorium. She and Suzanne separated to usher students into seats.

A heightened sense of excitement crackled in the air, like electricity before a thunderstorm. Intense whispering rippled along the rows. The occasional eruption of laughter was quickly squelched by unsmiling teachers. A hush swept over the student body as Dr. Tim Jordan mounted the steps and took his place center stage.

"As most of you know, Barrett Connelly is no longer with us. His body was found on the beach this morning. The police tell me he died some time before seven a.m."

Voices rose as students commented to one another. Tim lifted his palms, and the chatter faded at once.

"At present we are not concerned with how Barrett died. We'll leave that matter to the police and other officials. Rather, we—his teachers, his friends, and fellow classmates—have gathered here to pay our respects to a member of our community and to mourn his passing."

Mac Debrowski made a few general remarks about the tragedy of a young man's life ending before he could reach his potential. Then Tim asked if anyone would like to say a few words to honor Barrett. Bursts of laughter greeted this proposal. No one volunteered.

From her vantage point near the back of the auditorium, Gabbie observed a few of the girls sniffling and blowing their noses, including Lizzie Terranova. *So,* she thought, *some of them had found Barrett handsome and appealing. A romantic figure, perhaps, rebelling against the status quo. Or it could be they were moved by his sudden death.* She wondered if he'd dated any of the teary-eyed girls. If he had, no girl appeared to have played a major role in the last days of his life.

Her third period students were too charged up and eager to talk about Barrett's murder to settle down to a grammar lesson. Gabbie assigned it as homework instead and let them chat quietly among themselves.

Fourth period, Theo barely nodded to her when she entered the classroom. Her face looked pinched, her scowl was in place. *She's terrified for Charlie*, Gabbie thought.

This proved to be true when Theo jumped down Jed Lancaster's throat when he dared to suggest that Charlie Russell had done them all a favor by offing the school bully.

Sixth period was worse because this was Barrett's English class. Gabbie was taken aback when Heather and April suggested that the class plant a tree outside the cafeteria as a memorial to Barrett. The others quickly scotched the idea, and Gabbie was able to steer them to a lesson on writing a business letter.

When the bell rang, she gathered up her briefcase and parka and flew out of the building, eager to escape the oppressive atmosphere. It troubled her that one of her students had been murdered, another was a possible suspect, and a third—Theo—was making herself ill by fretting over Charlie.

As she walked toward her car, a slender young woman in a black leather coat dashed across the parking lot and made a beeline for her.

She extended her right hand. "Hello, I'm Aurora Dutson. I wonder if I could speak to you for a minute."

Gabbie had no choice but to shake the proffered hand. Puzzled, because the woman couldn't be a day over thirty, she asked, "Are you a parent? I don't believe I have a student named Dutson."

Aurora Dutson tossed back her long blonde hair and laughed. "I'm not a parent. I'm a reporter for *The Record*. And you are?"

Furious, Gabbie unlocked her car and spun around. "I've nothing to say. Please go away."

"But it's my job to ask questions." She whipped out a notepad and a pen from her huge leather bag.

"Not in a school, you don't," Gabbie snapped.

Aurora smiled, immune to Gabbie's hostility. "Were the students upset to hear that Barrett Connelly was murdered? I understand from his neighbors he was *persona non grata* among his peers."

"I've nothing to say." Gabbie got into the Volvo and slammed the door shut.

"Do you think this murder has anything to do with Cameron Leeds' death?"

Shocked, Gabbie opened the window and stared up at her. "No, I don't. Why do you ask?"

"Because Barrett and his friend discovered Mr. Leeds' body on the beach. Eight months later, Barrett's found shot to death in the same vicinity."

Gabbie glared at her. "Irresponsible assumptions give the press the bad reputation it deserves." She raised her window and turned on the ignition.

The reporter shrugged, put away her notepad and pen, and walked off.

Gabbie clutched her arms to still her trembling body. "Of course there's no connection between the two murders," she whispered, and took deep breaths to regain her composure.

When she was calm enough to drive, she put the car in gear and headed for town. She longed to block out her visceral reaction to the reporter's question, but that was impossible and stupid. If Gabbie had learned one thing from the upheavals of the past year, it was the importance of confronting any issue that alarmed her, immediately and head on.

Why had she'd been so upset by the suggestion that the same person had killed Cam and Barrett? Undoubtably, because it meant the murderer was agitated and wouldn't hesitate to kill again to protect himself. And she, who'd been instrumental in reopening the investigation to prove Cam's death was no accident, had better watch her step.

Gabbie didn't have the heart to go home to Cam, who was bound to bombard her with questions. Craving the noisy camaraderie of the living, she drove to Logan's Place. Even if the murderer were present, there was safety in numbers. Maybe, among all the comments and speculations about who killed Barrett, she'd pick up a kernel of vital information.

She opened the door to the bar and was enveloped by the sound of voices raised in lively discussion and the heady aroma of meatloaf.

"Gabbie, we're over here!"

She waved back at Reese and headed for the table, silently chiding herself for having allowed herself to grow fond of a potential murderer. No, Reese couldn't have done anything that horrendous. She greeted Terry and Jack and smiled when Reese introduced her to Sam and Cleary, two insurance agents who worked in the new office building just outside of town.

Terry winked as she sat down beside him. "I was telling the guys how I discovered Barrett Connelly's body when I was out running this morning. I'm the one who called the police. You can read about it in tomorrow's paper."

His boastful manner was irritating, especially since she knew Terry had almost thrown up at the scene.

Gabbie winked back at him. "I heard all about it... every little detail," she added meaningfully.

A look of alarm replaced the glow of excitement on his handsome face. She leaned over to whisper in his ear. "Don't worry, I'll keep your little secret."

He exhaled with apparent relief.

"What are you two going on about?" Reese demanded. When neither answered, he turned to Gabbie. "I thought you'd set your sights on Darren Rollins."

Gabbie felt the color rise to her cheeks as the men guffawed and slapped the table with delight. Her putdown of Terry had boomeranged. She remained silent as he told the rest of his story.

When he finished, she said, "That same reporter tried to question me in the school parking lot. Can you imagine the nerve?"

"She's only doing her job," Terry said.

"She's talking to everyone in sight," Reese said. "I wonder if anyone's told her most of the town's glad to be rid of that troublemaker."

"Reese!" Gabbie exclaimed.

"Well, it's true," Jack said. "The Connelly kid was nothing but trouble." He took a long draw from his beer bottle. His second beer, Gabbie noticed from the empty beside him.

Mike came over and Gabbie ordered a tuna fish sandwich and coffee.

Sam, a slender middle-aged man said, "I hear the Ross kid is missing. Or has he shown up at school?"

"No, he hasn't," Gabbie answered before anyone else could speculate.

"I wonder if he and Connelly had a falling out," Cleary mused. He was a handsome Black man in his thirties. "Maybe they got into a fight and Ross shot him accidentally. Now he's afraid to show his face."

"That's probably what happened," Jack said. "Did they find the gun?"

"I don't think so," Reese said. "Either the killer tossed it somewhere or took it with him."

"Or her," Terry said, glancing at Gabbie.

"Thanks for the equal opportunity," she said sarcastically, and they all laughed.

"Where can Ross be?" Jack asked. "I didn't hear that any cars are missing."

Sam shrugged. "Maybe he's dead. Or maybe he hitched a ride out of town."

"Nah, he's not dead," Reese insisted, "or they would have found the body by now. The kid's lived here all his life. He's bound to have plenty of hiding places."

Gabbie thought of Todd's shed in the woods but said nothing.

As though reading her mind, Jack asked, "You think he's hiding out in the woods?"

Terry pounded Jack's beefy shoulder. "Could be. Why don't you be a good citizen and join the search party out looking for him?"

Jack gave him a slow smile that showed the space between his front teeth. "Maybe I will. Maybe I'll do just that."

Despite her intention to listen and learn, Gabbie found the conversation had taken away her appetite. She asked Mike to wrap up her sandwich. The men laughed good-naturedly and were still discussing Barrett's murder when she left. She stepped outside as a chubby young man was about to enter Logan's. They nodded to each other, then Gabbie smiled because he looked familiar. Though his face was fuller, he resembled Cam.

At the same time, it must have dawned on him who she was. "Excuse me, are you Gabbie Meyerson?"

"Yes, I am." She grinned. "And you must be Roland Leeds. Darren mentioned you'd be coming."

He nodded. "You're leaving." He sounded disappointed.

"Yes. I'm going to the police station to see Darren."

"I just left him there, dealing with the frantic parents of a missing boy."

"Todd Ross's parents," Gabbie said. She hesitated, then asked, "Did the ME find out anything conclusive?"

"Yes," Roland began, then moved aside to let two women enter the restaurant. He led her around to the side of the building.

"Cause of death was a blow to the back of the head by a blunt instrument. The skull had been struck twice. It was the second blow that killed him."

Gabbie inhaled sharply. "I see."

"I'd love to sit down and talk to you at length," Roland said. "Darren tells me you convinced him to open the investigation into Cam's death."

"I suppose," she said, deliberately vague as she had no idea if Darren had told Roland of Cam's ghostly presence.

As though reading her mind, Roland crinkled up his face and burst out laughing. "I know about Cam. Can't wait to see him."

"Then by all means come for dinner tonight," she offered. "You and Darren."

"I'd like that." He extended his hand. She took it, meaning to shake hands, but he drew her hand to his heart.

"Gabbie, I can't thank you enough for caring. My brother's pulled some shady deals in his life, but he didn't deserve to be murdered."

"No, he didn't. See you around seven." She smiled. "You know the way."

Gabbie continued to smile as she got into the Volvo. Meeting Roland had the calming effect of a good massage. He'd struck her as intelligent, self-possessed, and capable of getting results. He was an ally, someone whom she and Darren could trust in this town overrun with possible suspects. Gabbie nosed out of Logan's parking lot, waited for a pickup truck to pass, then eased onto Main Street.

As she began her left-hand turn, she caught sight of a blue car in her rearview mirror. It came closer, bearing down on her tail. Gabbie stomped down on the brake as the small car, which had jumped the red light, squealed around her, overcorrected itself, then sped on its way.

Her anger changed to curiosity when she recognized the clenched white face of Sonia Russell. Gabbie took off after her. The chase ended a few blocks farther when Sonia suddenly veered right, into the parking lot of the brick building that housed the post office and the police station. She dashed up the four steps to the station. Gabbie waited until Sonia was inside then went in after her.

She was in time to hear Sonia say to the pretty Latina behind the glass, "I must speak to Darren."

The dispatcher looked up from her paperwork and blinked at Sonia. "Okay, but Chief Rollins is busy right now. Please take a seat."

"Busy!" Sonia put her hands to her head and shook it from side to side like an angry toddler. "I can't wait. Tell Darren it's important. Tell him it's about Cameron Leeds' murder."

Gabbie's mouth fell open. *Dear God, don't let it be that Charlie killed Barrett, after all!* The dispatcher glanced at Gabbie before saying to Sonia, "I'll tell the chief you need to speak to him. Be right back."

Gabbie sat quietly near the door, hoping Sonia wouldn't throw a fit and accuse her of having followed her. But she needn't have worried. Sonia remained stone-still until Darren entered the room from a side door. He approached her, his manner as gentle as if he were speaking to a small child or a gravely ill person.

"Hello, Sonia. I'm with some people now, but I promise to talk to you as soon as we're done." He swallowed. "Is Charlie all right, alone in your house?"

"This has nothing to do with Charlie," she snapped. "It has to do with me."

"Fine," Darren said. "We'll talk about it. I have a nice room where you can wait for me. I'll only be a few minutes." His eyes flitted to Gabbie, then he beckoned to Sonia to follow him into the inner offices.

His hand was on the doorknob, when Sonia said, "Didn't your secretary tell you? I came to talk to you about Cam."

Slowly, Darren turned to stare at her. "What does this have to do with Cam?"

Sonia's face crumpled. Tears streamed down her face. "It's been eating away at me. I can't keep it in any longer." Her shoulders heaved with sobs.

"I've tried to pretend it never happened. It was easy when everyone thought he fell off the bluff because he was drunk. But now everyone's wondering who killed him, so I have to tell you. It was me."

Darren looked stricken as he put a hand on Sonia's shoulder. "You're upset. I must advise you to call your lawyer before you say another word."

She brushed his hand away. "Of course I'm upset, and I intend to tell you everything, Darren Rollins, right here and now."

He nodded. "All right, tell me."

Sonia stared down at her bony hands clutched together as if she were praying. "That day I heard Cam was leaving so I went to the cottage. I was angry." She looked up at him. "I brought a gun. That gun, the one those monsters took from Charlie."

"You drove there?"

She nodded. "I parked on the road and began to have my doubts. I wondered if it was just some stupid rumor that Cam was going away. 'Sonia,' I told myself, 'You're the one Cam cares about. He's told you so often enough. Have faith, even though he's sowing his wild oats with that bitch next door.' But when I opened the front door and saw the suitcases, I knew it was true."

The dispatcher came through the side door. She was about to speak, when Darren's look stifled whatever she was about to say, and she left.

"Cam sat writing at his desk. He didn't hear me come into the den because he had a CD blasting. He was going away and treating me like dirt—just like every other man I ever knew. I was furious but I couldn't bring myself to shoot him, so I turned the gun around and swung the butt down on his head."

Sonia shivered. "He slid to the floor and lay there, next to the open drawer. I came around and saw his eyes were closed." She swallowed. "He didn't move. I could tell he was dead."

CHAPTER TWENTY-FOUR

Gabbie left the police station ten minutes later, still shaken by Sonia's confession.

"Relax. I don't think she killed Cam," Darren murmured as he escorted her down the steps.

"Roland told me it was the second blow that did it. Even so, what she did was awful."

He squeezed her arm. "Gotta get back to the Rosses. They're furious because their son is still missing. Then I have to question Sonia in her lawyer's presence. Not to mention the small matter of investigating Barrett Connelly's murder."

"And Cam's." Gabbie gave him a crooked smile. "Roland's coming to dinner tonight. You're invited too, but I see you're much too busy to make it."

His grin sent her heart soaring. "Are you kidding? I have to eat sometime. And besides, I want to check out a whole bunch of new facts with Cam. Though I doubt I can get there before eight."

"That's fine. It will give Roland more time with Cam."

He patted her shoulder. "Remember, no sleuthing between now and tonight."

"That's for sure. I've had enough excitement for one afternoon."

The delayed reaction of shock set in the moment Darren disappeared inside the station. Sonia's mad confession and all its implications flashed strobe-like across her brain. Gabbie's legs threatened to buckle. She grasped the wooden railing to keep from sliding to the ground.

She gulped down air until she felt steady, though her head continued to reel. *Sonia had struck Cam and left him for dead!* A spark of anger kindled deep within her, the likes of which she hadn't experienced since her former husband had tossed out their marriage along with the trash. Cam was dead because of Sonia. She'd left him vulnerable and unconscious, and the murderer had finished him off.

As far as Gabbie was concerned, Sonia was guilty. She wouldn't be charged with murder, though she'd set the crime in motion.

She walked slowly to her car, acknowledging the fact that she was more upset than she'd realized. For the first time since she'd left her old home, she sorely missed the few close friends to whom she could turn whenever she felt blue. A long, empty afternoon yawned before her. What to do? Where to go?

The answer struck her as she switched on the ignition. Gabbie smiled and headed for Tessa's beauty salon for a manicure and some gossip.

"You're not one for making appointments, are you?" Tessa greeted her as she entered the shop. The place was empty except for three customers.

Puzzled, Gabbie blinked. "Sorry. With all that's happening, I don't know what I'm doing from one minute to the next."

"So I hear. Playing detective and teaching must keep you very busy."

Gabbie waited for the smile that meant Tessa was teasing, but it never came. She glanced over at the manicurist reading the newspaper. Annoyed, she said, "I stopped by for a manicure, but if you're all booked up, I'll come another time."

Tessa nodded, as though ceding a point. "Don't be silly. Marie can take you right now."

Gabbie made no reply as she sat down in the chair opposite the manicurist. She could be as snippy as the next one. Still, she had no idea why Tessa, who had called only a few days ago to find out how she was doing, was now freezing her out.

She paid scant attention as Marie soaked and filed and painted her fingernails, all the while carrying on a conversation with another patron about how awful it was that a young boy in the high school was shot to death. Until Marie wondered—her voice lowered to almost a whisper—why on earth a policeman would come to the salon to question Tessa's husband about the murder.

Ah, Gabbie thought. *So that's it.* She sat quietly, letting her nails dry, and looked up when Tessa stopped beside her chair.

"Sorry. I didn't mean to snap at you before."

"We're all on edge," Gabbie said. She considered telling Tessa about Sonia's confession, then decided it was police business and not gossip – at least not yet. "Nobody can relax with a murderer or two loose around town."

"Well, my Don didn't kill anyone!"

Gabbie raised her eyebrows. "I didn't realize he was a sus-pect."

Tessa threw her a look of disbelief. "I bet! Interesting how things got all fired up after you moved into the Leeds' cottage."

Gabbie felt her cheeks blaze red with indignation. "Cam was killed and Barrett caused trouble long before I came here."

Her protest did nothing to soften Tessa's attitude. "Your boyfriend hassled Don twice last week. He sent a county homi-cide detective after him today."

Gabbie decided to let the "boyfriend" comment pass. "Why? Did Don have a run in with Barrett Connelly?"

Tessa hesitated, then said, "There was an incident last sum-mer. Connelly slashed the tires of our brand-new Mercedes. Don was livid. He went to the kid's father and demanded that he pay for new tires. The man laughed. Said he'd pay if Don had proof it was his son who did the slashing."

Mercedes? Where had Tessa and Don gotten the money for a Mercedes? "Did Don see him vandalize the car?"

Exasperated, Tessa exhaled loudly. "No, but someone saw him running like crazy a block from here. That same evening three other cars had their tires slashed. All three were parked behind the shops."

"Weren't the owners of the other cars angry as well?" Gabbie asked.

"Of course they were angry. They called Darren and he ques-tioned Connelly," she grimaced, "with the usual lame results. But the damage wasn't as extensive, and their cars were mostly old wrecks."

And they weren't as incensed, Gabbie decided. Still, Don had every right to be furious at a kid who had deliberately vandalized his new car. But why wait several months to take revenge?

She opened her mouth to ask if Barrett had done something recently that had angered Don, when a stunning redhead in her thirties, who looked as though she'd been poured into her black leather jumpsuit, burst through the door. She pranced around on high-heeled boots, fluttering her right hand like a banner.

"Come see what he gave me! A two-carat sapphire with diamond baguettes on each side!"

Everyone but Gabbie stopped what they were doing to mob the woman and admire the ring sparkling on her finger.

Tessa got there first. She held the woman's hand this way and that to catch the stones' facets in the light. "Kim, it's absolutely exquisite."

Kim threw her arms around Tessa. "It's all thanks to you. I followed your instructions, and they worked like a charm!"

"Of course." Tessa winked. "Listen to Mama Tessa if you want a make-up ring."

Intrigued, Gabbie asked Marie, "What's a 'makeup' ring?"

Marie cut her a sidelong glance. "When a husband misbehaves and wants to get back in his wife's good graces, he buys her a 'make-up' ring."

"I see," Gabbie said. "But what does Tessa have to do with it?"

Marie laughed. "She wrangled one out of Don years ago. Now she tells her good costumers exactly what to do if they want one, too. Funny thing is, it works every time."

"Hmm. I'll have to keep that in mind."

Marie winked. "First you have to get married."

"Oh."

"Sometimes it takes years before it works. Jane Walters got a ring recently. Adele McMahon did, too. An antique beauty with pavé diamonds."

Both Reese and Jack had sprung for expensive rings! She'd have to tell Darren so he could call on local jewelers and, hopefully, find out if either or both of them had paid for the ring in cash. "I wonder what bad deed their husbands committed," she mused aloud.

Marie waved her bony hand in the air. "I've no idea. It could be anything from screwing around to going fishing for a week instead of taking his wife on a vacation."

Gabbie handed her a tip then went to the desk to pay for her manicure.

"Come back soon," the receptionist called after her.

"I will," Gabbie said, and realized that coming to the salon had done her some good. She'd calmed down, and her nails looked nice. Best of all, she'd learned that Don, Reese, and Jack had all bought expensive items since Cam's death.

She drove to the supermarket, mentally listing what she needed: ground sirloin for meatballs, tomato sauce, onions and peppers, fresh pasta, salad fixings, appetizers, and ingredients for a simple cake. *Life marches on despite murder and other tragedies,* she mused as she yanked a cart free from the long line of wagons. People work, prepare meals, get together. She found the thought reassuring, as though there really was order in the universe.

Gabbie thought it best to leave the brothers' reunion until after dinner. It almost seemed like they'd silently agreed to hold off on discussing Cam's murder while they ate—the subject never came up. Instead, they talked about Chrissom Harbor, Gabbie's teaching, and Roland's work.

After coffee and cake, Gabbie shot Darren a knowing look. "You guys relax in the den while I load the dishwasher."

She grinned when, a minute later, Roland's voice rang out in surprise. By the time she joined them, the brothers were deep in conversation. Roland, it seemed, had adjusted surprisingly quickly to seeing his brother in ghostly form.

Perhaps it was the nature of his work. Digging up artifacts to study the history of mankind must have given him a broader perspective on life.

"I can't understand why she'd do such a thing," Cam was saying, his voice filled with self-pity.

Gabbie rolled her eyes at Darren and Roland. To Cam she said, "We've explained it, and you still don't get it. You don't want to get it."

"One last time," Cam pleaded. "Please."

Gabbie sighed. After listening to Darren's report of Sonia's lengthy confession, her anger toward the woman was tempered by a feeling of profound sadness.

"Sonia actually believed you meant it when you jokingly told her she was the one for you and the two of you would eventually marry. She was willing to wait. She was content to see you when you ran into each other in town."

"That's the part I have trouble with," Cam said.

"I know." Gabbie drew in breath and continued. "Because of her brutal father and the rape, Sonia hates and fears men. She's probably unaware that she does, because she's had a crush on you ever since you and Darren beat up the boys who attacked her. It suited her that you made no demands."

Cam nodded. "In other words, I was safe."

"Exactly," Gabbie said. "God only knows what romantic fantasies she wove in her head, fantasies unsullied by reality and sex, and kept alive by your promises."

Darren leaned forward on the couch. "Sonia got angry when she caught you kissing Jill one afternoon. She took to spying on the two of you and saw it happen repeatedly, but since you continued to tell her she was your girl, she convinced herself your relationship with Jill was a cheap affair. You were 'sowing your wild oats,' as she put it.

"What really set her off was hearing you planned to leave town. She was willing to put up with anything but you abandoning her. So, she got out the old revolver and drove to the cottage to find out for herself. She came here that afternoon, and guess what she saw?"

"Jill's car leaving the cottage," Gabbie said, "and suitcases in the hall."

Roland grimaced. "She assumed the two of you planned to go away together. It's a good thing she never went after Jill."

Gabbie said thoughtfully, "Jill knew Sonia was angry at her, but she never knew why."

"She went after me instead," Cam mused. "She couldn't bring herself to shoot me, so as soon as Jill left, she brained me with the butt of the gun."

"She thought she could trust you," Darren explained. "But you deceived her, just like those boys."

Cam thrust out his long arms in supplication. "Hey, let's not go overboard feeling sorry for her. Besides, how can you be certain she didn't kill me?"

Darren looked at Cam. "Because the ME said a powerful second blow with an object wider than the butt of a gun caused the fatality. Probably the Roman statuette, since they found traces of blood and, oddly enough, a hair on the back of it. They're checking now to see if they're yours."

Cam pursed his lips. "I used to love that little statuette. Any fingerprints? They would prove that Sonia killed me."

Darren shot him a look of disbelief. "Are you kidding? After eight months' time and all the traffic in this room? Besides, it doesn't make sense that Sonia would strike you with two different objects. And she says she didn't take your money."

Cam stared at him incredulously. "And you believe her?"

"Why shouldn't he?" Roland asked. "Sonia confessed to a murder she thought she'd committed. She was offended when Darren asked if she'd taken your money."

"Yep. Told me she was no thief," Darren said. "But she'd noticed the drawer full of cash. Which means your second visitor most likely killed you for the money."

Cam buried his face in his hands. "So, we're back to square one. No clues. No evidence. This murderer, whoever he is, must be damn clever."

"Or damn lucky," Roland said. "No doubt the person stopped by, saw you lying on the ground—dead for all he—"

"Or she," interjected Darren.

"Or she knew. Saw the money and started shoveling it into some kind of sack."

"Probably a pillowcase," Gabbie offered.

"Right," Roland continued. "You probably moved or moaned, indicating you were very much alive. At which point, he or she reached for the statuette and hit you again. And this time, finished you off."

Cam shuddered. "Sounds awful."

"It is awful," Darren agreed, "but I think that's what happened." He hesitated, then began haltingly. "There is one other thing."

"What is it" Roland asked.

"This is official police business, but it's pertinent and I trust you won't say a word to anyone about what I'm about to tell you."

"And whom would I tell?" Cam demanded.

"Sorry. Reese called me late this afternoon to say he had to get something off his chest. I told him to come over to the station and he did."

"And?" Roland prompted.

"He said he'd stopped by the cottage just after five that afternoon. To say good-bye to Cam."

Cam laughed. "He came to collect his money. The old coot is still lying."

"No point in my pressing that issue," Darren said calmly. "He said he entered the cottage, saw the suitcases but no sign of Cam, so he left."

Gabbie felt a surge of excitement. "Did he happen to notice the drawer full of money?"

"Afraid not. He noticed the bottom drawer stood wide open and empty. Reese figured Cam had gone to take care of some last-minute business. He said he couldn't wait, so he went on his way."

"Oh." Her enthusiasm dissipated as quickly as it had risen. "That's not much help then."

"It narrows down the window of time in which the murder was committed," Darren said. "Now we know it occurred some time between Sonia's attack and Reese's visit."

"Could be Reese is the guilty party," Cam said.

"Could be," Darren agreed, "and I have to factor that possibility in as well. I'll question everyone again and again, until someone reveals another bit of information." He gave Gabbie a half smile. "It's persistence and detail work that solve crimes."

"Do you think the two murders are connected?" Gabbie asked. The idea that they might be had been preying on her mind all evening.

Darren scratched his chin as he considered her question. "It's too early to say, but if they are, we've lost an eyewitness to Cam's murder."

"Unless Todd saw the murderer kill Barrett," she said, "and is hiding out, afraid to surface until you've caught him."

He frowned. "Exactly what I've been thinking. Which is why I'm leaving now to join the search party."

"I'll come too," Roland said.

She walked them to the door. Darren gave her a quick peck on the cheek. "Talk to you tomorrow. Keep the doors and windows locked, and don't let anyone in."

"Hah! As if I would."

Darren and Roland left, and Gabbie double-locked herself in. She checked the sliding doors in the den to make sure they were locked as well. Even Cam had disappeared to wherever he went when he wasn't at the cottage, which suited her just fine. She yawned as she climbed the stairs to her bedroom. She was tired and longed for the luxury of a good night's sleep.

But once she got into bed and turned off her lamp, it was as if she'd switched on the think button of her mind. So far, clues and witnesses to both murders were nonexistent. The police were almost certain the statuette and Sonia's gun were the murder weapons, but they lacked evidence pointing to the identity of the murderer or murderers. Gabbie had no doubt that Darren would coax more information from the various suspects when he questioned them again. Unfortunately, that would take time. She shivered. Meanwhile, someone else might die.

She considered Darren's list of suspects: Fred, Reese, Jack, Terry, and Don. Any one of them might have killed Cam. They all had reason to hate him, some more than others. Still, none of the five men—including Fred—struck her as a murderer.

Gabbie laughed aloud, chiding herself for being silly and naive. It was impossible for her or anyone else to plumb the hearts and minds of her fellow human beings. She hadn't the vaguest notion of what any of the suspects was capable of doing. Hadn't she read stories in the newspaper about religious leaders who were pedophiles and mothers who'd murdered their own children? She frowned. Not to mention her own husband, who had proven to be a thief and a cheat.

Her best bet was to rely on logic and observation. She had to consider what she knew about each of the men. Where were they at the time of the murders? Who appeared to be tense or ill-at-ease when the subject of either murder came up in conversation?

She suddenly remembered Terry had jumped like a rabbit when she teasingly threatened to tell the others what had happened when he'd discovered Barrett's body. He'd been relieved when she promised not to tell. She meant not tell that he almost threw up.

But what if he was relieved for another reason? Excitement coursed through her veins. He could have been glad she wasn't going to say something pertaining to Barrett's death. Not that she knew anything.

Only she did, she suddenly realized. She'd heard the shots.

She leaned back and closed her eyes, trying to recapture the moment when the first shot had awakened her. She'd given a start and snuggled under the covers. When the second shot had followed, she'd opened her eyes and glanced at her clock. It had been six twenty-one.

"Nineteen minutes before Terry found the body! I bet he killed Barrett!"

She forced herself to calm down and review the facts in an orderly manner. Terry had claimed he'd found Barrett at twenty minutes to seven. He must have killed Barrett, then pulled the body into the woods, continued running down the beach, and then turned around and pretended to notice the body at twenty to seven as he reported.

It all fit together! No doubt Barrett remembered having seen Terry or his car at the cottage the day Cam had died. Once Cam's death was officially declared a murder, Barrett realized that Terry was the killer.

Her excitement grew as all the pieces fell into place. Terry hated Cam. He'd as good as told her so himself. Plus, he'd beaten his wife, which indicated a streak of violence. Terry was strong enough to lift Cam and throw him over the bluff, and smart enough to cover his tracks. And—the final piece—he had no alibi for the afternoon of the murder.

"I must call Darren!" She reached for the phone, then realized she'd left the slip of paper with his cell phone number down in the kitchen. She pulled on her bathrobe, stepped into her slippers, and started down the stairs.

CHAPTER TWENTY-FIVE

The sound of knocking sent Gabbie's heart hammering against her ribs. She froze where she stood, midway down the staircase, and listened.

Nothing. Surely what she'd heard was a branch hitting against the cottage.

The noise started again, a quick rapping at the front door. She forced herself to place one foot in front of the other until she reached the hall.

"Who's there?" Fear cracked her voice.

"It's Todd, Ms. Meyerson. Open the door, please."

His palpable terror seeped through the wood. She hesitated, her hand on the doorknob.

Danger lurked outside. She'd be a fool to open the door. Todd was malicious. He'd done awful things to Charlie and to other kids. She had to consider the possibility that he and not Terry had killed Barrett.

"Please, Ms. Meyerson, I'm freezing and he's coming! Please open the door. I don't want to die like Barrett!" He sobbed, gulping in air.

Gabbie shot the bolt and opened the door. The cold nipped at her bare ankles and Todd stepped into the cottage. He stared up at her, mouth gaping, his eyes red from crying. She recoiled when she saw the gun in the deep fold of his trench coat. He held the gun away from his body as if it were contaminated.

"I found it. That's why he's after me."

"Who's after you?"

Gabbie moved to shut the door when a violent force shoved it against her. She stumbled backwards.

Jack McMahon entered. His massive shoulders and oversized face loomed over her, chilling her with terror and disbelief.

"Jack!" she cried as Todd shrank behind her.

Voice shaking with terror and disbelief, she said, "What are you doing here?"

"Don't play innocent, Gabbie. This is no time for games."

She shook her head. "You killed Barrett? But why?"

"Had to." He glared at Todd, an ugly frown giving his dull features a Neanderthal look. "And this little creep was spying. Well, we know what happens to spies." He lunged.

Todd spun around and ran toward the living room.

Jack moved lightning fast and grabbed Todd's arm. The gun clattered to the floor.

"Thanks. I'll take that." He picked up the gun and smashed the butt against the side of Todd's head. With a moan, Todd sank to the floor.

"No!" Gabbie resisted the urge to kneel beside the unconscious boy. She needed to stay on her feet if she hoped to get them out of this alive. She stared at Jack, still reeling from the shock that he and not Terry was the murderer.

"You killed Cam and Barrett and threw my paperweight at me!"

Jack looked down at the gun in his hands. Slowly he pointed it at Gabbie. "I didn't mean to hurt you, Gabbie. I don't want to hurt you now. You shouldn't have stuck your nose in what wasn't your business."

A shiver rippled through her body as she inched backward toward the den. She forced herself to speak in a conversational tone. "But why did you kill Cam? That afternoon he was going to give you your share of the money."

He blinked, looking puzzled. "How do you know?"

"Darren told me," she lied. "He found out about the cigarette deal."

Jack pursed his lips. "We were getting peanuts compared to what Cam made on the deal. Mr. Big Sport was giving me five thousand more because we used my truck."

He went on, aggrieved. "It's not like I meant to kill him. When I found him lying on the floor, I figured one of the other guys did him in, then panicked and left without taking the money.

"Then he moaned. I nearly jumped out of my skin 'cause I thought he was dead. So, I hit him with that little statue. It just seemed like the natural thing to do. So did picking him up and tossing him down to the beach."

The natural thing to do? Sickened, Gabbie backed up another foot. She forced herself to sound impressed. "And no one knew. They said it was death by misadventure."

Jack shot her a malicious smile. "Surprised, aren't you?"

She controlled her tremors as best she could. "What do you mean?"

"You know. Dumb Jack. Can't keep a business afloat. All he's good for is odds jobs and making deliveries. Well, I showed them. I didn't leave any traces that day, even though I had my worries about the statue." He laughed. "But no telltale finger-prints. I suppose I have the cleaners to thank for that."

Another step and she'd be in the den. "Except that Barrett saw you," she said.

"He did not! When word got out that Cam didn't die from any fall, he remembered he'd seen my truck here that afternoon. Smart ass kid. He thought he could blackmail me."

Again, Jack looked down at the gun in his hand. "I killed him with his own gun."

"Sonia's gun," Gabbie said. "That's what she used to knock Cam unconscious."

"Sonia?" He shook his head, amazed. "Well, I'll be damned."

This time when Gabbie moved, he noticed. "And where do you think you're going? I haven't forgotten all this is your fault. Adele and me would be leading the good life, if you hadn't stirred things up."

He raised the gun and pointed it at her heart.

Todd moaned, and Jack turned to look at him.

Gabbie dashed into the darkened den.

"Cam, come here, I need you!" she shouted. "Right now!"

A bullet whizzed past her ear.

She dove to the floor beside the desk as Jack stumbled into the dimly lit room.

"Cam, huh? Cam can't help you! Now where's that damn light switch?"

Gabbie bit her lip, afraid to make a sound. She heard a car on the road and thought she heard it stop.

Jack must have thought so too, because he went to the window and pulled aside the curtain to peer out. "Can't see a damn thing," he muttered.

It was now or never. "Cam! Cam! Show yourself now!" she shouted. "Arg," she garbled as Jack grabbed her arm, yanking her to her feet as easily as if she were a rag doll.

"Let go of me!"

"Sure I will." Jack tightened his grip and jabbed the gun into her back with his other hand.

Gabbie gasped as she arched her back in pain.

"Stay still," he ordered, "or I'll shoot you now."

Cam materialized, barely visible in the dim light.

Please God, she prayed, *don't let it be too late.*

"Nice going, Jack," Cam said. "You've got a real smooth way with the ladies."

"Who–who's there?" Jack demanded, his voice thick with fear. He eased the pressure of the gun against her back.

"Don't you recognize my voice?" Cam taunted. "Use the light switch to the right of the doorway, and you'll see me plain as day."

Jack put on the light. "N–no, it can't be." She felt his body tremble, felt the gun barrel knock against her spine. Carefully, she eased out of his grip. The gun fell to the ground.

He didn't seem to notice. His eyes bulged as he stared at Cam. "But you're dead!"

Cam nodded. "I sure am, thanks to you. Were you so desperate for the money you had to kill me?"

Jack covered his face with his hands. "I didn't mean to. I thought you were already dead."

"So, you finished me off and took the dough. Some good pal you turned out to be."

Jack didn't answer. Gabbie picked up the gun, hoping the shock of seeing the ghost of the man he'd killed had rendered him powerless.

No such luck. She stared, transfixed, as Jack's hands curled into fists, his face contorted with rage. "Think you were a good pal, Cam? You conned your friends and grabbed the lion's share of every deal."

"I set up the deals," Cam said calmly. "You made more money than you ever would have because of me."

"Always thinking you were so special. So damn sure your looks would get you any woman in town."

Cam laughed. "Jealous, Jack? Was that the problem?"

Jack snorted. "Me jealous of you? I'm alive and you're dead."

"And about to spend your life behind bars for two murders."

Jack lunged at Cam. A blast of icy air stopped him in his tracks. He huddled into himself, wrapping his arms around his shivering body.

Gabbie pointed the gun at him. "Jack, sit down on the couch while I call Darren."

Instead of obeying, he lumbered toward her, right arm outstretched. "Give me that. You don't have it in you to shoot me."

Gabbie stepped back. Her finger tightened around the trigger. "Keep away! I mean it!"

A noise from the hall startled them both. They turned and saw that Todd had knocked over the small table as he pulled himself to his feet. He had one hand on the doorknob.

"Stop!" Jack shouted at him.

"Run, Todd!" Gabbie shouted. "Call the police!"

She was caught off guard when Jack grabbed her forearm. The gun went off, shattering glass. Jack leaped back. He spun around, then chased after Todd, who had escaped through the door and into the night.

"Shoot him," Cam told her.

Gabbie lowered the gun and ran after them, determined to shoot Jack if he attacked Todd. The cold night air numbed her hands and face. She blinked, trying desperately to make out the two figures in the darkness.

Headlights flashed, car doors flung open. Darren and Lionel took off after Jack. Gabbie held her breath amid the sounds of grunts and groans and snapping branches as Darren and Lionel fought to subdue Jack.

"Easy, man," Darren said between breaths. "There's no place to run. Todd, get in the front seat of the car."

Gabbie heard Jack curse.

Lionel yelped in pain. "Put your hands behind you, now." She'd never heard Darren sound so stern.

The click of the handcuffs was reassuring, as was the sight of Darren ushering Jack into the back seat of the police car. Then he came toward her. Gently, he uncurled her fingers from the gun and bagged it. A moment later he was holding her in his arms.

"How did you know he was here?" she asked.

"I saw his truck on your driveway and knew that meant trouble. I peered through the window and was about to break in when Todd came running out."

He studied her face in the glare from the police car's bright headlights. As much as she wanted to turn away, she let him see her vulnerability and fear mixed with naked joy because he'd come in time.

"You'll be okay?"

She nodded, knowing he meant okay without him because he couldn't stay. "I thought it was Terry."

He laughed. "I thought it was Don." Darren brushed his knuckles along her cheek. "I'll come back tomorrow and take your statement. Now I have to take Jack down to the station and deliver Todd to his parents. Go inside before you freeze to death."

Feeling as weak as if she'd risen from a sick bed, Gabbie entered the cottage. Now that she was safe, the terror of what she'd been through nearly felled her. She wondered if she would have been capable of shooting Jack. Thank God, Darren had come in time. Her fingers trembled as she put on the kettle for a strong mug of tea laced with brandy.

It took several sips before warmth coursed through her veins, and she regained some of her equilibrium.

"It's finally over," she said aloud. "Now everyone can relax."

She went into the den. "Cam?"

"I'm here," he answered softly.

Her eyes scanned the room until she saw him peering out the sliding doors facing the Sound. "You–you're transparent! I can hardly see you."

He turned to her. "That's because I'm leaving this plane."

"For good?"

"Yep. It's over, as far as I'm concerned. Thanks, Gabbie. I'm eternally grateful."

"But–but," she began, not certain how to finish her sentence or how to explain the tears filling her eyes.

Transparent though he was, there was no missing the huge, audacious grin. "Don't tell me you've gotten used to my company and hate to see me go."

"Something like that," she admitted.

"Oh, you'll be fine without me," Cam said airily. "You have Darren."

She squirmed. "Do I?"

He came close enough so that the chill of his presence made her rub her arms. "Plus, he has you." He turned serious. "Don't screw it up, Gabbie, like I did with Jill."

"But–but," she began again, a trace of the old panic rising, "I'm only staying in Chrissom Harbor till school lets out. And Darren and I, we both have baggage."

Cam laughed. "Who doesn't? Tell Tim Jordan you want a job next year. You're a hero. The school board will make you a guidance counselor if they can't give you an English program."

Gabbie blinked. She could barely make out his form. "How do you know so damn much about the high school?"

"I made it my business to know everything about this town, and you should, too." He winked. "Being the great sleuth you are, you're halfway there."

A tear trickled down her cheek. "I'll miss you Cam. This place won't be the same without you."

No one answered. Just silence. He was gone and he wouldn't return. Gabbie reached into her pocket for a tissue and blew her nose. She felt sad and happy, agitated and relieved, and, most of all, exhausted. She climbed the stairs, longing for sleep.

Tomorrow the school would be buzzing about Jack's arrest for the two murders and the part she'd played in it. She grinned as she saw herself telling Tim Jordan she wanted to come back next year, after all. In which case, she'd find herself another place to rent—an apartment or small house closer to town—which she'd decorate and furnish according to her taste. It would be cozy and exclusively hers.

She got into bed and turned out the light. For the first time in ages, she had only good things to look forward to. And underlining it all was the knowledge that Darren would be close by.

She sighed. Of course, she didn't expect any more murders to occur in a small town like CH. But if they happened to crop up, she hoped Darren would let her help solve them. She yawned. Kind of like a consultant. After all, now she had experience in the field.

CHECK OUT MORE GREAT MYSTERIES FROM ROWAN PROSE

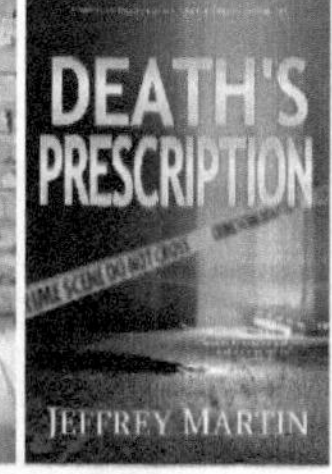

A former Spanish teacher, Marilyn Levinson writes mysteries, romantic suspense, and novels for young readers. Her Golden Age of Mystery Book Club series was a King Rivers Life Magazine's "Best of 2014," and on Book Town's 2014 Summer Mystery Reading List. She's an Agatha nominee, a Library Journal "Pick of the Month," on Goodreads's list of the 200 "Most Popular Books Published in 2017," a Suspense Magazine Best Indie, and was on Book Town's Summer (and) Fall Reading Lists. She also writes under Allison Brook. Marilyn loves traveling, reading, knitting, doing Sudoku, and visiting with her grandchildren. She is co-founder and past president of the Long Island chapter of Sisters in Crime. She resides in New York with her family. www.marilynlevinson.com

www.ingramcontent.com/pod-product-compliance
Lightning Source LLC
Chambersburg PA
CBHW021145310726
48971CB00002B/486